CONTENTS

ARCANE II: THE KING'S WHISPERER

PROLOGUE: ALIKA'S MEETING

Alika sat in the topmost room of the Mountain Base, her blood colder than the snow that fell on the mountainside around her. It was not the icy weather that chilled her though. It was fear.

She went to move closer to the fire, but her legs didn't respond.

A knock on the door. It opened a crack and a sliver of a man could be seen. The man was Faru, a Captain of the Kaofrelsi. One of the toughest soldiers Alika had ever met.

"He is here." Faru whispered, his usually gravelly voice sounding frightened and childish.

Alika tried to gulp down her growing terror. "I will go down to see Him." She shook. It took all of Alika's strength to push herself out of the seat and cross the room. When she glanced at Faru's face, she saw pity and fear in equal measure.

Faru went down the stairs first, his shoes clacking on the stone. Alika followed close behind, she could only hear her heart thundering. Faru stopped. "He told me to wait here. You must go to meet Him alone."

Alika could not even nod. Now that she was on her way, she just needed it to be over and she raced past Faru, into the wooden room at the end of the stairs.

In the centre of the room was a man dressed from head to

toe in white. He turned towards her as she entered.

"Alika." He smiled coldly. "Please lock the door behind you."

As Alika shut the door with a click, she thought of the previous failures who had been summoned to Him after they had made a mistake, each left with a hollowed, tortured look in their eyes that faded over time but never went entirely.

CHAPTER 1: AN UNEXPECTED PARTY

Mo was stretched out on the floor humming a song under his breath, too quietly for Jack to make out the tune. It might have been happy birthday, but it was hard to tell.

Ember flashed him a stern look and Mo stopped with a grin.

"Don't you think that it is time for bed?" She asked the two boys.

"Great, you're telling me what to do now as well." Jack retorted.

"No, it is just that I am tired."

"It's still light outside though."

"Well, I really think we should go to bed." Said Ember in her most prompting voice. Jack looked at Mo for his support but instead, Mo nodded.

"Yeah, let's just crash now." He said with an obviously fake yawn.

"Whatever." Jack muttered, getting to his feet and leaving his friends without a 'goodnight'. He felt guilty as he flopped down into bed. He knew it wasn't fair to get annoyed with Mo and Ember. They weren't the ones keeping him a proxy prisoner.

Since being let out of hospital, Alectus had made Jack

stay in the treehouse despite Jack insisting that he felt fine. If someone had told him during his time in the Wilderness that he would have a comfortable bed at night, three large meals a day and nothing to worry about, Jack would have thought it sounded like paradise. Now, he was less sure. When they had been in the Wilderness, Alectus' constant concern for their safety had been understandable but now that they were safely in Edenvale, it was painfully patronising. It seemed to Jack that he never got more than a few moments of time to himself without Alectus trying to control him.

To make matters worse, while he had been shut up indoors, Mo and Ember had been allowed to go and visit Teraturt and get involved with the daily activities of the Alforn. Out of spite, Jack hadn't opened the packets of sweets that they had brought back from Teraturt for him.

A door creaked. Stealthy, deliberate footsteps came out of Mo's room.

"Don't think Jack heard me leave." Mo whispered.

"Good." Ember breathed back.

Jack listened attentively. He was tempted to go and see what his two friends were doing but self-pity held him back. He remained in his room, the feeling of being left out allowing him to feel sorry for himself.

After a fair amount of rustling, Ember spoke again. "Ok, that is them all done I think." She sighed.

"Yeah, well, see you tomorrow." Mo whispered back.

Jack slept right the way through to midmorning the next day, he had been sleeping far more than usual yet somehow always felt tired, as though spending all day doing nothing drained him of energy. His constant weariness only fed his short temper.

When he entered the living room, however, Jack found something that finally lifted his mood for Alectus, Mo and Ember were all there in a circle around a considerable pile of presents.

"Happy birthday." Four voices sung in unison. Jack spun around to see Tom enter through the doorway pulling a simply colossal present behind him.

Jack stood dumbstruck for several moments, he had totally lost track of the days!

"Trust me, it is your birthday mate. We're not going to get you presents on some random day for a laugh." Mo said.

Jack nodded cautiously, still uncertain about whether he was dreaming.

"Open mine first!" Tom panted, dropping his present at Jack's feet and finally convincing him that this was really happening. Jack saw that the present was limp and human-shaped, and it was with trepidation that he removed the wrapping paper.

There was more than a little relief when Jack realised that the present was soft and not human-like to the touch. He unveiled the present from the feet up, discovering as he went that it was made from pillows and wearing his (Jack's) clothes. Tom had even painted Jack's face on it.

"Umm... thanks." Jack said, depositing the last of the wrapping paper on to the floor beside him. Thankfully, Tom missed the hesitation.

Jack held himself for a few moments before moving the creature onto the unoccupied seat nearest the door. Trying not to look at his voodoo doll, Jack moved on to Mo's gift.

Mo hadn't even wrapped his present, just lain a bit of paper on top of it. "What is the point of wrapping it at night when you will just unwrap it the next morning?" He said and Ember rolled her eyes.

When Jack removed the paper, he was perplexed. It appeared that Mo had given him a miniature wooden seesaw with a sand timer on one end and a chunky rock on the other with a bowl of water underneath. "Ember helped me build it." Mo stated.

"And what exactly is it?" Jack asked.

"It's an alarm clock!" Said Tom with the suddenness of realisation. Jack turned to see him giving Ember a high-five.

"I always knew you were the clever one." She said and Tom looked delighted. Desperate to show just how clever he was, Tom scampered towards the present.

"Look, you put some sand into the timer and, once enough of it has run out, the see-saw tilts." Tom pushed down the end with the rock. "And the rock rolls off into the water causing a splash which will wake you up!"

"Which means you can get up early enough to go running with me." Mo smiled.

Alectus cleared his throat.

"Once you're well enough of course." Mo added. Clearly Alectus did not think Jack was up to going running quite yet.

Jack had to restrain himself telling his father that he was totally fine. He didn't want an argument to spoil this morning. Instead, he knelt and examined Mo's present more carefully, the sand timer had tiny writing on the side, so you knew how much sand to add to measure a certain amount of time.

Next, once he was certain he wasn't going to snap at his father, Jack moved on to Ember's present, it was a wooden platform with an inordinate number of wheels on the bottom. Ember showed Jack how it could clip onto the front of her wheelchair. Jack didn't have a clue when this was likely to come in useful but promised that they could try it out that afternoon.

A few of the orphans, including Jasmine and Alvin, had stayed in Arcane along with Tom, Mo, Ember and Jack. They had all also gotten him presents as well, every one of which turned out to have been bought from Teraturt. On the one hand, Jack couldn't help but feel a little jealous as he imagined them all exploring while he had been stuck inside but on the other, he was elated that people had thought about him. He had never had a birthday present before.

The final gift was Alectus'. Clearly, it had been expertly wrapped but even so, Jack couldn't guess what it was. A couple of feet long, hard, and bumpy were all the clues he had.

Within moments, it had been unwrapped and, once again, Jack was left holding something he didn't know the name for.

"A Receiver-Transceiver." Alectus said, pointing. He brought out an identical one from the side of his seat.

"And what does a Receiver-Transceiver do?" Jack asked.

"They allow you to communicate. Receiver-Transceiver's (more commonly known as Rec-Trec's) are always made in pairs and whatever you write on yours, I can see on mine." Explained Alectus.

"So they are like really bad phones?"

"My word, I had forgotten all about the mobile phones!"

" 'The mobile phones'. You really have fallen behind the times."

"Yes, well I thought that it might help me keep track of you."

"I'm hardly going to get lost, am I? You still don't let me out of the house!"

"You are still recovering from your time in the hospital." Alectus said gently, too gently, almost baby-speak.

Jack had to take several deep breaths to calm himself.

He hadn't imagined how annoying being patronised could be. "Ok. Thank you for my present." He said as politely as he could manage. Really, he was furious. He couldn't believe that A-lectus had used his birthday as a way of controlling him even more.

Ember came to the rescue. "Can I show you something in Edenvale?" She asked Jack.

"Yeah, that would be great!" Jack said quickly, before A-lectus could comment.

Alectus half-opened his mouth. Maybe he realised how close Jack was to losing control at being kept inside. He could not miss the enthusiasm in his son's voice at the possibility of being allowed out of the house. Either way, with a small sigh, he shut his mouth again and nodded his permission.

"Can I come as well?" Tom asked quickly.

Ember hesitated and Jack realised that she wanted to say no but couldn't find the words. "Yes, I suppose." She said with a sigh.

"Where're you going?" Asked Mo, stealing a biscuit from Jack's stack of presents.

"The Monarch's Mark." Ember replied.

"Ah, excellent. I will come as well and then continue to my office in Teraturt." Said Lord Alectus. "I have a lot of work to do today but shall endeavour to be home for the birthday dinner."

"Well I guess you may as well come then." Ember said, pointing at Mo and sounding extremely irritated.

"I love feeling wanted." Mo smiled, stealing another of Jack's sweets.

Jack descended the spiral stairs as fast as he could without running. He was desperate to finally get out of the house. Once into the open air he took a deep breath and grinned to himself. Free at last.

The others reached him a few moments later.

Alectus made sure to walk close to Jack as if at any moment Jack would collapse onto the floor. As they walked, Alectus spoke at length about what was going on with his work, Jack listened half-heartedly "Chaos in my department at the moment! Not only are we having to prepare for the King's visit next week, but there are also some very odd decisions being made by the court... dismissing Karen Longton is madness, more experience than everyone else put together... talk of stopping the Cart network... wasting money on a new palace..."

Eventually Tom interrupted Alectus' monologue, "It is further than I remember." He gasped as they started climbing yet another hill. But Jack didn't mind, he was delighted to finally be outside, and it was cool underneath the thick brown branches of the trees.

"Yeah, I don't remember it being this far to the edge of the forest." Mo said as they reached the top of the hill. "Wait! I don't remember this at all." He continued, looking around him.

They had suddenly reached a large circular clearing on the top of the hill.

"Are we lost?" Tom asked, sounding nervous.

Jack gasped. There were markings on the ground. The Monarch's Mark!

"What?!?" The three boys said in unison, all noticing the brown lines. Since when had the Monarch's Mark been in the middle of the forest?

Sensing Ember and Alectus' silence, Jack looked to them for answers. Both appeared more than a little smug.

"How have they moved the Monarch's Mark?" Jack asked.

"Movement is a relevant concept." Ember said. She and Alectus both smiled as if they were both in on a secret joke.

"What's that meant to mean?"

"It means you are asking the wrong question. The Monarch's Mark has not been moved. The forest has moved."

"How?"

"The trees of Edenvale Forest are different to any others on Earth or Arcane and the Alforn have lived with and within them for time out of mind. If there is the need, the Alforn can grow a seed to a tree in a day. In a week, a land can go from treeless to densest forest."

"That sounds quite cool, if it's true, but why bother?"

Clearly Ember had been anticipating the question because she started speaking the second that the words were out of Jack's mouth, "The Darkest Day Dance!" She squealed. Jack had only seen her this excited once before, when she had built a drawbridge for their camp. "Every year, at the Winter equinox, the Alforn celebrate the longest night of the year with a Dance" She explained.

"Why would anyone want to celebrate the longest night of the year?"

"The Alforn prefer the night to the day. They work most of the morning, then sleep through until sunset then do whatever they please during the night!" Ember replied enthusiastically.

"That's weird." Tom said, scratching his head.

"Only because it isn't what we are used to. The Alforn are different to us, they have evolved down a separate route." Alectus explained. "See it is nearly ten o'clock now, the Alforn are halfway through their work shift while we are just starting. Oh no!"

"What?"

"I have to be in a meeting to arrange the King's visit and I was meant to be there two minutes ago, and no one can see me arriving from this way!" Alectus said very fast.

"Why not?"

"Well my office is in Teraturt and no one from Teraturt knows Edenvale exists. People will wonder why I am arriving from the middle of nowhere!"

And with that, Alectus hurried off towards Teraturt.

"Yes, so the Darkest Day Dance is tomorrow night!" Ember said eagerly. Clearly, she wanted to get everyone's attention back to the event at hand.

"Ok, so what are we doing here now?" Mo asked, laughing. "We are a day and a half early."

"Well, I just wanted to bring Jack really... help set up for the dance..." Said Ember, turning pink. "That is why the forest has been grown around the hilltop so that no one from Teraturt can see everything being set up." She continued, recovering herself slightly.

Unable to wait any longer, Ember raced across the clearing to an untidy pile of poles and sheets. Mo, Jack, and Tom followed her with significantly less enthusiasm and began sticking poles into the ground about roughly where they thought it would make sense for them to be. Ember on the other hand sat still, looking at all the different bits and pieces with an expression of first interest and then understanding.

It quickly transpired that the poles were all in the wrong place and the sheets didn't fit between them. Ember, with a frantic excitement, raced around, telling them to move certain poles and Jack was unsurprised to find that when they now tried to fit the sheets between them, everything slotted perfectly into place.

There were two more pavilions to be built and this time, they all let Ember tell them what to do from the outset and they were put up much faster. Even so, by the time that the third pavilion was up, it was midday and getting quite hot in the clearing.

Together, they headed back to Alectus' house for what Mo and Jack decided was a well-deserved lunch.

The cupboards had been emptied of food (mostly by Mo who ate more than Jack thought humanly possible) so lunch consisted of Jack's birthday sweets. Jack couldn't believe that he had spitefully refused the ones that Mo and Ember had gotten him because they were amazing; layers of fresh honey and dark chocolate called 'the Bees Knees', spicy flower-shaped chocolates called 'Chilli Lilies' and sticky-sweet marshmallowy clouds called 'Dream Creams'.

Feeling bloated, the boys lay back on the sofas. Jack had never seen Mo look more lackadaisical. Only Ember had any energy. "Come on!" She said, heading towards the door.

"What?"

"We still have lots to set up!"

"Do we have to?" Mo mumbled, shutting his eyes.

The change was instantaneous.

"No, you don't HAVE to! If you would rather just sit around here like a... a... a potato then that is FINE!" Ember shouted. "Coming?" She asked Jack.

Too startled to do anything else, Jack nodded and stood up, following her out of the treehouse. He noticed Mo and Tom were following him. They all exchanged looks but didn't say anything.

When they returned to the hilltop, they started sorting out the games, there were several that Jack recognised; ring tossing, tug-of-war and bobbing for apples but the one that he was most looking forwards to seeing was Barge-Board, Jack had never seen a game of Barge-Board but one day Mo had come back unable to talk about anything else, and Jack knew at once why it had caught Mo's imagination so tightly, as Barge-

Board was where two Alforn balanced on two separate, huge, floating logs on a lake and tried to knock the other one off. Of course, there was no lake on the top of the hill where the Monarch's Mark was so the three of them had to dig a vast hole that would then be filled with water tomorrow.

The frantic excitement that Ember had had throughout the day was nothing compared to the hysteria that filled her face when the finished setting up the games. "Now, it is time to sort out the dancefloor!' She said dramatically.

Jack, Mo and Tom were set to work, laying down a plastic substance on the floor to make it easier to dance on and then putting up translucent tables and chairs in the positions that Ember allocated. Ember, meanwhile, kept up a constant commentary of "Oh that will look beautiful in the starlight." and "I hope no one will notice the slope there." And (most commonly of all) "I hope I have left enough room for the partners to dance!"

Eventually, Jack couldn't take it anymore, he also felt that he was safe, Ember seemed to be glowing too brightly to snap into anger-mode. "Ember, not being funny, but there are hundreds of Alforn in Edenvale, why are we the only ones setting up?"

"They are going to come and help tomorrow."

"Why didn't we just do it all together tomorrow?"

Ember looked slightly hurt. "I thought you might be looking forwards to it." She said quietly.

"Not really, I just hope there is plenty of food." Jack joked, looking at Mo and Tom.

This was a mistake.

"WELL YOU CAN JUST LEAVE NOW THEN! THERE IS MORE FOOD AT HOME IF THAT IS ALL YOU CARE ABOUT!" Ember roared.

Jack backed up, which only gave her space to get more wound up. She continued shouting along the same lines of 'just leave now then' but with more and more expletives that Jack hadn't imagined her yelling at him before. Only Mo's expression of controlling explosive laughter made Jack certain that this wasn't a strange dream.

Eventually, Ember was all shouted out and stormed off.

"I think..." Mo began but then, unusually, lost his nerve.

"Go on, you may as well tell me what you think." Jack sighed.

"I just think she is really looking forwards to the dance is all."

Jack knew that Mo had really wanted to say something different but couldn't be bothered to argue.

Ember sat looking glum on the corner of the plastic sheet. Jack, feeling embarrassed, continued trying to work without really looking at her. Eventually, the third time he tried knocking in a hammer with a nail, he realised that his brain was far too unfocused to bother continuing with the project and crossed over towards Ember but the moment that she realised he was coming towards her, she spun her wheelchair around so that he couldn't talk to her.

"Look, I didn't mean to annoy you." He sighed.

Ember didn't respond.

At that moment, Jack began to feel rain spitting down onto his neck.

"Come on then you lot! It won't do to arrive at the Bar all soaked." Came a voice from the edge of the clearing. Jack spun around and saw Alectus appear on the other side of the clearing. "I must say I am terribly impressed with what you have done today." he said, indicating all that they had set up.

Jack looked at Ember, wondering if the compliment

would break her refusal to talk but it didn't seem to. She made a clear point of avoiding eye-contact.

Totally oblivious, Alectus began marching towards Eden-vale. "This way!" He said cheerfully.

"What's this way?" Jack asked, feeling relieved that they were doing something other than setting up for the Dance and that he could get some space between himself and Ember.

"Mr. And Mrs. Vality's Breakfast Bar." Replied Alectus, dis-appearing into the forest.

"So I'm well enough to go out for food now." Jack said to himself.

"Alectus, you do know that it is, like, evening." Said Mo.

Ember rolled her eyes, but Alectus smiled. "Well it goes back to what we were saying earlier about the Alforn working in the morning and being awake through the night. Their biggest meal of the day is about now to give them energy through the night."

"Suppose that makes sense." Mo replied. Jack knew that his friend was never going to complain at the idea of food, regardless of the time of day.

"Right, here we are!" Alectus said a short while later, stopping suddenly next to a colossal dark brown tree which had thin white lines on it, reaching down to the floor. With an effortless flick of his hand, Alectus turned the section of wood within the white lines into a small ball of etter and they all crossed through into the well-lit, homey, hollowed interior of the tree.

Jack was amazed to see at least a dozen tables surrounded by Alforn of all different ages, the three tables closest to him hosted separate families. There was another one that had Alforn that were about the same age as Jack, although more than two feet taller. The other tables all had groups of people deep in conversation, Jack guessed that they were clubs of some sort.

"Ah! Alectus! So good to see you." Said a red-faced Alforn who was particularly huge. He wore an apron with 'Mr. And Mrs. Vality's Breakfast Bar.' written across the chest "Table for six, wasn't it?"

"Yes, thank you Gerald."

"Who is the sixth person?" Ember asked, making Jack jump, he had forgotten that she was there.

"Dr. Nabielle." Said Alectus. "I hope you don't mind me inviting her?" Alectus asked, turning to Jack.

"No, not at all." Jack said instantly. Seeing as she had saved his life only a couple of weeks earlier, inviting her to his birthday dinner didn't seem like an unreasonable idea.

As they walked past the various groups, Jack's guess that they were clubs turned out to be correct; on one table, all the members had the same book out and were analysing it, on another, everyone was discussing new building regulations and even the small snippet of conversation that Jack overheard was enough to make him yawn.

Suddenly, one of the building-regulations-people rolled his neck and looked around him. He spotted first Alectus and then Jack. He quickly called a halt to the building-regulations discussion and everyone on his table fell silent and stared open mouthed at Jack. Then, noticing the silence that had fallen on their neighbouring table, the book group turned and saw Jack. They also stopped speaking and stared round-eyed at him.

The trend rolled around the room like a wave until everyone was quiet and staring. Suddenly, from above him, Jack heard someone clapping, he looked up and saw the heart-shaped face of Dr. Nabielle.

Slowly at first but building momentum like a tsunami, everyone else joined in. It was soon so loud that Jack could feel the tree shake.

Jack saw Ember looking as embarrassed as he felt, Tom looking shy and Mo obviously loving the attention. Eventually, Lord Alectus made himself heard, shouting that they needed to go and have dinner.

Looking delighted, Mr. Vality lead them up towards the table where Dr. Nabielle sat.

Jack, who was at the front, heard Mr. Vality muttering under his breath. "Spiffing, absolutely fantastic, we are going to be full for weeks, everyone wanting to discuss it all over again!"

"Not one for the limelight?" Dr. Nabielle laughed as Jack sat down, he knew that his face was still furiously red.

"Not really."

"Yeah, me neither, I hate being the centre of attention." Said Mo as he took the seat next to Jack.

Mr. Vality was all a flutter as he wrote down their order for drinks. "Going to be full for weeks." He said happily to himself once more as he waltzed away.

Ember's return to talking didn't appear to extend to Jack and she pointedly sat as far away from him as she could. As Tom took a seat between Jack and Dr. Nabielle, he spoke breathlessly about his own birthday, even though it was nine months away. Still not pausing for breath, he moved onto the Darkest Day Dance. He was as excited about it as Ember although his reasoning was obvious – he was going to be allowed to stay up all night if he wanted.

Suddenly, Mo grabbed Tom's arm, making him go quiet. A look of wonder was on Mo's face, Jack followed his gaze and saw Mr. Vality and a female Alforn (presumably Mrs. Vality) pushing a sturdy metal trolley. Despite the trolley's robust appearance, however, it was audibly groaning under the weight of the vast amount of food it was supporting. There were at least a hundred small, elegant dishes. Jack, who had only ever eaten school-style food, sweets and whatever they had man-aged to forage in the Wilderness, didn't know where to look or what to think, there were buttered prawns, smoked salmon on biscuits and neat chicken skewers.

"Tuck in." Alectus smiled. Jack didn't have to be asked twice, he grabbed food indiscriminately and piled it onto his plate. Mo, Tom, and Ember were not far behind while the adults showed a little more restraint. Mr. and Ms. Vality looked delighted, taking the total silence for pleasure.

Eventually, the trolley was empty, and Jack looked at Mo and laughed. He couldn't believe what had just happened. He was dimly aware of the trolley being pushed away and then, he heard it before he saw it, another trolley take its place. Jack's mind refocused and he saw that this one was loaded with bur-gers and bacon and sausages on the top shelf while on the bot-tom were baps and a vast array of sauces.

Jack couldn't believe his eyes when he saw Mo heaving more food onto his plate, there was no way that he could eat anymore and yet he could already feel his stomach thinking about just one sausage.

Half an hour later and Jack had managed four sausages, two burgers and plenty of bacon. Now, amongst his tiredness, he felt a strange feeling of accomplishment.

The trolley squeaked as it was wheeled away, the sound faded and then got louder again. A third trolley came into view, bending under the weight of the vast number of puddings that it held, a great chocolate birthday cake taking pride of place.

This time, Jack really couldn't eat anymore and even had to donate his slice of cake to Tom who, remarkably, was still going.

"Wow!" Exhaled Mo. "I knew that the Alforn were more advanced than us." He sighed happily as the third trolley was wheeled out of sight.

Jack felt too tired to say anything in reply.

It was the change in tone that alerted him.

For several minutes, Jack had sat half-asleep in his chair letting the white noise of conversation flow over him but now he saw that Ember was speaking to Tom, leaving Dr. Nabielle to talk with Alectus. Clearly, they were discussing something more important than the phenomenal food.

Careful to remain looking drowsy and unfocused, Jack started listening attentively to the conversation across the table.

"Of course, dismissing Karen Longton has been the biggest shock recently but it is far from the only one. King Taigal has been making insane decisions for the best part of a year now." Said Alectus.

Dr. Nabielle took a moment to answer. "It is curious." She said carefully. "Of course, it might be simply that the King is growing up, testing out his strength as teenagers do, but there is a pattern here, over the last month; Karen Longton, Anne Pilkington and Denis Rote have been dismissed. All of them were powerful, competent, experienced Council Members."

"Yes, it is remarkable really." Said Alectus, nodding his head. "If someone wanted to weaken the Government as much as possible, they would be the three I would get rid of." He said with the slightest trace of humour.

Dr. Nabielle showed not the remotest flicker of a smile.

A meaningful pause.

"No! You can't really think that someone would try and do that? Surely it is just the typical incompetence of the King and the politicians!" Said Alectus, cottoning on.

Jack finally turned towards the conversation just in time to see a darkly significant look on Dr. Nabielle's face.

She caught his eye, and, in a flash, the normally smiley doctor was back. "Now that the food is done, it is time for presents!"

"Oh no... you don't have to... not at all." Jack stammered. Seeing as Dr. Nabielle had recently saved his life, it just felt wrong for her to be giving him presents.

"You haven't seen what it is yet." She said with her blue eyes twinkling like the sea. For a moment, she rummaged around in her handbag. Then, with a flourish, brought out a handsome, transparent compass with two needles, one red the other blue.

She handed it to Jack who took it from her with extreme care, turning it over in his hands. It was beautiful.

"What's that?" Asked Tom, his voice straining with curiosity. Jack saw that he was pointing to two small marks above the North on the compass, one mark was sapphire blue, the other ruby red.

He was just about to tell Tom to be quiet, afraid that Dr. Nabielle would take offence at the highlighting of such a small imperfection when she said something that took his breath away. "Those are Tracking Diamonds."

"What?" Mo and Ember gasped together.

"Tracking Diamonds. Wherever the Diamonds are moved to, the needle points straight there no matter how far away the Diamond is taken."

"Wow." They all breathed together.

"No, I can't." Said Jack suddenly. "I can't take this. Not from you. Not now."

"It would make me happy to give it to you. It would make you happy to have it. The only reason you can't take it is pride. Idiots alone value pride above happiness."

Feeling like he had been trapped in ropes made of

words. Jack could only nod and smile his gratitude. He wiggled the blue tracking diamond out and moved it once in a circle around the compass, watching the blue needle follow it around. Then, with extreme care, he returned the tracking diamond to its hold in the compass before doing the same thing with the red one.

On the walk back, Mo and Tom took turns holding the Diamonds then running away and hiding at which point, Jack, looking at the compass, would point straight at them.

By the time that Jack got into bed that night, he was delighted. It had been the best birthday ever and he had, just about, managed to stop himself ruining it by not getting annoyed at Alectus' present.

CHAPTER 2:
TERATURT

When Jack woke the next morning, he immediately felt the top of his bedside table for his Tracking Compass. He couldn't resist moving the red Diamond around and watching the ruby needle twirl after it.

"Y'alright?" Mo asked, bursting through Jack's door with Tom close behind him.

In his surprise, Jack dropped the diamond and it bounced away under his bed. "Oh, great." Jack muttered, getting down on all fours to look for it. Mo joined in. Tom, however, picked up the compass and followed the needle until, a few seconds later, emerging with the beautiful, red diamond. Jack sat there feeling like an idiot. Mo, on the other hand, roared with laughter until he had to sit down on Jack's bed and get his breath back.

"What did you want to say?" Jack asked.

"Oh yeah right," Mo sighed, recovering himself. "Ember is about to head up and do some more setting up for the Darkest Day Dance. Thought we should go help. Otherwise, the chance of us not living 'til tomorrow is a bit too high for my liking."

"You're probably right." Jack said trying to sort out his bed hair. "I'll meet you downstairs in a few minutes."

"Do you think she will mind if I don't come?" Tom asked. His voice making it only too obvious that he wanted nothing more than to stay where he was.

"I'm sure she will be fine." Jack replied.

Ten minutes later, with his hair flattened and a piece of bread in his hand, Jack followed Ember to the Monarch's Mark. He was delighted to see that it was already swarming with Alforn decorating the pavilions in bright colours. They all smiled and waved at Jack, Mo, and Ember as they joined in. As they got on with helping, Jack noticed that they were treated with an unusual combination of awe (because of rescuing the Amulet from Carsicus) and parental protectiveness (because they were about the same size as Alforn six-year-olds).

The work was much easier than yesterday's and Jack quite enjoyed painting the different designs. A group of particularly colossal Alforn were busy carrying buckets of water as big as boats up the hill and filling in the hole that Jack and the others had dug yesterday so that Bargeboard could be played that evening. Just as Jack began to get those rumblings of midday hunger, one of the Alforn shouted that they were done. There was nothing left to set up! For them, it was time to go home and sleep until the evening.

Jack, Mo, and Ember began following the Alforn back towards the woodland but, suddenly, Mo stopped. "There isn't any food at home." He said, a flicker of excitement beginning to light his face.

"I'm sure that we can find something." Jack shrugged, unsure why Mo was smiling, having no food was not normally something that would delight his friend.

"Well, what I was thinking, was that we could go to Teraturt." Suggested Mo.

"Mo, be sensible." Said Ember sharply. "The Alforn have remained undetected for thousands of years, if you keep going to Teraturt and back eventually someone might follow you and discover them!"

"But Alectus does it the whole time."

"And have you seen how careful he is to avoid being followed?"

"We'll be just as careful." Mo promised. "Anyway, *you* must have seen how good the Alforn are at hiding, even if someone were to follow us back from Teraturt for some reason, there is no way that they would find anything except trees. What do you think Jack?"

Jack shivered. He didn't want to think about how furious Alectus would be if he found out Jack had snuck off to Teraturt. But then Jack straightened. The only reason that Alectus insisted he stay in Edenvale was because he needed to build up his strength but seeing as Jack had spent the last day and a half working, he thought that more than enough evidence that he was well enough to go to Teraturt.

"Are you coming?" Jack asked, turning towards Ember, hoping she wouldn't shout at him, but instead she only mumbled something about wanting to get ready for the Dance. Jack opened his mouth to point out that that was hours away but then shut it again without saying anything, he felt as though he was still on dangerous ground from the day before.

The walk to Teraturt was a mile up and down hills but to Jack it felt no distance at all, and as if he was walking on clouds. Finally, he was getting to do the things that had been closed off from him since leaving hospital.

Just as Jack was about to ask how much further it was, they reached the top of a hill and the town of Teraturt was laid out below them like a map. "Those two houses are where everyone in Teraturt thinks that Dr. Nabielle and Alectus live!" Mo said, pointing to two impressive houses on the closest side of town, "and there's the sweet shop!"

Mo began running down the slope and Jack did his best to chase after him, but Mo was fast, very fast. By the time that they passed Alectus and Dr. Nabielle's supposed houses, Jack was fifty metres behind. Soon, he was chasing Mo along winding dirt roads which had squalid houses on either side. Jack was so preoccupied with racing after his friend that he didn't even bother to stop and look at the other people walking down the road, the first human adults he had seen (other than Alectus and Dr. Nabielle) that didn't want him killed for two months.

As they ran, the houses on either side of the road became steadily bigger and better maintained. The road itself was no longer mud but cobbled stone. There were also small shops every few hundred metres.

Finally, Jack saw Mo stop and push open the door to a brightly painted shop.

With a hand pressed firmly to his side, massaging a stitch, Jack entered the shop. There was a tinkle as the door swung open. If anything, the interior was even more colourful. Jack looked towards the dark wooden floor and blinked furiously, letting his eyes have a break.

Mo ordered two extra-large 'bees-knees' from the surprisingly slender man behind the counter, "That will be six King's Notes please."

From his pocket, Mo pulled out six paper slips, "Alectus gave us some when we came last time, and I didn't spend it all." He explained. They went up a narrow staircase. The upstairs was thankfully a bit more tired looking.

When their orders arrived, Jack felt as though 'Massive Hornet's Entire Legs' would have been a more accurate description because they were about a foot long. Although, as Mo was quick to point out, the name didn't have the same ring to it.

As they ate, Jack couldn't help continually looking around at the normal people enjoying their food, he hadn't seen this many adults at once since leaving Earth. The realisation that two months had passed since his arrival on Arcane surprised Jack, it felt as though time had flown and yet in that time, he had become a totally different person.

Once they had eaten plenty, the two boys headed out into the street.

Jack turned right to go back the way that they had come but Mo gave him a look that said, 'are you mad?'

"What?" Jack asked.

"We have a whole afternoon to explore, why go home now?"

"Ok, but let's make sure we are back plenty before A-lectus or we'll both be in for it."

"Don't worry, we've got ages."

Mo continued down the street, curiously looking from side to side. "We didn't come this way with Alectus." He explained. As they walked, Jack became aware that the houses were getting steadily grander. Suddenly, the houses stopped, and the two boys arrived on the Highstreet.

"What the..." said Mo, his mouth open.

The street was wide and marble. Jack couldn't see a single blemish anywhere; it was surgically clean.

"Oi, look at this!" Mo gasped and they crossed the street to a shop that glistened. Around the tall windows were white pearls. The shop was a Jewellers and even Jack was amazed at the range of gleaming watches and necklaces. There was nothing that didn't sparkle.

The two boys were startled as the door tinkled open and a lady emerged in a shimmering silver dress that made Jack think of a fish. She crossed the Highstreet into a circular skyscraper with 'Fiyas Lawyers' written on the side. The skyscraper had lines of incredible colours running into each other forming complex patterns.

The two boys continued down the Highstreet in a trance-like state. Everyone else was dressed to impressed, there was not a single button out of place or untucked shirt or tired looking dress. They were so struck by what they were seeing that Jack and Mo didn't think about how out of place they must look. As they progressed down the Highstreet, the shops only got more glorious, all trying to outdo each other. The shops were not the only things trying to stand out though, as Jack looked around, he felt a growing sense of demonstration. He began to realise that people walked slightly too slowly, spoke a tiny bit too loudly, all begging to be noticed. Now that the feeling had materialised, it grew into unease. Everything was too theatrical. Jack didn't like it.

They kept walking but nothing broke the pattern.

Suddenly, Jack spotted something that stood out like a banana in a pile of apples, there was a glistening blue signpost with dazzling white signs to different shops except for one plain, weather-stained, wooden arrow. Jack pointed it out to Mo, who was clearly beginning to feel the same as him. They dashed towards it and saw in simple black writing the word's 'Teraturt Library' pointing down a smaller, slightly crooked street.

The two boys hurried down the street in search of a place where they would feel more comfortable. At first, the houses were much the same as the Highstreet but the further that they went along, the more home-like the houses became. Finally, they turned a corner and there, at the end of the road, stood the library. It was everything that Jack had wanted, perfectly imperfect, once white stone walls turned grey with age, moss tugging at the corners, the bushes at the front needing a cut. There was even a spider-web across the top of the door!

"D'you think it's open?" Jack asked.

"Only one way to find out." Mo replied, taking the lead and pushing the doors inwards.

When he passed through the chipped doors at the front of the library, it felt to Jack that he had finally got out of the spotlight of a play and into the backstage.

A friendly voice called something from the desk, but Jack could not make out the words, he turned to see a wizened old woman so shrunken by age that she barely appeared over the top of the desk.

"Oh, hello..." said Jack instinctively. Mo stamped hard on his foot and Jack gasped but not from pain; he had suddenly realised that he had spoken in English not Arcanian!

"Hello." Mo said in Arcanian and the lady smiled.

Trying to atone for his mistake, Jack said in the best Arcanian that he could manage "We were looking for a book."

The old lady smiled as she hoped off her chair and came around the desk. "Well in that case, you have come to the right place. Could you be any more specific?"

"Awah... wa..." Said Jack, he hadn't thought this far ahead.

"We were wondering if we could find some history books." Mo said quickly.

"My favourite." Grinned the old lady. "If you would follow me young gentlemen." She said before hurrying off with remarkable speed past rows and rows of books. Jack began to feel like he was back in the memory library with Errion.

"Excuse me, Mrs. Deraton, could you help me find a book on Kaur's?" Another voice asked suddenly from down a row of books, making Jack jump.

"Of course my dear girl." Said the librarian. "Follow us if you would. These boys are looking for history books and the books about Kaur's are right next door."

The girl emerged from the shadows and Jack saw that she was a few years older than him, eighteen perhaps, and almost identical in height. Her blond hair was pulled into a long pony-

29

tail. "Hello, I'm Polly." She said brightly.

"Hey, Mo and Jack." Mo smiled, pointing at each of them in turn. Jack gave an awkward grin of recognition, hoping that Mo's unusual accent would go unnoticed.

"Come on, this way." Mrs. Deraton the librarian said from a little further on.

Jack felt awkward as they continued through the library. He could not think of a single thing to say.

He was greatly relieved when the librarian pointed the girl down one aisle and himself and Mo down another on the opposite side a bit further on. "Well, looks like we now have to do some reading on history."

"Excellent." Said Mo, choosing a thick volume before seating himself against the bookcase.

Just before the librarian left, she turned to Jack and said, "We have some books on English here as well, a few aisles down, although, thinking about how well you spoke it, maybe you don't need to read up on it anymore. It almost seemed as though it was your first language."

Jack felt his heart flip in his chest, his slow wit had already roused the suspicions of one person in Teraturt. What would happen if his stupidity led to Edenvale being discovered?

Thankfully, the librarian said no more and simply returned to her desk.

Trying to calm himself, Jack pulled down a random book and began flicking through the pages without processing any of the words. However, as he continued feeling nervous, he thought he could do with moving around for a bit.

Curiosity guiding him, he proceeded to the aisle that the librarian had said the books on English were. He opened a small volume called 'A beginners guide to the history of English.'

"The language we believe to be called 'English' is a most curious one, the origins of which none can be sure. Many scholars believe that the language in fact originates from a planet other than Arcane! All that is certain is that oftentimes important objects, particularly those supposedly related to the legends of the Crown and the Amulet, are found with writing near them in this curious language. From time to time, places are described that appear to have no similarities to any on Arcane. This is the perfect book for beginners looking to develop a deeper understanding of this mysterious dialect.

Jack returned to Mo with his book and settled into a comfortable position.

Half an hour later and Jack was beginning to get bored, his mind kept slipping from the words. "Should we start heading back now?" He asked.

Mo only held up a finger.

"We need to get back before Alectus!"

"Let me finish this chapter." Mo said, not looking up. Jack had never seen him so still.

Jack stood up, planning on putting his book back. But, when he reached the end of his aisle, he suddenly heard whispering, "Now or never. Got to do it now. C'mon, don't be a coward. He will be so impressed!"

Jack peered through the bookshelves and saw Polly pacing. She continued whispering to herself as she walked. Then, in a flash, she steeled herself and marched from the library. Jack wanted to go back and get Mo but knew that he risked losing Polly so instead, fantastically curious, he followed her out, shoving his book into a gap in the shelves, nowhere near where he had gotten it out. During the weeks he had been forced to remain in Edenvale, his need for adventure had returned, and was now stronger than ever.

Polly turned sharply left out of the library down a dark, narrow passageway between fences. Jack darted after her, flitting from shadow to shadow as the passageway got steadily darker and narrower.

As Jack began to get closer, Polly stopped sharply and glanced behind her. Jack ducked down, pressing himself against the fence. He took three slow, deep breaths before looking further down the alleyway. Polly had gone.

Nervously, Jack pressed on down the alleyway. Where Polly had disappeared, there were routes leading off either side and no trace of which way she had gone. Jack was slightly relieved but, mostly, disappointed. He had lost her. The adventure was over...

Then, he heard whispered voices from further down the dark alleyway and, with butterflies of excitement, he continued towards them. The alleyway now grew lighter and broader, and Jack saw that at the end was a wide, open space. He reached the end of the fence and peered around the corner.

Derelict concrete tower blocks surrounded an overgrown square. They were all abandoned with smashed windows and lifeless faces. In the very centre of the square were a man and a woman.

Jack gasped with shock. Polly was nowhere to be seen. Instead, in the middle of the square, were Alectus and Dr. Nabielle!

Dr. Nabielle looked up sharply, hearing Jack. Jack pulled himself around the corner but thought that, just for a second, Dr. Nabielle had seen him.

Jack sat still as a statue, holding his breath.

He listened with all his might but couldn't hear any footsteps coming towards him and he finally let out the air that had been trapped in his lungs. Alectus broke the silence.

"It was only agreed for definite this morning, the King is to arrive in Teraturt a week tomorrow." Alectus said in a tired voice.

"You remember the plan that I suggested."

"Yes, clearly I remember the plan, you badger me about it so often that I can't focus on anything else."

"That's because it is much more important than everything else."

Alectus let out a great sigh.

"I know that we need to do it, but the risks just seem too high, Jack has only just gotten to safety and I just can't throw him straight back into danger."

"I know what you are thinking, and the answer is no, Alectus. We are not getting involved in politics and treachery."

"We **MUST** do it." Alectus whispered with terrifying ferocity. "It is the only way that we can guarantee Jack's safety, convince the King that Jack is on *his* side."

"You have always been perilously close to the dishonesty of politics. Don't overstep the line, Alectus." Said Dr. Nabielle with icy calmness.

"Can we at least compromise, at least don't tell the King about Carsicus." Whispered Alectus and Jack was alarmed to hear how much desperation was in his father's voice, he was begging.

"In a time of universal deceit, telling the truth is a revolutionary act."

"To hell with truth!" Growled Alectus, the fury entering his voice once more. "This suicidal obsession you have with being better than everyone else puts your life on a knife edge. That's your choice. But you will not put Jack in the same position."

"That is not your decision."

"Of course it is, he is a child!"

"A child who survived more than a month in the Wilderness, who protected the Crown from Carsicus."

"But still a child!"

"A person who has earned the right to make his own decisions."

"NO! I am not going to let him put his life in even more danger. Not now, not ever!"

"Alectus, we must be better than those we are trying to replace, surely you see that."

"NO!" roared Alectus.

Jack heard footsteps crossing towards him and only retreated into the shadows just in time to hide from Alectus who swept round the corner in a towering rage. Alika followed behind, her expression neutral. Just as she passed Jack, she turned to where he was hiding and winked before continuing down the passageway, back towards the Highstreet.

Jack sat in the darkness for several moments, questions racing around his head. Why had Alectus and Dr. Nabielle met so far from Edenvale? What did Alectus mean 'even more danger'? And why had Dr. Nabielle let him hear the conversation?

Needing to talk to someone about what he had just heard, Jack hurried back to the library.

"Jack!" A voice whispered from a bush just as Jack was about to enter through the chipped doors.

"What?" He exclaimed as Mo emerged from the undergrowth. "Why on earth are you hiding in a bush?"

"I was just coming out to see where you had got to when Alectus and Dr. Nabielle came out that alleyway, so I had to hide from them. Where did you go?"

As quickly as he could, Jack explained everything that he had seen.

"Crazy." Mo smiled once Jack finished. "Sounds fun though."

"Do you think it is something to do with Alika?"

"Probably. She is evil enough to worry about. And she has the Crown now so is going to be very powerful as well."

Jack sighed thoughtfully, his eyes unfocusedly taking in the sinking sun.

"Alectus!" He said sharply. "We need to get back to Edenvale before he does or we will be in big trouble."

Mo took the lead, jogging steadily on the route back to Edenvale. Jack followed doggedly behind. They ran past the sweet shop... past the houses where Dr. Nabielle and Alectus were meant to live... up the steep hill to the forest edge... over the Monarch's Mark, now covered in the bright pavilions that they had set up, and finally back to Alectus' treehouse. All the time, Jack kept peering over his shoulder, worried that Alectus would be behind them and see the pair running back. However, all the way to the treehouse, he didn't see a single person or Alforn. Mo banged hard on the door, and they heard Ember coming down the ramp in her wheelchair.

When Ember pulled the door open, Jack was startled to see that she was in a green dress that she must have bought in Teraturt.

"Cheers." Mo said, entering the treehouse.

Ember didn't seem to notice; she was staring fixatedly at Jack. What she wanted, he couldn't guess.

"Umm... thanks." He said awkwardly. She let the door slam behind him.

"You won't guess what we saw in Teraturt!" Mo said, pulling his shoes off. Ember didn't reply.

When he looked up, Mo quickly changed tack, "I'll be in my room." He said, disappearing up the stairs.

Jack stood frozen, all too aware of Ember's eyes on him. Several moments passed. She wanted him to say something but the awkwardness that the pair had felt on Earth seemed back in full force. "Well what we saw in Teraturt..." Began Jack, hoping to thaw the atmosphere.

"I don't care what you saw in Teraturt!" Ember shouted, turning her wheelchair around and running over Jack's foot on her way back up the ramp.

Jack stood still, more lost than he had been in his life.

Eventually, he headed up the stairs to Mo's room. "Did you hear that?" Jack said dejectedly, sitting down on his friend's bed.

"Yeah." Mo replied sympathetically.

"I just don't understand."

"You'll work it out."

"Yeah." Jack sighed. "Some day far, far in the future..."

Alectus returned a few minutes later. Ember was the first downstairs and opened the door for him. "Wow, that is the perfect dress for the dance." He smiled.

"Thank you!" Ember replied loudly and Jack was reminded of the Highstreet where everything was slightly over the top in order that it was noticed.

"I need to go and change, and you two as well." He added, pointing at Jack and Mo as they arrived at the door.

"We don't have anything smart though..."

"You should, I put a suit in both your wardrobes a couple of days ago."

"Thanks." Said the two boys before heading up to their rooms.

"Don't think I have opened my wardrobe in the last couple of days to be fair." Mo grinned as he entered his room.

"Charming."

CHAPTER 3: THE DARKEST DAY DANCE

The blue suit Jack found in his wardrobe annoyed him, he felt that Alectus should have asked before going into his room and putting stuff in his wardrobe. But it didn't seem worth the hassle to complain about it so instead Jack added it to the pile of frustrations he had towards his father.

"WHAT HAVE YOU DONE?" Alectus' voice echoed up the stairs just as Jack began tying his tie. Worried that he was in trouble, maybe Alectus had found out about them going to Teraturt, Jack dashed down the stairs.

It quickly became apparent what the problem was, and Jack was relieved. He saw Mo standing in a red suit, but the trousers were slashed at the knees.

"I don't want to look like everyone else." Mo shrugged.

"Urggg..." Alectus growled with frustration. "Well, I suppose it is all done now and we should get a move on or we'll be late as well as untidy." He said, opening the door so fast that Jack was surprised that the hinges didn't break.

Jack, still trying to tie his tie, followed Alectus out the door. Ember soon raced past him, matching Alectus' pace at the front of the party. She looked far less enthusiastic than Jack had expected. Slightly guiltily, he remembered that her lack of enthusiasm probably stemmed from whatever she had gotten angry with him about earlier.

"I know that Ember bit you head off for saying it, but you

were right..." Mo whispered in Jack's ear.

"About what?"

"There will be loads of food."

Jack broke into a smile, at least Mo had something to look forwards to.

They were among the first to arrive at the Monarch's Mark, the few Alforn already there were all young families, although even the children were close to six foot with shoulders the same width as a bear's.

For the time being, the youngsters had total monopoly over the dancefloor, and the band were still setting up, so Mo and Jack settled into a comfy pair of chairs around a table laden with food. Ember took one, disapproving look at them before wheeling off.

Jack kept half an eye on her, watching her circle the party, pretending to examine the pavilions and check that they were set up correctly. It was obvious that she had nothing to do and simply wanted to appear busy. Eventually, once she had triple-checked everything, Ember wheeled reluctantly over to the boys. They looked at each other but Ember showed no interest in joining in the conversation and soon even Jack and Mo stopped talking, it felt too awkward to ignore the frostiness that was heavy in the air.

Jack could hear Alectus' voice through the general murmur of conversation. "More madness going on in the Government, the King has approved the cancellation of the Cart network, apparently it is too expensive and energy draining. I can try and speak to him about when he comes to Teraturt next week but can't imagine he will listen to me."

"While it is quite absurd, it hardly affects us, does it? It isn't like we can order a cart and head off." Replied the Alforn that Alectus was speaking to.

"I suppose not." Alectus sighed. "Still, I am losing count of all the silly decisions being made."

The Alforn turned away.

"It is almost enough to make me wonder if Dr. Nabielle is, as usual, right." Alectus muttered to himself. Jack sat up and saw that Mo had been listening just as intently as himself, they exchanged a look. Even Alectus was beginning to think that there was something suspicious going on with the King.

Jack tried to catch Ember's eye, but she still resolutely refused to acknowledge his existence.

So the trio sat in silence. Jack began longing for the relationship that they had all shared in the Wilderness.

Thankfully, people soon began to show up, both the children who had come to Arcane from the Orphanage and the Alforn who lived in Edenvale. Tom came to sit with Mo and Jack, thawing the frosty tension like a fire. Many of his friends came with him and some even began speaking with Ember although most kept their distance from her – remembering her as the stern, authoritative leader that she had often been a month earlier.

Right on time, the band of Alforn began to play. Of course, neither Jack nor Mo had heard any of the Alforn music, it was very different to anything Jack had heard before. The lead singer was a giant even among Alforn, probably ten-foot-tall and, unsurprisingly sang with more power and energy than Jack had ever seen before. Also, presumably because of her vast lungs, she was able to hold notes far longer than humans which gave, to Jack's ears, the music a unique twist.

The flow of Alforn arrivals didn't slow for the next two hours. Jack watched with a smile as many of the Alforn headed straight to Lord Alectus and asked him to dance. He didn't have a break, going relentlessly from one partner to the next. Still, he danced with a smile on his face non-stop.

Soon, the moon was out and shining bright. The stars

were quick to join it with their own cold light. The music had become louder and faster, frequently punctuated by jovial shouts and screams.

"Did you really fight Carsicus?" A voice demanded suddenly.

Jack looked around and saw an Alforn almost as short as himself, which meant he was probably six or seven years old.

"Yeah." Jack replied simply.

"What happened?" The young Alforn asked curiously, beckoning some of his friends over to listen as well.

"Umm... well we knew that Carsicus wanted to destroy the Amulet, so we just held him off long enough for Alectus to come and stop him."

The Alforn all looked slightly let down.

"Oh c'mon!" Mo laughed before launching into a blow-by-blow account ever since they had arrived on Arcane.

"Wow!" gasped the crowd when Mo finally finished. "You sound really cool; do you want to play a game with us?" The first Alforn asked.

"Ok!" Mo said, looking interested.

"My name is Gally." Said the young Alforn.

Jack and Mo both followed Gally across the floor, which was rather dangerous as giant Alforn were waltzing around surprisingly fast.

Suddenly, realising that they had left Ember behind, Jack turned to look at her. She was glowering at him, and Jack instinctively dropped his gaze. He wished he knew what her problem was.

Bang! Jack was knocked over like a bowling pin. In his distraction, a particularly huge Alforn had crashed into him. The Alforn pulled him back to his feet, almost wrenching his arms out of their sockets as he did so.

"Thanks!" Jack gasped, his back and head aching from where he had fallen.

"Dangerous this." Smiled Mo, as he dodged another Alforn by a hair's breadth.

Eventually, without another collision but with several close shaves, they reached the pavilion with the games inside. Gally's friends were already there.

"Meet Elodie, Babble, Wallop, DJ, EZ, Tilday, Trixy and Micah." Gally sang. Jack blinked several times, trying to put eight names to eight identical faces.

A sudden motion in the corner of Jack's vision made him glance sharply towards it and he saw one of Gally's friends hurl a bright red ball at a tower of metal cans and half of them came down with a crash.

"Great job Trix." Gally said excitedly.

"Oh, that was nothing." Mo said with a competitive smile. "Surely you want to see how a real master does it."

Jack was relieved to see that the young Alforn seemed to get the innocent rivalry that Mo was setting up. They hurried over and reset the tower before giving the red ball to Mo.

Mo tossed the ball lightly from one hand to the other. Then he closed one eye and lined up the shot before grinning like a lunatic, turning his back, taking three large paces away from the cans and, with a quick look over his shoulder, throwing the ball like a missile at the base of the tower. The bottom can skidded across the table while the ones above it seemed to freeze in mid-air before crashing down onto the wooden surface below.

"Wow!" All the young Alforn whispered in unison, giving Mo nine strong high-fives.

"Your turn." They said, turning to Jack, already replacing

the tower. Jack went red, how could he possibly match what Mo had done?

"What are you doing playing children's games?" A voice asked from the edge of the pavilion.

Jack saw two Alforn girls standing there, they looked a year or so older than himself and Mo but short for their age (still a good six inches taller than Jack though).

"Just showing them how it's done." Mo smiled, taking the ball from Babble.

The two girls stood still, not sure what to say to that.

"Are you going to stay here and watch, or would you rather go and dance?" Mo said, unable to keep the mischievous look out of his eyes.

"Hey, dancing sounds good." One of the Alforn said in mock surprise to her friend.

"Let's go." Mo smiled, turning and throwing the ball into the tower and once again causing all the metal cups to crash onto the table. He let the Alforn lead him out of the tent.

Which left Jack with her friend.

Screwing up his courage, Jack managed to gasp. "You want dance?" In his best Arcanian.

"Yes please!" She said enthusiastically and Jack felt a little more at ease.

Copying Mo's example, he let her lead him out of the tent and onto the dancefloor.

"Ok, do what I do." She said, looking far more self-assured than Jack felt.

It was like being caught inside a tornado alongside a speaker, the music was playing, and Jack was twirled and spun, pulled and pushed with the beat. Every step, he thought that he was going to end up on the floor on his backside, but his partner always seemed to just about keep within his limitations and Jack found himself smiling, his awkward self-awareness slipping away. It felt as though he became one with that sweaty mass of people dancing and laughing within the clearing.

Time flew past, at some point, he and Mo swapped partners and at another he tripped headlong over some old Alforn's outstretched foot. However, when the music began to quieten, Jack was alarmed at how much he had wanted to continue.

"What's happening?" Mo asked as he slipped his way through the crowd towards Jack.

"Not too sure. Is someone getting up on stage?"

"Yeah it's Dr. Nabielle. She isn't that far away, how can't you tell that that is her?"

"I can never make out..." Jack began but was cut off when Dr. Nabielle began speaking from the podium.

"Hello, hello, hello!" She called out to the crowd.

"Lelho!" One Alforn shouted back before staggering sideways and toppling onto the floor.

"Is he ok?"

"Yeah, it's just Ulwell. Had too much to drink again."

"Just help me to my feet." The man on the floor gasped. "And then grab me another drink, there's a good lad, another drink's what I need – that'll sort me out."

"Well I can see at least one of you is having a good evening." Dr. Nabielle said from the front, her eyes glittering. "And I hope that the rest of you are enjoying it just as much just ... in a different sort of way."

There were plenty of nods from the Alforn around Jack.

"Good. Well as you know, someone has to give a speech

every year at these things, and I am delighted that you chose me for the … seventh year in a row." There was scattered laughter at this. "But seriously I thank you for choosing me, just don't do it again because I will have run out of things to say." Again, a general snicker from the crowd. "But this year I do have something very important to say to certain people."

The crowd went quiet, caught by surprise. There had never been anything important said in these speeches before.

"Firstly, sometimes fate calls on one person and requires of them far more bravery and sacrifice than those around them." Jack felt that just for a moment her eyes turned to him. "It also has a curious trick of choosing just the right person for its task."

Before Jack could turn to Mo and say anything, Dr. Nabielle continued.

"Secondly, the line between protection and possession is blurred and all too easily stepped over and sometimes the only way to keep something is to not be possessive of it."

What did that mean?

"And finally, Ulwell, you really do not need another drink."

There was a significant pause before the laughter this time as though the crowd needed some time to leave their state of deep concentration and realise that something amusing had been said.

Whilst her audience were remembering themselves, Dr. Nabielle left the stage, using their distraction to leave unnoticed.

"Crazy!" Jack laughed.

"Was a bit." Agreed Mo.

The two boys distractedly made their way back to where they had been sitting earlier. Ember was still there.

"Would you honour me with a dance?" A smooth voice said from nearby, as Jack and Mo sat down. The speaker was a skinny male Alforn probably seven-foot-tall. For a moment, Jack was a bit startled but then realised that the Alforn wasn't looking at him, he was looking at Ember.

Ember gave Jack a hard, critical look. He nodded and smiled encouragingly, and Ember turned, allowing the Alforn to lead her off into the midst of the dancing couples. Jack watched her go and saw that she didn't look as happy as he would have expected. In fact, if anything, she appeared frustrated.

He watched closely. The dance turned Ember abruptly towards him. Jack grinned towards her. He was happy that she was finally getting to dance, the thing that she had been most looking forwards to for two days now. But she didn't return his smile. If anything, it only antagonised her further.

Suddenly, a theory that would explain Ember's unexpected actions towards him formed in Jack's head. It made him flush with embarrassment. Needing a distraction, Jack got quickly to his feet and started wandering around, looking at the Alforn playing the games that he had helped set up. But he couldn't concentrate on that... What if Ember had wanted him to ask her to dance... Jack messed his hair up and then flattened it, fidgeting like Mo.

He needed a distraction...

Suddenly, he noticed lights flashing randomly and brightly far in the distance. His prayers had been answered.

Quickly, he hurried back towards Mo. They had something to investigate.

CHAPTER 4: SHADOW

When Jack returned to the group, he saw that Mo was deep in conversation with Tom. One thing that Jack was certain of was that Tom was not going to come with them.

Unable to think of any other plan, Jack spotted Ember in the midst of the dancing couples and pushed his way towards her.

"Can you talk to Tom quickly for me? Distract him." He said when he finally reached her.

"Why?" She asked, clearly surprised that Jack had broken their unwritten pact of silence towards each other.

"Please, please just trust me. It's important."

Ember looked straight at him, and Jack had a feeling she was seeing more than just his face. "Ok." She said quietly.

It only took a moment for her to cross over and distract Tom. Jack swooped in, tapping Mo on the shoulder. "C'mon, we need to go check something out."

"Whassat?"

"Flashing lights in the East. They look like they might be Sceptre's."

"Let's go grab Ember and have a look." Mo smiled.

"It might be easier if we do it with just the two of us." Jack said awkwardly.

Mo waited a moment, considering what Jack had said before shrugging and heading off towards the forest.

Checking over his shoulder, Jack saw Alectus dancing with a giant elderly Alforn whose grey hair tumbled the whole nine feet from her scalp to the floor. No one else was looking their way.

Excitement bubbling in his stomach, Jack followed Mo in slipping away out of the firelit clearing and into the silent darkness of the forest. A heart-beat quickening sense of danger began to build in Jack's stomach as they crept through the forest. Neither of the boys made a sound on the loamy floor.

After a few minutes, the ground suddenly seemed to fall away beneath Jack's foot and a second later, he withdrew it and realised it was dripping wet.

"I think we are at Paradise Lake." Mo whispered. "This is where the Alforn normally play Barge-Board."

"In the nick of time." Jack whispered sarcastically back.

They were careful to skirt a fair distance from the edges of the Lake before continuing towards the Sceptres flashing in the distance.

"How much further?" Mo asked eventually, his voice a whisper even though there was no obvious reason to keep their voices down.

"Not far, I think. Yeah look!" Jack whispered excitedly back, pointing to where the lights had appeared once more, streaking through the darkness at the top of the next hill. They hurried towards the streaking flashes of light... up the steep hillside below the lines... the trees were thinner on the hilltop, so Jack and Mo watched from the denser forest a little lower down, lying on the floor so that they were all but invisible in the deep darkness of the forest.

Four sceptres were fighting: An aggressive green, a menacing, midnight blue and a sinister scarlet were all swinging against the fourth, against a foe terrifyingly dark and powerful, a sceptre so black it drained the night of colour.

The shadow holding the stygian blade moved faster than a striking snake, blocking all three blades in turn as they attacked.

The shadow darted forwards and with a harsh grunt, the green light went out. The blue and scarlet seemed to back off. Jack and Mo remained frozen.

As one, the scarlet and blue rimmed sceptres swung at the shadow who slipped easily out of the way. Jack saw the blue rimmed sceptre smash into the black and then get wrenched from its master's hand. Now only the scarlet sceptre remained in the fight against the shadow. One, two, three strokes the shadow parried and then with frightening ease slipped behind the owner of the scarlet sceptre and ripped the weapon from their grasp.

Now that the sceptre lights had dulled, it seemed to Jack that the night became suddenly very dark and very cold.

Beckoning for Mo to follow him, Jack began to sneak towards the hilltop, hoping to see more clearly the nature of the shadow and its foes.

"Stop skulking out there and come sit with us." The shadow growled in Arcanian from the clearing. "Otto, set a light overhead."

A ball of scarlet etter suddenly appeared over the shadow and Jack saw for the first time that it was a man with shoulders like a bull. "Come, sit." The shadow said once more.

Jack thought about running but knew the speed of this shadow and that to flee would be folly so instead he put his head back and strode into the clearing, hoping that no one could hear his heart hammering beneath his chest. Praying that his faux-confidence would trick the shadow into thinking he had back up.

"Your friend can come too." Growled the shadow and Jack saw Mo emerge from the clearing.

The owner of the black Sceptre was a shadow no longer. He had a tough face and arms scratched and scarred in lines Jack knew had been drawn by the Sceptre's of previous foes. It was the eyes more than anything that spoke of a battle-hardened character though, dark brown like mud but with the hardiness of stone.

Still trying to bluff confidence, Jack started up. "What were you doing fighting up here?"

The shadow stared at him, and Jack felt the shadows ferocious eyes boring into his soul like a spiritual drill, searching and finding his fear and once it had been found, Jack soon looked away.

"Just like your father." The shadow growled and for the first time Jack realised he spoke with a lisp. "He would stick his nose where it doesn't belong and demand to know what I was doing without respect."

"What were you doing up here though?" Asked Mo. Jack glanced nervously across at his friend, to push the matter with a man this brutal seemed stupid.

Again, the shadow stared hard at Mo who refused to look away. For the first time, the shadow's face showed some flicker of emotion. What the emotion was, Jack couldn't tell.

"We were sparring. Keeping our reactions sharp." Rumbled the answer eventually.

"You mean you weren't really fighting?"

"Just practicing... just practicing." The man said flexing his fingers. "Now sit, you are making the place look untidy."

Feeling more than a little awkward, Jack took a seat on the ground.

"I'd have thought Lord Alectus' son would have the manners to introduce himself." Said the owner of the black Sceptre after a pause.

Slightly abashed, Jack said quickly "Yes, sorry, my name is Jack, and this is Mo. "

"I am Shadow." Said the shadow, "And these spoilt incompetents that I was sparing with are Otto, Jacob and Marieta." The three others raised their hands in turn and didn't appear to show any objection to being referred to as 'spoilt incompetents'.

"I didn't know that there were other people in... OWWWWW!" Jack squealed as Shadow stomped on his foot. "What was that for?!?"

"Stay here." Shadow growled at the others. "You. Follow me." He said pointing at Jack. Nervously, Jack followed Shadow a fair distance away from the others except for Mo who followed closely behind.

"This is why I hate children. They never use even the little brains they have." Shadow muttered under his breath as soon as they were out of hearing range. "And I thought I told you to stay over there." He added, pointing at Mo who shrugged. "Are you just going to talk about Edenvale in front of everyone you met? I imagine that Lord Alectus, arrogant git that he is, at least told you that talking loudly about Edenvale is an idiotic thing to do. Been kept a secret for thousands of years but tell a child where it is, and it remains hidden for less than a month."

"Oh yeah." Jack said, feeling slightly embarrassed.

"How comes you know about Edenvale then?" Mo asked Shadow.

"Dr. Nabielle showed me as part of a deal. Great woman she is..." Shadow said open-endedly. Then, regaining his normal demeanour, turned to Jack, "If you are going to start using your brain half as much as your mouth then you can come sit with us. And remember, mention Edenvale to no adults other than me, Alectus and Dr. Nabielle or I'll have to slap some sense into you."

"Yes sir." Jack said immediately.

Shadow grunted dismissively.

When they got back, the three others were huddled in a group and the quick silence that suddenly fell between them made Jack certain that they had just been talking about him.

Sensing the pause, the boy with the scarlet sceptre stepped forwards, he was tall and athletic with short hair spiked up like a scrubbing brush. "Hey, my name's Otto. I'm a final year at the University."

"The where?" Mo asked. Jack heard Shadow sigh.

"The University." Olivia said loudly, clearly thinking that Mo had misheard.

"I didn't know that there was a University in Arcane." Jack said, trying to keep the conversation rolling.

Again, Shadow groaned. "Thought you said you were going to start using your brain." He whispered. "Sorry, Jack and Mo here are from a very quiet village so have probably never heard of the University." He told the others.

"Lord Alectus' son has never heard of the University?" Otto said in surprise.

"That's what I just said you deaf dimwit. Should've clobbered you over the head when we were sparing, would've cleared some of the earwax out."

Otto tilted his head to the side thoughtfully but didn't push the point.

"I'm Marieta." Said the short, freckly girl whose dark blue sword hung by her side. "I also go to the University, studying English."

Jack looked at Shadow, he was very confused but didn't want to say anything that would result in a sharp comment.

"Same for me." Said the other person in the group. "

'cept my name is Jacob not Marietta."

"Basically, they're a load of spoilt softie's who live in Teraturt and they can all leave now." Said Shadow. "Before Jack says anything else stupid." He added in a whisper.

"Why were you sparing at night-time?" Mo asked as the others moved away, his voice more curious than accusatory.

"Less chance of people coming across us and skulking around to watch. Takes a special type of nosey to come all the way up here in the dark then hide behind a tree and watch."

"We didn't come here on purpose. We were just a bit bored at the Darkest Day Dance."

"No one willing to dance with you. Can't say I am surprised."

"Don't see anyone dancing with you tonight either." Mo pointed out.

"Dancing is just fighting without the chance to hurt people." Shadow growled, putting his sword away. His voice left no doubt that the opportunity to hurt people was a major bonus to any sport.

Even Mo didn't know what to say to that and there was a moment's silence.

But then Shadow spoke again, and the normal hardness of his voice faded a little, "I used to dance when I was younger to improve my footwork." Then Shadow shook himself and his voice became heartless once more, "that was a long time ago. I was young and stupid, didn't know the first thing about life. Bit like you two. Dr. Nabielle was saying that she reckoned you would go along with her plan in a heartbeat."

"What plan?"

"Can't tell you. Dr. Nabielle insists that we wait for A-lectus to agree to it first. Which means we will be waiting for him to kick the bucket because he'll keep you wrapped up in cotton wool the whole time like all parents do."

"**EINOR!** What are you telling him?" A voice called sharply from across the clearing.

Jack turned and saw Lord Alectus. His heart dropped. Now he really was going to be in trouble.

"I haven't told the kid anything." Replied Shadow lazily.

"Jack, what has he been telling you? If he has said anything that he shouldn't have..." Alectus continued as he crossed over towards the trio.

"What are you going to do? Have a go? You won't do anything..." Shadow said, still looking relaxed but Jack noticed that he tightened his grip on his black sceptre.

"Why would I waste my time with a washed up junky like you?"

"You have always thought you are so much better than me, haven't you?"

"Yeah, because I am." Said Lord Alectus weakly. "Right, come on you two, we are leaving."

"Why should I?" Mo asked, crossing his arms.

Jack looked frightenedly between his father and his best friend. Too scared to do anything else, Jack went over to Lord Alectus. Mo, looking slightly disappointed, followed Jack.

Alectus set the pace, clearly enraged. Jack was beginning to feel very tired but knew that Alectus was going to insist on a full explanation before he was going to be allowed to go to bed.

Soon, Jack was leaning on Mo for support because he was so exhausted. Of course, if Alectus turned back and saw his son unable to keep up he would help him home, but Jack didn't want his help. He wasn't going to allow anyone to feel sorry for him.

Even despite Mo's help, Jack found it harder and harder

to keep up. Only anger and frustration with himself kept him pushing onwards. They walked past the clearing where the Monarch's Mark stood. They could hear the music and joyous shouting voices. Even if he had been allowed, Jack had zero wish to go and join in.

As soon as they were back in the dining room of Alectus' treehouse, the shouting started.

"Why? How? How could you possibly think that disappearing off was a good idea? What if you had gotten lost? What if... if..."

"If we had actually had a good time without adults trying to stop us?" Said Mo who Jack was alarmed to see wore the expression of someone going to battle.

Alectus fell silent with anger as if there were too many impassioned replies that they were caught up in the bottleneck that was his throat. Eventually, he managed, "Go, get out! Go to the hospital, Dr. Nabielle will look after you for this evening. We will find somewhere new for you to stay from tomorrow. You are not welcome in my house anymore."

"You can't send him away!" Jack shouted.

"No! I won't have it; he is rude, and he is a bad influence on you, always taking you towards danger."

"It was me who saw the lights, Mo didn't even do anything except come with me."

"I don't care." Growled Alectus. "Get out..." He said, pointing at Mo.

"No..." Began Jack once more but Mo put his hand on his friends' shoulder.

"Look, it's fine, I don't want to stay here anyway. I'll spend tonight at the hospital with Dr. Nabielle." Said Mo. And then, whispering in Jack's ear so that Alectus couldn't hear, "And I will ask her about the plan that Shadow mentioned. She wants to tell us anyway."

"I'll come with you." Jack replied.

"No, you need to be here. Make sure that Alectus is out of the way." Mo whispered back. All the time Alectus looked down at Mo through his nose.

Jack sighed in agreement.

"I don't want to see you come through my front door ever again." Called Alectus as Mo left and headed through the woodland towards the hospital. In return, Mo put up a hand gesture as he walked away.

Jack and Alectus stood in silence for several minutes, both attempting to work out what to say. "Should we sit down?" Alectus suggested eventually.

Jack instantly felt relieved that he was speaking at a normal volume.

Carefully, he took a seat, not taking his eyes off Alectus.

"I know that you think I have been a bit over-protective." Alectus began. Jack scoffed, he felt that was an understatement. "It is just that I want to keep you safe."

Not a very sincere apology, thought Jack.

"But now that Mo is gone, hopefully you will stop doing dangerous things. That boy is a bad influence."

Jack bolted to his feet before storming away, up the spiral ramp, blood pounding in his ears like a battle drum. He couldn't hear any of Alectus' shouts to come back. His father could annoy him with belittlements and pedantic controlling. But he wasn't going to get away with calling Mo a 'bad influence'. This had been building for weeks now, it seemed as though everything that Alectus did, everything he said was designed with the sole purpose of annoying Jack as much as possible.

Insane with rage, Jack punched a tree wall with every

sinew of muscle in his arm. Pain shot up his hand, one of his knuckles had broken for sure. Jack felt wetness forming on his lower eyelids and that only made him angrier.

Suddenly, light spilled onto the landing as Ember opened her door. "What did you punch the wall for?"

"Oh, Ember." Jack sighed, needing someone willing to understand him. He stepped towards her.

"Stay there." She said, her voice sharp. "Don't come any closer."

The intense cold in her voice froze Jack in his tracks. "But I need to talk to someone..." He said sadly.

"Oh, you need some attention, do you? Someone to care enough about you to see what you want? I do wonder what that would feel like..." Every syllable was bubbling and bursting with red sarcasm.

"What do you... oh..." Jack said, cottoning on.

"Yeah, finally." Ember said, slamming her door. Jack crept towards it, putting his ear against the frame. He could hear the unmistakable sound of weeping. It made him sick with shame.

"Oh, Ember." He said to himself as he returned to his room and collapsed on his bed.

He missed Mo. He had ruined his relationship with his father. But worst of all was Ember, he had treated her so badly; firstly the Dance, he hadn't paid close enough attention to see the blindingly obvious evidence that she had wanted him to ask her, then, when he had realised, he had been too cowardly to ask her. Worse than that, he hadn't even faced it in any way other than looking for a distraction. Finally, worst of all, she should have come with them to the lights in the distance. They were a team; him, Mo and Ember and he had used her to distract Tom so that he could satisfy his own need for adventure.

Jack didn't find sleep until sunrise, kept awake all night by a cocktail of shame and pain, his knuckle was agonising.

CHAPTER 5: THE FINAL FALL BEFORE THE BOUNCE

"Bwoah!" Exclaimed Jack as he spluttered awake.

He sat up from his drenched pillow to see Ember looking at him. Weird dream.

He went to pinch himself. "Ahh!" He gasped; his knuckle felt like it was on fire.

"You are awake." Ember said, breaking into a smile. "Can I sit on your bed?"

"Yeah." Jack replied, slightly surprised but scooting to one corner as Ember pulled herself onto the middle of the bed.

"I am so sorry. I have been a..." Jack began.

"Yeah, you have a bit."

"Sorry."

"It's alright. Water under the bridge."

"Water under the what?"

Ember laughed and rolled her eyes. "Water under the bridge. It means it is all done, we can move on."

"Ok, right, because the water has moved past the bridge."

"Yeah, exactly. I made some breakfast if you want some."

Jack hesitated – he still felt a little guilty about accepting anything from Ember so soon after last night.

"C'mon." Ember said as she slid back onto her wheelchair. "What did I *just* say?"

"Ok, water under the bridge." Jack agreed. "I would love some breakfast."

"So, what did happen in Teraturt?" Ember asked with a cheeky smile as they headed down the spiral ramp.

As Jack explained everything that he and Mo had seen, he had to fight the urge to jump for joy at the return of Ember to the person that she had been in the Wilderness.

Alectus arrived downstairs soon after, he must have heard the talking voices. "Dr. Nabielle convinced me to let Mo back." He said, looking less than delighted.

"Yeah she did!" Said a familiar voice from the doorway, Jack turned to see his best friend striding into the room, his endearing, crooked smile spread from ear to ear.

At once, Jack's joy became mixed with anger that Alectus appeared to find no gladness in Mo's return to his home. His father was so obsessed with keeping him safe, he seemed unable to look out for his happiness or the happiness of those closest to him.

Jack did not say any of these things as he regarded Alectus, instead he added them to that steadily growing pile of frustrations that he held towards his father.

"Well, I need to leave for work now." Said Alectus. The clipped tone of his voice grated Jack's ears and make his blood boil once more. There was a vindictive sense of pleasure as Jack heard the door close. Then, Jack heard a rattle and a click.

"No. Surely not." Ember muttered under her breath, wheeling over to the door. She pushed down the handle and leant against the door. It didn't move. She pushed harder and it still did not budge. "It's locked." She muttered.

"Let me have a go." Said Mo, crossing the room towards

her. He tried and Jack could see his muscles straining as he put his back into trying to force the door open. Jack knew that if Mo couldn't open the door, he wouldn't have a chance. Suddenly, he spotted a seemingly blank piece of paper on the windowsill that hadn't been there last night. It was folded precisely and Jack knew at once it had been left there on purpose.

Interested, he unfolded it.

Door locked. You are only to leave the house under my supervision.

Alectus

"You've got to be joking me." Mo said shaking his head as he read the letter for the twentieth time. "Only allowed out under my supervision." He sighed, mimicking Alectus' voice. "I'm not going to let him tell me what to do." Mo said determinedly, trying to force the window open.

Jack joined in, trying to prise a different window open but to no avail.

The two boys moved randomly from one window to the next, testing them.

"Can you give us a hand?" Mo asked Ember, sounding irritated.

"It's not going to work."

"And why is that?"

"Have you met Alectus? Do you think that he is going to leave any stone unturned or rather any window unlocked when it comes to keeping Jack inside? You can bet he has triple-checked every possible way of getting out."

"Why do you always have to be right?" Jack sighed with a

trace of humour, sliding into a chair, and pulling his breakfast towards him. "Mate, just give up." He said, turning to Mo but Mo didn't seem to hear him.

Instead, he ran across the room to where the spare keys hung from the wall.

"Still not going to work!" Ember laughed, "you have to use them from the other side."

"Oh I can't wait to take that grin off your face." Mo muttered, crossing over to the black backpack that he had brought back with him from the hospital before rummaging around and pulling out a chunky black object.

"What? How did you get that? It was in my room..." Jack gasped because Mo had just pulled a Rec-Trec, Jack's birthday gift from Alectus, out of the bag.

"It's not yours you muppet. The Rec-Trec's basically all look the same. Now, how do I turn it on?" Mo asked, feeling around the sides for the on button.

"How'd you get it?"

"Present from an admirer."

"What?"

"Sarah came to the hospital last night and gave it to me."

"Who's Sarah?" Jack asked.

"One of the girls you were dancing with last night."

There was a loud snort and Jack turned to see Ember laughing. "You didn't even know what their names were!"

Jack shook his head.

"Ah! Got it!" Mo exclaimed as the Rec-Trec flickered into life. "Right, now we just need an enthusiastic volunteer."

"Come quickly, home alone and need some help." Mo read out as he typed.

"Oh no, you can't send that." Ember said at the same time as Mo pressed send.

"Now we wait and see." Mo smiled.

He had barely sat down when there came a hard knock on the door, "Mo, are you in there?" A voice called.

"Man, that was quick." He laughed, bolting back up to his feet.

"Yeah, I live three trees down. Oh, the door's locked."

"Yeah, we know."

"We?!?... Who else is in there?"

"Just Jack and Ember from last night." Mo replied casually.

Then, from the other side of the door they heard retreating footsteps. "What, where's she going?" Jack asked, perplexed.

"I don't think she wanted us here." Ember replied, pointing first at Jack and then at herself.

"Oh brilliant, now we are stuck." Jack sighed.

"Not necessarily." Mo grinned.

"What?"

"You'll see, oh you will see."

Mo returned to his bag and fished out a second Rec-Trec.

"Is that another..."

"Yep."

"Don't tell me you were given it by..."

"Yep. Anna, who was the other one we were dancing with..." Mo said, glancing at Jack. "...came and gave this to me about twenty minutes after Sarah had given me hers. Right, let's try this again, come quickly home alone and need some help."

Once again, the wait was no more than a minute until they heard knocking on the door.

"Hey, Mo, are you there?"

"Yeah, this stupid door is stuck for some reason. If I slide the keys under it, can you try unlocking it from that side?"

"Umm... ok." Came Anna's slightly confused voice from the other side as Mo slid the keys to her.

There was a rattling in the lock before the door swung open.

"Cheers." Said Mo.

"Thank you." Said Ember.

"What?" Anna gasped, seeing Jack and Ember. "What are they doing here?"

"Well, they live here." Mo replied shrugging.

"Fine. I'll see you around." Anna growled, throwing the keys back at Mo who caught them with ease.

As Anna stormed off, Jack caught Ember's eye and they broke into a huge, shared grin.

"Right. What's the plan?" Mo asked, looking very unperturbed by what he had just done.

"I would really like to go and meet Einor." Ember answered.

"Who is Einor?"

"That is Shadow's real name, Dr. Nabielle told me a bit about him."

"Why do you want to go and meet him?"

"Think about it, he knows Dr. Nabielle's plan and the only reason he didn't tell us yesterday is because he was meant to wait for Alectus to agree to it."

"Yeah so..."

"Well, if he and Alectus had an argument he probably isn't in the mood to be doing favours for Alectus."

"It's definitely worth a shot."

"Yeah, let's do it."

Still chortling to himself at how they had managed to get free, Jack walked between Mo and Ember, retracing the route that they had walked last night.

As they passed through the dense woodland, Jack realised that this was the very first time he had seen this bit of Edenvale in daylight, it seemed crazy that after so long trying to find it, he had explored only a small fraction of the forest. Maybe it was just because he knew that this wasn't an ordinary wood, but Jack did begin to feel in his stomach that this place was special, that these trees had seen so much of the world that they held a wisdom of their own deep within their bark. There was a sense of almost magisterial power too, a knowledge that this place had been here long before the creatures that called it home and it would still be standing when they had all gone.

"That's the hill where Carsicus is being held prisoner." Mo said pointing a few minutes later, interrupting Jack's thoughts.

"Where? I can't see him..." Said Ember.

"Well he is inside the hill isn't he?"

"I was only joking." Ember sighed. Jack realised that he had never heard Ember joke before. She must be in an even better mood than he realised.

Soon, they were walking up the hill where they had seen the Sceptre's the previous night.

"Wait, is Einor going to be here?" Jack asked as they climbed.

"Oh yeah, he can't exactly just live on this hilltop."

"Great. You lot are back." A grumpy voice said from behind them, and they turned to see Einor walking up with hill.

"What do you want?"

"Firstly, I just want to say that it is an honour to meet you sir." Ember said politely.

Einor spat on the ground. "Honour exists only in the minds of children and cretins." He growled. "Now what do you want?"

"I just wanted to ask about your reign as the Warrior of the World." Ember said in a soft voice. Jack and Mo looked at each other. Had they misheard?

Judging by Einor's reaction, they had heard just right. "How do you know about that?" His expression was not friendly.

"Dr. Nabielle told me." Ember explained and Jack was amazed at how strong her voice sounded.

Einor's expression softened slightly, and Jack remembered the admiration for Dr. Nabielle that Einor clearly held.

"Ok, if I tell you about my reign as Warrior of the World, will you leave me alone?"

"Yes." They all choroused.

Jack settled down into a comfortable position. Einor remained standing and Jack was once again reminded of how broad his shoulders were.

"So, the Warrior of the World is, in theory, the best fighter in Arcane. Each year, there is a competition where each of the seven Kingdoms within the Realm puts forwards a Champion and the winner of the competition, the Champion of Champions, takes on the Warrior of the World. And, if they win, they become the new Warrior of the World."

"I grew up in Sjor, the smallest of the Kingdom's. I was seventeen when I was chosen to be the champion for Sjor. A few months later, after winning the tournament, I took on the Warrior of the World."

"Did you win?"

"Yes." Einor replied and Jack was struck but how flat his voice sounded as though he couldn't have cared less about whether he had won or not. "Yes, I became the Warrior of the World before my eighteenth birthday. The youngest ever. I defeated three Champions of Champions before Vermhell beat me." Einor's voice was still firm and unexcited, simply stating facts but he did lift his arm up to show a thin scar running the whole way from his wrist to his shoulder.

"Did Vermhell do that?"

"Yes."

"It doesn't look like a sceptre cut to me."

"It wasn't. It was a whip."

An uncomfortable silence seemed to settle and make the clean midday sunlight seem out of place and disrespectful.

"Didn't you try and win it back, become Warrior of the World again?"

"No. I couldn't. I had to flee. There was a lordship offered for anyone who captures and kills me. Still is actually."

If this information bothered Einor, he didn't show it.

"Was there no one you left behind? No one you cared about?" Ember asked softly.

"Only one. But I killed him before we left."

"Bit of a strange decision." Mo grinned, clearly thinking that Einor was joking.

With a motion so fast that it seemed a blur, Einor extended an arm and slapped Mo hard around the face. Mo got up quickly rubbing his cheek but with a firmness in his eyes. "Sorry. I didn't realise." He said and Einor stared at him hard before nodding.

"How... How... If you don't mind me asking... How did it

happen?" Mo stammered.

"No." Said Alectus and there was a tremor of fear in his voice. This was a man who showed no fear in the fact that a lordship was promised to whoever could kill him and yet the memory of what had happened evidently filled him with terror.

Jack was at a loss of what to say, what to do, so he just sat there staring at the floor. Trying to imagine what could have happened that would reduce Einor to fearful silence.

"Einor, could you tell us the plan that you mentioned yesterday?" Mo asked.

"So that's why you came – I did wonder. I didn't tell you yesterday because I had agreed to wait until Alectus agreed to the plan but, right now, I could not care less what that posh, stuck-up snob wants so I don't see why not... fire."

"What?"

"FIRE!" Repeated Einor, pointing and Jack saw that there were bright red flames at the top of a hill on the other side of Edenvale.

"You three stay here. I have to go and put it out. We can't risk people from Teraturt seeing it and coming to investigate, there is too high a chance of them discovering Edenvale."

With that, Einor dashed into the forest. There was a split-second when Jack looked at the two others before they all darted after Einor, chasing him down the hill and into the woodland. Immediately, the gap between Jack and Mo started to grow rapidly. No matter how hard Jack pushed his legs, Mo just got further and further away. In turn, Ember was rapidly falling behind him.

"Jack!" She shouted. He didn't want to turn around, he needed to keep Mo in sight. "Jack!" She shouted again and, remembering the day before, he glanced a look over his shoulder to see that she was beckoning him backwards.

He made the decision quickly, he decided to trust that Ember understood the situation and needed him to come back so, reluctantly, he turned and ran over to her.

"What?" He panted.

"Look, carefully, over there, the hill where Carsicus is being held prisoner."

"I can't see anything." Jack murmured back. But then he saw a dark patch move on the slope. "What is that?"

"I don't know. But we need to go and find out. Everyone from Edenvale will have seen the fire by now and be putting it out. We are probably the only ones who are seeing *this*."

Knowing that she was right, Jack now began running away from the fire and towards the hill. He could hear Ember only a little way behind. Unlike on the loamy surface in the woods, on the grassy planes she was not too much slower than him.

As they drew closer to the prison, the black shape became clearer but still Jack couldn't work out exactly what it was. Then it lifted a large piece of skin which Jack realised was a wing and his brain formulated the rest of the creature, it was a crow but nearly fifteen-foot-tall and with the wingspan of a small plane. Jack saw that it was using its huge feet to dig out the side of the hill, each of its talons were spades. Already there was a hollow like a bomb-crater.

Suddenly, the creature turned to face Jack. With a start, Jack saw that its eyes were golden, just like Carsicus'. This creature must be one of Carsicus' Rafiki's trying to free him!

"It's almost through. We have to stop it." Ember gasped as she reached Jack. No sooner were the words out of her mouth than the bird's foot slipped, and Jack saw that it had finally gotten the whole way through the hillside.

The sight of Carsicus climbing out of the side of the hill, his hands in Andagaldur cuffs but now climbing into freedom made Jack snap and before he knew what he was doing, he was tearing across the ground. Carsicus was now totally in the open air. Jack put on an extra burst of speed. He saw Carsicus get onto the crow's back. The crow spread its wings and begin to leave the ground. With a guttural scream, Jack threw himself at the creature's legs, reaching them just before they flew out of reach. The extra weight made the crow lurch dangerously to the side.

Carsicus began leaning down, trying to get into a position to prise Jack's hands off but there was no need, Jack could already feel his hands slipping... slipping... and then he was falling.

The ground screamed up towards him and then the world went black.

CHAPTER 6:
THE PLAN

'Oh. Not again.' Was Jack's instant thought when he woke because he was once more lying in the hospital with Dr. Nabielle, Alectus, Ember and Mo around his bedside.

"I can't believe you actually tried to fly on a massive crow."

Jack groaned; in the light of day, it didn't seem like the best decision. He rolled over and realised that his body felt-fine, Dr. Nabielle had once again used her almost magical level of healing to fix him.

"What were you doing up there anyway?" Alectus asked.

"We wanted to see Einor and find out what the plan was."

Alectus gave a growl of frustration. "So this is your fault." He said, turning to Dr. Nabielle. "Before your plan even starts it has placed Jack into a nearly fatal situation."

"Yes, and if it never starts, we will all be in a totally fatal situation before the summer."

"There is **NO EVIDENCE** for that."

Dr. Nabielle didn't even give a verbal reply, just a disbelieving stare. Alectus looked around him, as if looking for someone to back him up but, of course, nothing came. Instead, he turned to Jack, "And how could you be so stupid as to leave the house **AGAIN**?"

"You don't own me; I should be allowed to leave the house

when I want. I am my own person."

"You're my son."

"I wish I wasn't. Although let's face it, I barely am. I didn't see you for my first thirteen years of life. Because of you, I grew up in an Orphanage. I grew up alone." All the anger and frustration that had been building towards Alectus for a month now had culminated in this. "You left me to fend for myself, without family. I didn't even know what it felt like to be cared about until I met Mo. And for what? So you could come here and look for 'some clue about Conscience and Temptation'. You didn't even find anything!" Jack finished with a hysterical laugh.

Alectus seemed lost for words and despite the resentment Jack had built for his father, he was uncomfortable watching the pain that he was clearly inflicting. Alectus opened his mouth, but no sound came out.

Then, he spun on his back foot and stormed from the hospital into the surrounding forest.

Mo and Ember sat in stunned silence. Dr. Nabielle was watching Jack with great interest. "What are you going to do?" She asked.

"What do you mean?"

"Are you going to stay here or go after him?"

Jack didn't know. When he had first discovered that Alectus was his father, it had been the best feeling in the world, the first time he had known family, but there was too much anger there now, too much indignation. How had something so brilliant fallen apart so quickly?

"What should I do?" Jack asked Dr. Nabielle.

"Well, like everything in life, it depends if you care enough. If you want a relationship with Alectus badly enough, you need to go and talk with him, if not..."

But Jack was already out of the door sprinting through

the forest. He was going to keep his family. He cared enough. He hadn't said anything untrue, but he was willing to forgive all his complaints to keep his father in his life.

Jack didn't have to run far to find Alectus who was squatted against a tree looking at the forest canopy.

"Hello." Jack said timidly, clearly startling Alectus who had been too preoccupied with his own thoughts to hear Jack approach.

"Hello." Alectus replied, his voice just as uncertain as his son's. "I am sorry. I messed up. Dr. Nabielle was right, I wasn't just trying to protect you, I was trying to possess you."

"I messed up as well, I should have been more open with you. I'm sorry." Jack said, before sliding down the tree to sit next to Alectus. "Dad, I never asked, what happened with mum?" The question had played on Jack's mind for weeks, but he hadn't been able to bring himself to ask until now.

Alectus took a moment to answer. He wiped his eyes. "I don't know for certain, but I think she must have... passed on."

Jack felt his throat go dry and block any words that formed in its base.

With a gulp, Alectus continued, "You were a baby when Errion visited me and insisted that I come to Arcane and try to work out what was going on with the Amulet and the Crown. Your mother seemed a bit off, but it was only a week after you were born, I just assumed that she was exhausted. But maybe..." Another gulp, "maybe she didn't get better... her family were rich and respectable, not like me. I thought if I left your life then you would have a better future, with them, I never dreamed that they would leave you at the Orphanage, so I went with Errion to Arcane, hoping you could have a better life without me in it."

"What was she like?"

"I... I have never met anyone quite like her, she was the

cleverest person I knew. The bravest too and the kindest, she always, always put other people first. And she brought out the light in everyone, even the most torn up people seemed to come to life when they were around her."

After that, there was nothing more for Jack to ask because there was nothing else he wanted to hear. The blurred image of his mother that he had carried in his mind since childhood had been given some detail for the first time.

The afternoon became evening, and the woods became cold but still neither Jack nor Alectus moved and the animals in the wood seemed to be silent in solidarity with them. Only when evening slipped into night did Jack and Alectus stand without speaking and return to the hospital where Mo, Ember, and Dr. Nabielle were waiting for them.

Mo and Ember seemed unsure of what to say or do but Dr. Nabielle was wearing her biggest, brightest smile. "Wonderful, wonderful." She beamed. "You should probably get back into bed." She said, indicating Jack. "You are still on the mend, although I imagine you are quite bored of hearing that by now."

"Yeah, just a bit." Jack agreed but, nonetheless, returned to the bed.

"Alectus, time is running short, what do you say about telling them the plan now, both with and without your ... suggestions."

Alectus sighed. "I don't know. I... It just seems too risky."

"What would my mum have said?" Jack asked, looking Alectus straight in the eye. With a small, almost imperceptible, nod of the head, Alectus finally agreed to let Dr. Nabielle explain.

"Fantastic!" Said Dr. Nabielle giving Jack a broad grin. "I'll start and if you want to add anything at any point, Alectus, then please do."

"Well, as you know, the King is arriving in Teraturt in six days' time to meet Alectus and discuss thoroughly boring things. My plan is to ask him to allow you, Jack, to go to the University."

Jack looked at Mo and Ember, all surprised.

"Umm... and is that it?"

"Yes."

"It's just that we expected something a little more... complex I suppose." Ember explained.

"The more parts that there are to a plan, the more things that can go wrong."

"Fair enough."

"Dr. Nabielle, you haven't told them why they are going to the University."

"Oh, yes, I knew I had forgotten something. As you have probably already heard, there have been some most unusual decisions being made by the King over the last few days. So, the reason that we are sending you to the University is because we need someone that we can trust to keep an eye on him. It should be easy to keep track of who is talking to the King because there is a dome around the University so the students can't get in and out once term has started, so there are a limited number of people who can speak to him."

"The King is at University?"

"Yes."

"Strange."

"What subjects will we be studying?" Asked Ember, looking curious.

"Ah, yes, slight snag... er... Jack is going to be the only one who can actually study at the University."

"Why's that?"

"Well the University only let people in who can control etter in." Replied Dr. Nabielle apologetically, "people who can enter the second level of the Deep to be precise. Anyone less powerful as an etterician wouldn't be able to keep up in certain classes."

"I'm not hanging around here while Jack gets to go on an adventure!" Mo answered indignantly.

"Who said that you were staying around here? You two will go with him if he goes."

"But you just said only etтericians can go and Jack is the only one who can control etter."

"No, only etтericians can *study* at the University but every student has two servants to help them out, ironing their clothes, bringing up their food..."

"ARE YOU JOKING?!?" Mo gasped, his mouth falling open.

For a moment, Jack managed to contain his laughter, but it soon escaped him as he imagined Mo ironing his uniform for the evening.

Ten minutes later, Mo was still shaking his head and Jack was still cackling although his sides ached.

"Oh it's not that funny." Ember barked severely. Jack and Mo shared a look and managed to restrain their feelings at least for the moment. "What is Jack going to be studying and how are we going to get to the University?" Ember asked.

"Jack will be studying English because firstly that is what the King is studying and secondly because I would hope it won't require too much effort on his part. As to how you will get to the University..." Dr. Nabielle and Alectus looked at each other and Jack knew this was something they had discussed many times before, "the original plan was to take a cart the whole way to the University which would have been simple, easy and convenient. Unfortunately, as you may have heard, the King decided to disable the whole cart network yesterday, which means we will have to go on foot, and it is several weeks walk." Said Dr. Nabielle.

"And, to make matters worse, Carsicus has escaped." Added Alectus with a sigh.

"What does that have to do with anything?" Jack asked, more than a little confused.

"Well *if* there is someone who has the King's ear, Carsicus is as good a bet as anyone and if he has managed to guess our plan, he will be watching the path from here to the University."

"Carsicus knows the King?" Jack, Mo, and Ember exclaimed together.

The two adults nodded their heads, "Carsicus doesn't just know the King, they grew up together. Apparently, King Taigal calls Carsicus his big brother." Sighed Alectus.

"How did that happen?"

"A lot of children spend time at the Monarch's Court." Said Dr. Nabielle, "all the children of the Lords of Arcane and the children of the leaders of all the political parties, which did include the Kaofrelsi before they were exiled, are expected to have their education at the Monarch's Court. Carsicus' father was one of the Consuls of the Kaofrelsi, meaning Carsicus lived at court until his father died three years ago, when Carsicus took his place."

"What do you mean Consuls?"

"Consul is the highest rank within the Kaofrelsi, there are always two and at the moment, they are Alika and Carsicus."

"But that can't be right!" Ember said at once and everyone turned towards her.

"Why not?" Jack asked.

"Because of what you told me, remember, when Halmer was listening to Carsicus' conversation, Carsicus said that 'our glorious leader knows that the Amulet and Crown exist."

There was a moments silence before Jack spoke again, "that was a while ago now, I don't know maybe Halmer misheard."

"There have always been two Consuls leading the Kaofrelsi since Haldred fled into the Wilderness at the very start of the Second Age. There is no reason that they would have changed it since." Said Alectus.

"Anyway, maybe Carsicus was just referring to himself as 'the glorious leader,' it sounds like the sort of big-headed thing he would do." Said Mo and everyone burst into laughter, with the obvious exception of Dr. Nabielle who remained very still, the only noticeable change was that her face had drained of colour.

"Are you ok?" Jack asked suddenly, noticing the change that had come over her.

"You are sure you heard Carsicus say about a Glorious Leader?" Dr. Nabielle asked Ember again and there was an icy cold in her voice that killed everyone's laughter in their throats.

"Fairly. Why?"

"Because that was how Haldred styled himself when he ruled the Kaofrelsi."

"But that was hundreds of thousands of years ago."

"Haldred's body was never found and there were rumours that he had found some way of preserving life. At least that is what some of the deserters from his army said. None of them ever said what it was though, if they were asked, they would go white with fear. Many of them never spoke again."

It seemed to Jack that the wind began to howl outside and the room became a little darker. He found himself pulling his bed sheets up to his chin childishly.

"Are either of you coming with us?" Ember asked.

"I can't because people would talk if I left Teraturt and the last thing we want is to raise everyone's suspicions even further." Said Alectus.

"The original plan was that I would accompany you, I am head of Medicine at the University so need to be there for the start of term anyway. But, after what Ember said about Carsicus mentioning a Glorious Leader, I need to investigate. You won't be going alone though, Einor will go with you."

"Einor?" Jack asked in surprise.

"Well, he is one of the best fighters in the Realm so you should be safe with him."

Alectus let out a derisive snort. "Providing he doesn't ditch them in order to go searching for any Briar."

"What's Briar?"

"That potion stuff that Mo drank while we were in the Wilderness."

"Why would Einor ditch us to go and get some Briar?"

"Because he is an addict. He has been ever since he arrived here six months ago, just sits up on the hill drinking the stuff and occasionally fighting whoever he can find." Alectus said, making no effort to keep the spiteful sense of superiority from his voice.

The others all gave him strong disapproving looks and Alectus shrugged. "It's your decision."

Jack felt delighted at those words, Alectus allowing him to make an independent choice was something he had been dying for for ages.

"Although, you haven't yet heard my suggestion to the plan. I beg you consider it. It will make it so much safer."

No one answered for a moment and Alectus seized the

chance to press on.

"My proposition is that instead of brazenly asking the King to let Jack into the University, we are a bit cleverer, we situate someone in a concealed spot near to the King and then get them to fire at him."

"No way!" Jack said. "How would that even help?!?"

"Let me finish." Alectus said quickly. "The person we put there would miss on purpose. Then, straight away, Jack would help rush the King to safety, which would make the King feel very grateful to him and, when Jack asks to be allowed to go to the University, there won't be any question that the King will let him in!"

"But what about the person who fired at the King, surely they will be caught."

"Well, there is one person that should be safe, Einor." Said Alectus. "He will be able to battle his way out easily and it doesn't matter if people recognise him, he is an outlaw anyway."

There was a long silence once Alectus had finished speaking, everyone thinking hard.

"I prefer Dr. Nabielle's plan." Ember said eventually. "It comes down to what she said earlier about the more parts that there are to a plan, the easier it is for it to go wrong."

Jack sat there nodding his agreement. "And..." He found himself adding, "in the time of universal deceit, telling the truth is a revolutionary act. Everything that we are doing here is because the King is acting suspiciously, surely we should be as open and honest as we can be when trying to find out what is going on."

As Jack had been speaking, he had had his gaze in the distance to allow his brain to think deeply, without distraction, but now he looked at those around him, he saw Dr. Nabielle looking strongly approving, Ember and Mo both impressed while Lord Alectus' face blazed with pride.

"You know what, I think I agree with your plan after all Dr. Nabielle." Said Alectus.

"There is one more thing" said Ember, "going back to what you were saying earlier, why did the Kaofrelsi go from a political party to being exiled beyond the Wall?"

"The Kaofrelsi had been growing less powerful for a while, and all the other parties and powerful people disliked them, they were too proud and self-righteous. Carsicus realised that he was slipping further and further from the King, away from a position of influence, so made a mad, desperate attempt to kidnap the King to make him listen. Of course, his plan failed, and the other Lords insisted he was exiled."

"Why would the King carry on trying to listen to Carsicus after that?"

"As I said, he called Carsicus his big brother and at the time tried everything he could to forgive him and keep him at court, but the other lords insisted he was sent away. But, if they found a secret way to communicate, there is every chance that Carsicus does have the King's ear.

Moments later, with heartfelt hugs, Ember, Mo and A-lectus left the hospital and went back to Alectus' house. Dr. Nabielle requested that Jack stay the night in the hospital, and he didn't mind either way.

"Jack Tourn." Dr. Nabielle said, her face serious.

"Yes." Jack replied, worried that he was in trouble.

"You are one seriously impressive human being."

During the night, Jack's brain kept trying to envision what asking the King for permission to attend the University would be like but every time it got to the actual asking, the dream fell apart because Jack had no clue what the king looked like, all he remembered was Carsicus' description of the king as "a child, and a weak one at that."

The next morning, when Jack went to open the door to go back into Alectus' treehouse, he almost got his nose broken by Mo who had just thrown the heavy door open.

"Oh, hey." He said light-heartedly, as though nothing had happened.

"Where're you going?" Jack asked, trying to sound just as casual as Mo.

"Teraturt. While you are meeting the King, Ember and I are going to be in the crowd and everyone has to be dressed really smart and, don't know if you remember, I sort of cut holes in my suit trousers, so Alectus reckons I need to get a new pair."

Jack grinned, the memory of being told that Ember and Mo were to be his servants and Mo's reaction to that revelation was still more than enough to bring a smile to his face.

"Git." Mo muttered although his eyes showed that he was also finding more than a little humour from it now.

"Are we good to go?" Ember asked, rolling down the ramp.

They took a slightly longer route to Teraturt than Jack and Mo had last time because it was easier for Ember to push her wheelchair on the grass than on the loamy floor in the forest. Still, they were soon on top of the hill that overlooked the town. "This time, can we stay away from the Highstreet?" Asked Jack.

"Why?" Ember asked at once.

"It's hard to explain." Jack sighed. "It just seemed a bit too posh to be believed. It was weird"

"I can't say I am surprised, Teraturt is a very rich city

according to Dr. Nabielle, it made its money from mining Andagaldur and shipping it around the Realm and because everyone needed Andagaldur so badly, they paid vast amounts for
it..." Said Ember before continuing about everything she had
managed to learn about Teraturt. As she spoke, she was so like
her old self that Jack began to feel like he was back in the Wilderness and broke into a broad smile. "...all the same, I would
like to have at least a look at the Highstreet." She finished.

Feeling like it was the least that he could do. Jack tilted
his head to the side and said "actually, maybe we should go and
have a look. It will probably be really different to normal because they will be getting ready for the arrival of the King."

"Truuue." Agreed Mo with a shrug.

Ember caught Jack's arm so that they were a few paces
behind Mo. "Thank you." She smiled gratefully at him, and Jack
felt better than he had in days.

"C'mon you two." Mo grinned mischievously and Jack had
a strange urge to throw something at him.

Soon, they were walking along the dirt road towards the
sweet shop. "No, we aren't going in there." Ember said as they
reached the shop front, practically dragging Mo away from it.
"We have things to do." And they continued onto the more
built up and posher part of town. Many of these houses had
children's drawings hung out the window, showing the King
smiling and waving. Jack really hoped that the King didn't look
at some of the pictures too closely because some of them were
terrible enough to get charged with treason. Still, Jack wasn't
complaining because they smashed that sense of exhibition
that last time had hung heavy in the air.

"I don't see what you were complaining about." Ember
said, shaking her head and sounding like a grandmother.
"Feels quite normal to me."

"Yeah well it was different last time." Jack replied defensively.

"Mo, what do you think of this place?" Ember asked, pointing at a clothes shop. Jack had almost forgotten that the entire reason that they were here was to get Mo a new pair of trousers.

"Nah, looks like a place my dad would get clothes from." Mo replied dismissively.

"Oh, now that's more like it!" Mo smiled, pointing across the street.

"No, we can't go in there, that is a fancy-dress shop." Ember said, sounding exasperated but Mo was already hurrying across the street.

"Really that boy!" Ember muttered under her breath as Mo entered the shop. Jack had to bite his lip to stop himself laughing. Sometimes he wondered how it was possible that Ember and Mo were the same age.

The inside of the shop was very peculiar, it didn't look like any shop that Jack had even been in before, nothing was hung up, instead, clothes were piled on top of each other around the outside of the room so that the walls were all obscured.

"Anything I can do for you young sir's and miss?" A voice said suddenly from near Jack's right ear, causing him to jump about two feet into the air. The man who had spoken was the strangest looking person Jack had ever seen, every single strand of hair on his head was a different colour, his face itself was a mass of contorted lines and stripes, then from the neck down he was wearing a onesie of bright, almost luminous, pink.

"What the ..." Ember whispered to the other two.

Mo, who unsurprisingly was the least taken aback, said with tongue in cheek, "Yeah, can I have on of whatever it is you are wearing please."

"Certainly, you can have this very one."

And the strange looking man reached to the top of his head and started pulling. Jack began wondering if this was a dream but the looks of utter bewilderment on Mo and Ember's faces seemed to confirm that they were also witnesses to the insanity that was happening.

Their expressions only grew more exaggerated as the hair began to separate from the man's head and the lines slid off his face and with a crackling sound, the onesie separated along the seams so that the man could remove it. And, before Jack could say anything, the costume was on the floor and the man before them was dressed in blue jeans and a white top, plain as porridge.

"Dibs!" Shouted Mo, throwing his arm out to stop Jack moving towards the costume. Laughing like a maniac, he worked his way into the outfit.

"What d'you think?" He asked, spreading his arms.

"I wish I had a camera." Jack said mournfully to himself.

Mo would obviously been happy to spend the whole afternoon dressing in absurd outfit after absurd outfit, but Ember and Jack eventually convinced him to leave the shop, carrying a bagful of odd hats and socks that they had bought with a fistful of King's notes to avoid being rude.

Whilst Mo had been trying on the costumes, the street outside had grown much busier and not just with adults going to work but younger children out on the street as well, walking next to their parents.

"Let's go to the Highstreet." Ember prompted. "There will be somewhere for you to get new trousers there, surely."

The two boys followed slightly reluctantly, not keen to return to the strange stage-like atmosphere. But, as they continued towards it, Jack felt no unease building up in his gut.

The addition of the drawings hanging out of house windows and children in the streets seemed to break that sense of pretence that had prevailed two days earlier.

Even once they were on to the Highstreet itself, Jack felt comfortable and was now able to enjoy looking around him at the mighty glass towers and glittering shopfronts. However much Jack was enjoying looking around though, it was nothing compared to Ember who was simply awe-struck. She darted from one shop to the next to the next like a cat in a crowd of pigeons.

"C'mon, let's just get some trousers and get out of here, man's hungry." Mo muttered but Ember was too far away to hear him.

Thankfully, she soon reached a shop and shouted across to the two boys "this one looks like it'll do." before going inside. Mo and Jack followed her into a bright, open sort of shop. There was one assistant inside who was busy serving a customer but gave the three of them a nod of acknowledgment as they entered.

"What do you think about these?" Ember asked, pulling a pair of trousers off their peg.

Mo grabbed them, quickly put them against his waist, checking their length, saw that they weren't too long and said "yeah, fine, let's get them."

"Don't you want to try them on?"

"Nope, they're fine, let's pay and go." Said Mo, already crossing over to the counter.

"There are changing rooms here, they might not match with the rest of ..."

"Ember, it's fine." Mo answered, his stomach giving off a loud rumble.

Mo quickly paid the man behind the counter before leading the other two out of the shop. "Right, let's head back and get some food." He said as soon as the door had closed behind them.

"But we only just got here." Ember complained.

"Well, I am heading back but you two can stay here if you want, that's cool with me."

"We'll see you at home." Jack said, startled that the words had escaped him. Ember gave him a surprised look and Mo nodded before turning and walking back in the direction of Edenvale.

"So, where do you want to go?" Jack asked awkwardly.

"There's a coffee shop over there that looks nice." Ember said, pointing.

"Sounds good." Jack agreed although privately thought that the coffee shop looked no different to the hundreds that they had already walked past; it had a glass front with 'Teraturt Tea and Coffee' written on the side.

He pulled out a seat and Ember stopped her wheelchair next to a small round table outside the shopfront. A short man with a mighty, ginger moustache and sideburns hurried out to greet them and hand over a pair of menus.

Ember quickly opened hers and began to read but Jack had something on his mind as he watched her reading.

"Umm... Ember, did you... before the dance... were you hoping that I would ask you to dance?"

Ember kept her face hidden by the menu. "Maybe a little but I don't mind really. If you didn't want to, I didn't want to force you. Anyway, I thought we said that it was water under the bridge."

"Yeah, ok, water under the bridge." Jack said but he was beginning to wonder if, maybe, he would have liked to ask her to dance.

CHAPTER 7: THE KING

During the five days until the King's visit, Jack's nerves increased steadily, he needed to prove to the King that he could enter the second level of the Deep, otherwise there was no chance of being allowed to go to the University.

To begin with, he had hardly been able to enter the Deep at all, he was so out of practice having not used his power at all since battling Carsicus over a month ago. He had gotten a little better and could now get in and out of the Deep without too much bother, but the second level was proving harder to access than he had expected, he could get in only about half the time, which left far more up to chance than anyone wanted. To make matters worse, there was a limit to how much practice was helpful because each time tired him out so much that it got steadily harder after every attempt.

On top of all that, Jack was struggling to sleep at night and waking every morning to find himself exhausted, every time he closed his eyes, his brain imagined a faceless King yelling at him 'get into the second level! Get into the second level!'

The morning before the King's arrival, Jack was sat by Heaven Lake, watching the Alforn playing barge-board because it was the best way he had found of relaxing himself. Despite this, he couldn't help fretting about that afternoon, what if he said something stupid and made the King suspicious? Every time he thought about speaking to the King, it felt as though someone slipped an ice cube down his throat.

A great splash as one of the Alforn fell into the water

brought Jack out of his stupor but didn't make him feel any more confident about what he had to do. The realisation that all of this, everyone here, was relying on him only added to the pressure.

"Go on, get him." Mo shouted from the edge of the lake as one of the Alforn swept at the legs of the other causing her to topple into the water to a scattering of laughter and applause, but Jack remained quiet.

"You'll be fine." Ember said turning to him, correctly interpreting his silence.

He tried to smile at her but knew that it was more of a grimace. "I'm going to go and get changed." Jack said quickly. Ember nodded sympathetically while Mo kept his eyes firmly on the game.

As he walked through the quiet forest, Jack realised that his breath was fast and ragged, and his heart hammered as though he was sprinting.

He was paying so little attention to where he was going that he walked straight into the front door of Alectus' house. When Alectus opened the door, Jack saw that he was already dressed in an immaculate suit, but it somehow made him look pasty and unhealthily pale. A far-cry from his normal tough, broad-shouldered warrior like appearance.

It took Jack several minutes to get dressed because of how badly his hands shook. This only added to his worry, what if the King noticed how worried he was? Would that be enough to arouse suspicion?

Wanting to be with someone, Jack headed back downstairs to the living room where he saw Alectus was fiddling with his tie, still looking slightly unwell.

"No, no, no." Alectus muttered, taking the tie off before tying it exactly as it had been before. Then, he leant close in to the mirror to examine it, as if determined to spot something wrong with it.

Unable to find anything, he sat down heavily in a chair before bolting back to his feet as if someone had left an unturned pin on the seat. He then strode up and down the room, playing with his hands, oblivious to the fact that Jack was there.

"Are you nervous?" Jack asked, his own nerves making him speak more loudly than normal.

Alectus jumped in the air out of shock. "Yes, I am a little bit. A little nervous I mean." He said with an anxious giggle that took Jack by surprise.

Suddenly, Jack felt significantly calmer. Seeing someone who was usually as calm and composed as Lord Alectus being all jumpy because of nerves was strangely reassuring.

"Are you nervous?" Alectus asked.

"Yeah, yeah I am a bit."

"That's ok, nothing to worry about, we all get nervous sometimes. Even me … ahahaha"

Whether it was what Jack had said calming him or some other reason, Alectus now did sit down properly and finally stopped playing with his hands although he remained looking a little pasty and when Mo and Ember knocked on the door, he nearly jumped out of his skin.

"Well, I think that it is a bit time to go." Alectus said five minutes later.

"What?"

"Sorry, I meant about time to go."

"Ok, no harm in getting there early I suppose." Jack shrugged because they still had three hours until they were meant to be there, and it was barely a fifteen-minute walk to Teraturt.

"My exactly thoughts." Alectus said nodding as he stood up.

As they left the treehouse, the stillness that Jack had gained when watching Alectus worry began to disintegrate but rather than nerves, he could feel the butterflies of excitement. Unable to contain himself, Jack did a little bit of shadow boxing as they walked. It was time. As is so often the case, the build-up to an event is ten times more terrifying than the event itself.

When they arrived, guards arrived to take Jack and Alectus onto the stage.

"Good luck. You will be fine." Ember said, pulling Jack into a hug.

"Yeah, don't pants it up mate."

"Mo!"

And, before Jack could say anything to them, he was hurried onto the stage to stand next to Alectus.

From the moment that they arrived onto the stage, they were busy; Alectus and then Jack shaking the hands and being introduced to members of the King's entourage who had arrived before him.

Jack soon forgot the names of the important people he was meeting, never mind their role in the government although he had had to work hard to avoid breaking into a grin when Dr. Nabielle had come over and said, "I am one of the King's medical team. Who are you?"

Finally, after what felt like an eternity, Jack realised that there was no one else coming up onto the stage to introduce themselves.

"Try and stand up straight. The King is going to be here soon, and you need to make a good impression." Whispered Lord Alectus who, Jack was alarmed to see, was once again looking nervous to the point of appearing ill.

Jack looked down at the crowd for Mo and Ember, he spotted them and gave the biggest smile that he dared. Ember waved wildly back. Mo stuck out his tongue. Just as Jack felt he had looked towards his friends for too long, he saw them rudely barged out of the way by an escort of guards. The guards surrounded a tall, thin man with a long black ponytail.

"Is that the King?" Jack asked, thinking that the man looked nothing like the weak child that Carsicus had described.

"No, that's Sturgis, the King's secretary. But that means that the King is not far behind."

When the man reached the stage, he headed straight for Alectus. "My Lord." He said with a bow, his voice greasy as a mechanics spanner.

"Royal secretary." Alectus replied, his voice clipped and sharp.

"The King will be here shortly."

At that very moment, there came the roll of drums from drummers around the edge of the Highstreet that Jack had been too busy to notice. The guards began separating the crowd through the middle. Jack didn't need Alectus' whisper in his ear to know what was happening. The King was coming.

Jack could hear Alectus next to him taking deep breaths, doubtless trying to slow his throbbing heartbeat. The tension in the air was so thick that Jack felt as though he could cut it.

Then, around the corner appeared a baby-blue carriage pulled by two enormous horses. One was white as snow and the other dark as night.

Suddenly, the horses came to a stop and a square in the top of the carriage swung open. Then, slowly and splendidly, a head appeared at the top of the carriage, quickly followed by a body.

The King sat in the throne on top of the carriage, looking out at the crowd. He wore an ornate golden crown on his head and around his shoulders was a luxurious red cape trimmed with a dark leathery material that Jack didn't know. "Dragon hide." Alectus muttered in his ear, pointing at the cape.

Jack was too shocked to reply.

At a flick of the King's hand, the carriage began rolling forwards again, through the gap that had been cleared in the crowd. The crowd itself was finding its voice, people talking excitedly to their neighbours or waving at the King, shouting "Errion bless you, your highness!"

As the King drew closer, he only became more magnificent, there was no hint of the weak child that Carsicus had described, his shoulders were broad, and his golden hair sparkled regally in the sunlight.

Soon, the King had reached the stage. Several carefully placed attendants raced towards the carriage to help him down and crowded around him as he climbed the stairs on to the stage.

"My King." Alectus said, dropping to his knees and exposing his neck. Jack did the same, not enjoying the sense of vulnerability at all but then, he supposed, that was the point.

"Rise, rise Lord Alectus." Said the King, his voice jumping in the middle of the sentence. Clearly, his voice had only just broken and was still adjusting. "And your son too, please, you are too kind."

In his surprise at the King's voice, Jack had lost track of the words and it was only when Alectus tapped him with his foot that Jack stood up straight again. "My King." Jack said, all too aware of his own accent, desperately trying to sound more Arcanian.

If the King noticed Jack's accent, he didn't show it.

Jack, however, was less discrete with his surprise when he looked up and saw the King. The broad shoulders that he had noticed from far away were now clearly fake, Jack could see the padding within the cloak that gave the impression of muscle, the golden hair was obviously dyed, the roots were brown, while the high neck of the cloak hid the King's weak chin from a distance but up close, it was blatantly obvious.

Jack had to give his head a little shake to recover himself and the King narrowed his eyebrows slightly but said nothing else to Jack before moving along to where some members of A-lectus' office were standing waiting to greet him.

"That went alright." Jack whispered to Alectus.

Soon, the King was back and smiling – clearly one of the people he had greeted had managed to say something amusing.

"We have some things to discuss, should we go to your office?" Although it was phrased as a question, Jack knew that it was nothing of the sort. The King didn't ask questions or make suggestions, he gave orders.

"Of course, your highness." Replied Lord Alectus, who could not sensibly say anything else.

The guards swarmed around them like a bunch of big, burly, heavily armed bees and once again, pushed a path through the crowd who all waved. The vast press of people around him prevented Jack from seeing where he was going, and he only realised that they had reached the building where Alectus' office was when the guard in front of him came to a hard stop.

"This way your highness." Said the oily voice of Sturgis, the King's secretary. Sturgis and the King led the way into the building while Jack and Alectus followed behind. The guards all remained by the door preventing any of the crowd following the King into the building.

Soon, the four of them were climbing and climbing up flights of stairs. Jack was dying to ask Alectus if anyone on Arcane had built an elevator but restrained himself – the last thing that he wanted to do was let the King hear something that would raise his suspicions. Although, Jack now realised, the King had a bigger problem, he was red as a traffic light with sweat pouring off his forehead and down his weak chin, the dragon skin coat that he was wearing was warm and heavy.

"Would you like me to carry your coat your highness?" A-lectus asked.

"I am the King! I can carry a coat! I am..." But King Taigal didn't finish his sentence as he suddenly staggered to the side, into the wall.

"I KING!" He muttered drunkenly to himself as he tried to climb another set of stairs, but he only made it halfway before staggering to the side once more. Thankfully, Alectus was lightning-fast and quickly caught the King before he hit the ground. Jack saw that the King's eyes were closed and his arms limp. Clearly, he was unconscious.

"Quick, go and get Dr. Nabielle!" Alectus shouted and Jack wasted no time in sprinting back the way he had come but he only had to go down one flight of stairs until he found Dr. Nabielle, already with water in her hand.

"Where is he?" She asked.

"Upstairs." Jack replied, shocked, how could Dr. Nabielle know what was going on? But before he could ask anything, she was gone, racing up to King Taigal.

Still confused, Jack now followed her to where he had left Alectus and the others.

He saw that Alectus had carried the King down to a section of flat, taken his coat off and propped him up against the wall while Dr. Nabielle was helping him drink from the bottle she carried. Then, she pulled a packet of small white tablets from her inside blazer pocket, adding two of them to the bottle of water.

"Wait! What is that?" Sturgis asked, his greasy voice full of suspicion.

"Salts to help re-hydrate him."

"Why do you have them on you?"

"I am a doctor. You wouldn't believe the number of people who fall ill on a hot day simply by not drinking enough."

Dr. Nabielle now turned away from Sturgis, back to her patient and it was clear that that was the end of the conversation. When she coaxed the liquid down the King's throat, Sturgis made a little twitch but didn't say anything.

Then, the King let out a small moan before opening his eyes a bit. "What happened?" He mumbled.

Alectus opened his mouth to explain but Sturgis beat him to it. "You got a bit too hot and passed out, so I carried you down here and took your coat off before going and getting Dr. Nabielle who gave you some water."

Jack looked in disbelief at Lord Alectus and Dr. Nabielle, nothing that Sturgis had said was true in any way!

"Get out." The King mumbled, pointing at Sturgis.

"What?" Sturgis asked.

"Get out. You are fired. I never want to see you again." The King said, his voice becoming stronger and his anger obviously swelling like a bullfrog. **"I am the KING!** I don't need people looking after me!"

As if in defiance of the words coming out of his mouth, the King began to cough and splutter, and it took him several seconds to recover.

Uncertainly, Sturgis began to walk away. He looked over his shoulder. "Go on." The King said and Sturgis disappeared down the stairs.

"My office is upstairs." Alectus said, trying to sound in control.

"Ok." The King grunted, lifting himself to his feet.

"It would be an honour, your highness, if you let me carry your coat." Dr. Nabielle said quickly. The King looked at her suspiciously but then nodded.

Alectus lead the way, the King following slowly behind, gripping the banister so hard that his hand was white while Jack and Dr. Nabielle followed behind. Eventually, after several pauses, they reached the top of the stairs – Alectus' was the only office on this floor.

"Lord Alectus." The King gasped. "After I leave, I want you to remove that banister and burn it. You can replace it with an identical one if you wish."

"Of course your highness." Alectus said evenly, as though that were a totally normal request from a King. Jack looked perplexedly at Dr. Nabielle but she shook her head, she would not explain now.

Alectus now led them through the heavy wooden door to his office. Jack had never seen anything like it, the walls were all glass and Jack could see the people below scurrying around like ants. He squinted but could not make out Ember's wheelchair or Mo's grin in the crowd.

"Thank you again for coming your highness." Alectus said as the King settled himself in the only chair in the room, leaving Jack, Alectus and Dr. Nabielle to stand before him.

The King waved his hand dismissively. "It is part of the duty of the King to travel around his Realm to all the different Kingdom's." He sighed as though it was a particularly hard part of life. "How have you found the staff here?"

"Very good your Highness, very professional."

"That's good. Just remember that I have the power to give them er … extra encouragement if they require it."

"Of course, I will let you know if their behaviour drops below my standards." Alectus said.

"It isn't your standards that matter though, it is mine my Lord." Said the King, trying once again to show that he held the real power.

"Yes your highness, that is what I meant of course, make sure that they do not fall below your standards."

"Good. I have read all the reports that you have written." Said the King. Jack had to stop himself smiling because the King sounded so proud of himself for having read all the reports, like any other kid his age being proud of having done all their homework. "And good thing that I did because plenty of those around me frequently missed out vital information. You can never rely too much on others." Said the King.

"No your Highness. Especially when you have a brain like yours that can pick things up that no one else can." Alectus answered, really lathering on the flattery. The King didn't seem to notice anything out of the ordinary.

"Too true, my Lord, too true. Now, how can I help you do your job? Is there anything you need pushing through? Or maybe some advice…"

Jack saw Alectus twitch slightly and felt a strange sense of vindication in the realisation that it was now Alectus' turn to get frustrated at being patronised.

"No advice your Highness…" Began Alectus but Dr. Nabielle quickly cut him off.

"What about that problem that you mentioned to me?"

"What problem?" Alectus asked, his surprise clearly not an act.

"The one about Jack needing a place to learn about the

Kingdom but we couldn't work out where he could go. He can't stay here; you need to be able to get on with work."

"Oh, yes, right." Alectus said, deciding to go along with Dr. Nabielle's plan, whatever it was.

"Somewhere to learn about Arcane away from here." Said Dr. Nabielle, her eyes flicking to the King. "Where could he go?"

"The University." Said the King suddenly.

Dr. Nabielle turned to Jack, her mock surprise exaggerated to the point of sarcasm. "What a great idea." She said, turning to the King who shrugged as if to say, 'well what did you expect?'

"Can he enter the second level of the Deep?" The King challenged.

"Yes, your highness, he can demonstrate if you would like."

"No need, no need, I will take your word for it Alectus. Of course, I can go into the Deep and check that he truly is in the second level, but I don't deem it necessary."

Alectus and Dr. Nabielle made small bows towards the King.

"If that is all my Lord." Said the King, standing up "the mindless masses below will be getting restless, don't even have ability to entertain themselves. We should go down, smile and wave a bit and then I can head back to my palace."

"Certainly, your Highness."

This time, the King took the lead down the stairs. Jack followed shaking his head, all that effort practicing entering the second level of the Deep for nothing! When the King emerged into the sunlight, the crowd began shouting and cheering loudly again. He acknowledged them with a superior wave and began climbing into his blue carriage which had been brought to the front of the building.

Just as he went to close the door, Dr. Nabielle caught it. "Your cloak your Highness." She said.

"I hope it was as much of an honour as you had hoped for, being allowed to carry it." Said the King.

"Oh, more than I could have dreamed of." Said Dr. Nabielle, pretending to wipe a tear out of her eye but, as the King turned away, she caught Jack's eye and winked, and Jack finally broke into the smile he had been threatening to all day. It was done. He was going to the University.

CHAPTER 8:
TIME TO GO

When Jack woke the next day, he was worried for a moment that it had all been a dream and that he still hadn't been allowed to go to the University. He was only convinced when he entered the main living area and saw Mo and Alectus frying sausages together – clearly their argument had been dealt with. "Thought I would sort you out a cooked breakfast to celebrate." Alectus said. "Afraid I can't eat with you, need to get into Teraturt for nine o'clock this morning. Lots of work to do, we have really fallen behind because of needing to sort everything out for the King's arrival. The building of the podium alone took..."

Unable to help himself, Jack began to yawn.

"Sorry." Alectus smiled.

Ember arrived just as Alectus left. "Morning." She said sleepily. "Now, tell us everything about the King again."

Jack recited all he could remember for the hundredth time, each time Ember and Mo found something new in the story to digest. When Jack finished, Mo started with a disbelieving grin. "Do you reckon he could get any further up his own..."

A cough made Mo stop what he was saying. They all turned around to see Dr. Nabielle stood in the doorway with a broad smile.

"So, what did you think of our Royal Highness?" Dr. Nabielle asked.

"Bit of a weirdo." Jack said quickly.

"We might need to dig down into his character a little more than that, seeing as he is the person you are investigating."

"He is really, really petulant." Ember said.

"What's a petulant?" Jack asked.

"Someone who is petulant throws their toys out of the pram quickly, can't stand things going wrong." Said Ember.

"Yes, you're exactly right Ember, he is very petulant. We saw that when he fired Sturgis without thinking. Knowing the King, he has probably already reinstated Sturgis as the Royal Secretary, it's rare a week goes by without the King firing one of his advisors before reinstating them the next day. Now, that's a good start. What else?"

"He is very proud." Mo said quickly.

"Probably the main one. Excellent thinking. The King is nothing if not proud. Jack, you saw him insisting that Alectus burn the bannisters, he can't bear the fact he needed to rely on something to help him. It was demeaning and embarrassing for the King who thinks he is so brilliant to not be able to make it up the stairs without holding onto the banister." Said Dr. Nabielle.

"And what else, there is one more, key thing that we are missing."

The three of them went quiet, all thinking hard. Jack was focusing on how happy the King had been with himself when he had suggested Jack go to the University but couldn't find the words.

"Is he... a bit ... insecure?" Mo asked uncertainly, like someone nervously exploring a cave without a torch, trying to press forwards without tripping.

Dr. Nabielle didn't answer verbally but her smile was all that it took to confirm that she agreed wholeheartedly with Mo whose confidence in his own idea seemed to grow. "Because, if you think about how happy he was when he suggested that Jack go to the University that only makes sense if he was insecure, him coming up with an idea that he thought was brilliant made him feel as though he had achieved what was expected of him for a change."

The whole time that Mo was speaking, Jack was interested to hear his friend's words flowing more quickly and louder as he became increasingly confident.

"You are spot on there!" Dr. Nabielle said enthusiastically when Mo finished. "King Taigal has always worried that he won't live up to what his mother did when she was Monarch and is always trying to prove that he is just as good as her, by coming up with clever ideas. It's a pity that they almost never work..."

Jack felt an unexpected stab of pity for the King, who was only a few years older than himself and yet not only had to rule the Kingdom but try and rule it as well as his mother who, as Alectus frequently mentioned, was the best Monarch since the end of the Second Age. That was a lot of pressure for anyone.

"That is all that I wanted to say really." Said Dr. Nabielle turning and heading for the door but, just as she pushed the door open, she looked over her shoulder and said with a smile, "Oh, and one more thing, Alectus and I decided that there wasn't much point waiting around so you will leave tomorrow at sunrise. I suggest you get packing!"

Jack looked at the others in disbelief, despite Dr. Nabielle's smile, it was clear that she wasn't joking, they were leaving in less than a day! By the time Jack's brain had digested the information, Dr. Nabielle had gone.

Without another word, Mo and Ember left for their rooms. "Where are you going?" Jack asked.

"You heard Dr. Nabielle, we need to get packing!" They said together.

The three of them therefore spent the morning in and out of each other's rooms, throwing stuff into the three large suitcases that they had found in the attic.

When Jack finally finished, he settled down on his bed and tried to force his brain to accept the fact that they were leaving the next morning because it still seemed like a dream.

"Mo, seriously listen to me!" Came Ember's voice from the other room.

"No, you do appreciate we have to carry all of this?"

"Let's see what Jack has to say about it."

"Fine."

Jack heard a pair of footsteps coming towards his room and he pushed his eyes open and sat a little straighter on his bed. Moments later, his door swung open and Mo and Ember marched in.

"How is your sense of smell?" Ember asked before Mo could get any words out.

"'bout average I suppose."

"Well then how do you feel about the fact that Mo is refusing to pack a change of clothes?"

Jack shrugged. "We are going to be outside the whole time …"

"Oh, you two are both hopeless!" Ember exclaimed, wheeling quickly out of the room.

"Also, that isn't quite true, I am packing a few pairs of socks to stop blisters."

"Mmm, good point." Jack said, getting off his bed and

scooping odd socks off the floor before shoving them uncere-moniously into the suitcase.

Alectus arrived back earlier than usual. "I wanted to spend some time with you before you all left." He explained.

After dinner, he insisted that they all unload their suit-cases and go through everything that they had packed before repacking. He insisted that Mo bring at least one change of clothes. As for Jack, Alectus couldn't help fretting. They emp-tied and then refilled his suitcase three times without adding a single item.

Eventually, Jack convinced his father that they were just wasting time and together, they headed downstairs to where Mo and Ember were in the living room reading.

"Can't believe I am going to have to go a month without a book." Mo sighed, not looking up.

"Well you managed it fine when we were in the Wilder-ness." Jack replied. Mo gave a small grunt of acknowledgment but again didn't look up.

Just as they were putting everything away after dinner, there was the sound of the front door being opened and hur-ried footsteps up the stairs. Jack turned to see Tom emerge into the room, a look of consternation on his face. "Is it true? Are you leaving tomorrow?" He panted and Jack realised with guilty shock that in his excitement at departing so soon and with so much to do, he hadn't said anything to Tom.

"Yeah, we are."

"How long are you going to be gone for?"

Jack looked at Alectus, he hadn't thought this far ahead having been so focused on actually getting to the University.

"Most people don't go home until the Midwinter Holidays which aren't going to be for a good couple of months after you start and we need you there as much as possible, keeping an eye on the King. Of course, you might have to stay there a lot longer than that. We will just have to wait and see."

Jack turned back to Tom who he was surprised didn't look too startled by the news.

"When are you going tomorrow?"

"Early, before sunrise."

"Well I guess it is goodbye now then." Said Tom and Jack was blown away by how grown up his younger brother sounded.

"Yeah, I suppose." Jack replied.

And Tom ran into him, wrapping him into a tight hug. When his younger brother let go, Jack realised it was time to go on an adventure again.

Alectus woke Jack, Mo, and Ember just as the first ray of sunlight broke over the horizon. Their stuff was all ready to go by the door and they simply threw it onto their backs and headed out. A strange feeling tingled in the back of Jack's mind as he walked past familiar trees on familiar paths but now they were the start of a long journey. They were meeting Einor at the hilltop where Jack and Mo had first met him.

As Jack drew closer to the former Warrior of the World, he saw that he did not look happy. "Why have you brought so much stuff?" Einor said gruffly.

"We only packed the stuff that they need."

"Isn't that cute, daddy packing everything that his baby needs." Einor said sarcastically. "Let me have a look in the bag, see what we can take out."

But before Jack could hand the bag to him, Einor had already snatched it and yanked it open. Einor went through quickly throwing items out onto the grassy floor, Jack saw all his clothes except his socks, most of his food and all his hygiene equipment dumped onto the discard pile.

All the while that Einor was going through his stuff, Jack stood in disbelief which was mirrored by the others.

"Right, yours next big mouth." Alectus said, taking Mo's bag.

This seemed to bring Alectus to his senses. "Be sensible for once, they need some other clothes."

Einor shut Mo's bag with a snap and stared back at Alectus. "We are going to be walking for at least a fortnight. We don't want anything other than the bare essentials. It isn't some leisurely stroll around Edenvale. Anyway, it won't harm them to do without everything for a change, might toughen them up a bit."

As usual, Einor either didn't notice whether he was offending anyone or just didn't care.

"Look here..." Began Alectus.

"Shut up. I know what I am doing. Say your goodbyes and go home." Einor said, cutting him off.

"You don't boss me around." Began Alectus, taking a step towards Einor.

"Oh for goodness sake you two." Said a clear voice and Jack saw Dr. Nabielle arrive on the hilltop. "When will you start acting like adults and stop arguing?"

Both Einor and Alectus fell silent, looking embarrassingly like two naughty schoolboys. Jack half expected them to point at the other and say, 'but he started it miss.'

"Right, now that the adults have started acting their age, we can run through the plan one last time; Einor will take you three." She pointed at Jack, Mo and Ember "to the University. Term starts in three weeks so if the journey goes as expected you should get there around a week before you need to. Hopefully, I will arrive soon after but if I don't, remember to get as close to the King as you can and listen for anything out of the ordinary. Jack, getting involved in everything you can will give you the best chance of picking something useful up. Let Alectus know on the Rec-Trec if there is something particular to look out for."

"Ok." Jack said nodding.

"And remember what we discussed about the King's character. It might help you work out who it is that he is willing to listen to."

"Got it." Mo said, looking and sounding extremely excited.

Dr. Nabielle then knelt and reached into her pocket, bringing out a small piece of folded paper, she unfolded it a dozen times, spreading a large map across the floor. She drew one of her long, elegant fingers delicately along the contours, almost as though she was trying to feel and understand their route. Suddenly, she looked directly at Jack leaving him in no doubt that she was evaluating him, trying to work out if he was up to this journey. Subconsciously, he pushed his shoulders back and stood a little straighter.

With a deep breath, she seemed to finally decide that he could handle it.

"Alectus, Einor and I have decided on your route. From here, you will head due North through the forest, around the outskirts of Teraturt. Then, once past Teraturt, you can turn East, towards the river. From there, hopefully, your route will be straight forwards as the river leads straight to the gates of Scholar's City.

"The river curves a lot." Said Mo analysing the map. "Why can we not head through the woods in a straight line to Teraturt? It would take half the time."

"I wish that was possible, there are cart tracks that are

direct lines through the woods between Teraturt and Scholar's City, from the days when Teraturt was simply a small mining town busy digging out Andagaldur that was then sent by cart to Teraturt."

"So why can't we just take them?"

"We need to get going." Said Einor, looking frustrated.

"Why can't we just follow the cart tracks?" Mo asked for the third time.

"It is time to go. All you need to know is that you **must** stick to the river. Whatever happens, don't go into the forest."

"But Carsicus will surely be watching the river, it must be safer to go through the woods, the chances of us meeting him in there are really small but all but guaranteed if we follow the river." Said Ember and Jack found himself nodding.

"You have Einor to protect you if Carsicus finds you." Said Dr. Nabielle. "Now it is time to go." She said and at once, her eyes filled with such sadness that Jack forgot about their route entirely.

"What's wrong?"

"I have to go as well on a mission of my own, try and investigate what you overheard about the Glorious Leader."

"Good luck."

"See you in three weeks then I hope. And don't go into the forest." She said with a smile that looked more like a grimace before turning and walking away. In the silence that followed, Jack knew that the others were all wondering whether they would ever see Dr. Nabielle again.

"Well, that's that I suppose," said Alectus. "Now it is time for goodbyes." He continued as he pulled Jack into a spine cracking hug.

Jack pulled away feeling embarrassed, but his feelings were spared when Alectus pulled the other two into embraces as well (although clearly less tightly).

Einor stood a fair distance away shaking his head as though he had never seen anything this pathetic before.

"Take the stuff that we don't need with you." He said bluntly to Alectus who opened his mouth as if to argue but after a moment closed it again and nodded. "Come on you three."

With one last quick embrace of his father, Jack joined the others in walking off towards Teraturt, starting their journey to the University.

Just before they got out of shouting range, Jack heard A-lectus' deep voice shout "Einor!"

The former Warrior of the World turned to face the Lord before Alectus shouted thickly, as though the words caught in his throat. "Good luck and keep them all safe."

Einor rolled his eyes without answering. "Pompous prat." He muttered to himself before continuing to stride away. Jack glanced over his shoulder twenty times before they reached the woodland and each time saw Alectus waving whilst holding all the kit that Einor had thrown from their bags. He wondered how just a few days earlier he had had a row with his father and almost forgotten how much he loved the only biological family he had.

CHAPTER 9: ABANDONED

The path that they followed was pleasantly dark underneath the thick trees. It was still early enough in autumn that the path itself was free from fallen leaves and the white stones marking the edges were clear on the muddy floor. They were heading due North so occasionally the bright morning sun would dazzle through the trees to their right. The path deviated slightly from side to side but, Jack noticed, always seemed to be heading downwards.

About mid-morning, the group came to its first rest of the day. "The right turning, when we loop around Teraturt and towards the river, is still at least an hour away." Einor explained. "In the meantime, we don't have a huge amount of water so don't have more than a couple of swallows." He told the others before passing a water bottle around. Jack drunk as much as he could in his two swallows.

Too soon for Jack's liking, they were on the move again and he could feel his legs starting to get rubbery, but it was bearable at the present. He was grateful that Einor had prevented him from taking anything other than the essentials as his backpack somehow appeared to have gotten heavier whilst they had been walking.

Still, he wasn't impressed when Einor called from the front saying that they needed to hurry up in order to reach the right turning before lunch.

"Can we have a break?" Ember panted a few moments later. Einor paused and looked up at the sky, seeing the position of the sun.

Einor turned and gave her a hard look before grunting that they could have another short stop.

They all took seats on the floor across the path. Einor got the water bottle out. "You two can have the rest." He said pointing to Jack and Ember. "Mo and I won't need any more before we reach the river." He added before Mo could complain.

Jack greedily drained half of the water bottle. He went to pass the rest to Ember, but she wasn't paying attention to him, instead focusing intently down the path.

"Einor, get off the path!" She whispered suddenly. Jack looked up just as an elderly couple joined the main path from a smaller one and began walking up the hill towards them. Neither of them seemed at all threatening and Jack was, for several moments, confused about why Ember had been so desperate for Einor to hide and why Einor himself had sprinted like the wind into the woods before throwing himself into a dense clump of bushes.

Finally, Jack remembered about the Lordship that was offered to whoever turned Einor in. It still took him by surprise to recall that they were travelling with a fugitive. He had grown used to Einor as a grumpy, irritable, menacing character but one that was on their side nevertheless.

"Beautiful morning." The old man said cheerfully as he approached, bringing Jack's focus back to the world around him. "Doesn't quite seem fair that you youngsters are going down the hill whilst we have to walk up it."

"You will be able to go down on your way back to Teraturt." Mo replied with equal cheer.

"Tha's true I suppose. Well, enjoy your walk." Said the old man, passing them and continuing off up the path. His wife, however, stayed still for a second longer and Jack saw that she was looking interestedly at the pile of bags that they had dumped on the side of the path, the four bags that were there, surrounded by the three of them.

Maybe he was being paranoid, but Jack thought he saw her eyes raise and look curiously into the woods where Einor was hiding. Then, the next moment, the lady was gone, following her husband.

"Do you think that those two were just out on a walk?" Jack asked the others.

"Probably." Was Ember's response but the slow, drawn-out pronunciation of the word made Jack think that she was far from convinced and, like him, had noticed the suspicion of the old lady.

Once the old couple were out of sight, Einor crawled back out of the undergrowth and joined the others on the path.

Having not noticed the interest shown by the old lady, Einor confidently swung his bag back onto his back and went to continue confidently along down the path.

"Einor!" Ember called.

"What? We can't wait around here any longer." Einor replied sharply.

"That wasn't what I was going to say, the old lady who walked past seemed to be looking for something. I think that we ... or at least you ... should stay off the path. We can't risk you getting recognised."

"Sensible." Einor nodded. "It's not like it will be difficult to keep up with you three even if I were to be walking on quicksand."

Jack found it easy to ignore the comment, but Ember rolled her eyes and Mo also looked a little frustrated. He couldn't help but wonder how long the group would be able to avoid arguing for.

Now as they walked, Einor stayed just out of sight in the thick trees but close enough so that he could hear the others if they called for help. Ember still had the remainder of the water bottle and Jack began to wish that he hadn't already downed his share.

They reached a right turning without meeting anyone else although several times, they had thought they had heard noises ahead and dashed into the forest as a precaution. Even though Einor was hidden, so that the public was no threat, Ember kept reminding them that Carsicus might have placed spies on the path to try and prevent anyone leaving Edenvale, including them.

"How much further from here to the river?" Mo called into the forest.

No one answered.

"Are we close to the river?" Mo called again, slightly louder this time.

Once more, there was no reply. He turned to the others, "I don't want to shout any louder, we don't want everyone within a hundred miles to hear us."

"It's fine, this must be the correct turning, we have been walking for at least an hour and I haven't seen any other one it could have been." Ember said, doing her best to sound confident.

"How much energy do you think you have, Mo?" Jack asked, taking the role of leader again.

"As much as normal."

"Would you be able to run a bit further down the path and see if there is another right turn a little further on?"

"Ok. Will be about half an hour." Mo said, already turning and jogging down the path.

"Where do you think Einor has got to though?" Ember asked as soon as Mo had gone.

"No idea, hopefully he has just gone to scout ahead a little bit and check that there isn't anyone unfriendly waiting for us."

"Mmm... I just hope he hasn't snuck on up to Teraturt."

"Why would he do that?"

"Remember what Dr. Nabielle said about his addiction to Briar?"

"No way. He wouldn't do something that stupid, not now. Surely." Jack replied but even as he spoke, he remembered thinking the same thing about Mo a month before.

Heavy breathing barely five minutes later announced Mo's return.

"Did you find a turning?" Jack and Ember asked together.

Mo shook his head in response. "Not a turning, no. I found a cave instead, well more like a mineshaft actually, I think it is just a side entrance to the big one that you mentioned, where they dug out Andagaldur and sent it off to Konungur."

Ember looked at him in disbelief, "we weren't looking for caves or mineshafts, we need to know if there is a turning towards the river." She said, exasperated.

"We could go and check it out though." Jack said and Ember turned her look of incredulity on him. "Think about it, it's only a five-minute walk and we don't want to take a turning until we know it's the correct one. I say we leave a note, telling Einor to wait for us here, while we go and check out this mine. Then, once we have checked it out, we come back, meet Einor here and head off."

"This is so stupid! Let's just take this path, it goes roughly the right direction anyway, instead of messing around looking at stuff that is in no way helpful!"

"I vote we go and have a look around. You heard Einor this morning, we will get there a week early anyway we may as well do some exploring." Mo said.

"Fine!" Ember replied, her tone making it all too clear that she didn't think this plan was fine at all.

They left a scribbled note on the side of the path and continued down the hill. The mineshaft was a little way into the woodland, Jack was surprised that Mo had noticed it as the entrance was wooden and camouflaged by the forest. The entrance was just big enough for all three of them to enter at once into a large, dark cavern. The ceiling sloped upwards, following the hillside above it and Jack reckoned that the far end of the cavern was at least thirty feet high.

In the opposite wall were three corridors cut into the stone. Jack led the way towards the middle one and the other two followed him but just before they entered, Ember came to a sudden stop. "We've had a look around now. Let's go back. Einor might be waiting for us at the turning."

"I doubt it." Was Mo's reply. "We've barely been gone ten minutes and besides, all we have seen so far is this big cavern. We haven't explored any of the tunnels yet."

"Let's just have a little walk down here and then we can head back. Mo's right, we haven't been gone more than ten minutes. And I don't care too much about making Einor wait for us if he is just going to disappear off without saying anything."

Ember sighed. "Well go on then." She muttered.

The three of them then pressed on down the tunnel, Mo at the front, Jack, and Ember next to each other a little further behind.

"How old do you think the tunnel is?" Jack wondered aloud.

"Ten to fifteen years I guess." Said Ember. "Look, the wood is starting to decay and break apart but is still holding for the moment." She explained as she snapped a little bit of wood off and let it drop on the floor. "Also, Dr. Nabielle told me it was about ten years ago that the mines were all abandoned."

"I wish that she had been able to finish saying why they had been abandoned."

"It was probably a bad collapse or something like that." Ember said knowledgeably. "Dr. Nabielle refused to tell me anything about it, so I am assuming it was nasty."

For the first time, Jack began to wonder how safe these tunnels were. There was a deep silence that made it clear that the other two were thinking the same thing. But none of them said it aloud.

"There's light ahead." Mo called suddenly from the front. A moment later and he came to an abrupt stop.

"What on earth are those?" He asked curiously and Jack saw that they were in another dome but this one wasn't empty, instead, around the outside were metre tall odd looking metal machines with hand driven pumps on one end and claw-like hands on the other.

Mo rushed over to the nearest one and began turning the pump. The claw-like hand immediately began moving up and digging out bits of rock.

"Sounds like there's water inside." Mo said and Jack realised he could hear the sloshing of liquid.

"That'll be hydraulics." Ember said thoughtfully. Jack could almost hear the cogs in her brain whirring as they manufactured a mental image of the inside of the machines.

"Wakey wakey." Mo whispered to Jack, shaking him by the shoulder and Jack suddenly realised he had been staring at Ember thinking for a bit too long.

Mo, who wore a too-knowing smile on his face, and Jack began playing with the machines, seeing who could dig fastest into the rockface. Ember meanwhile was busy disassembling a nearby machine and analysing each bit as she broke it loose.

"Mate, look at how far we have dug!" Mo said excitedly. Suddenly, the two boys looked at each other, the realisation of how long they had been here for hitting them simultaneously.

"Ember, we've got to go! Einor has probably been waiting for us for ages."

Quickly, the three of them darted down the stone corridor, out into the main cavern and into the open.

As soon as his head left the shelter, Jack felt a fat raindrop splatter onto his head. "Great." He muttered sarcastically as he looked up at the murky grey sky. Even as he looked, he could have sworn that he had seen it getting darker and darker.

"C'mon." Mo shouted, almost pushing Jack down the slope towards the path. They went along as fast as they dared but the wet, autumn leaves that covered the floor were now slippery as ice.

Eventually, they re-joined the path and ran up the hill as fast as they could to the turning. Mo arrived first and stood looking puzzled, turning his head frantically from side to side. "Einor isn't here." He called eventually.

Jack continued up to the turning nevertheless and saw for himself that Einor was nowhere to be seen. "How could we have been so stupid!?" Ember said angrily as she arrived. "How could we have been so bloody stupid?!" She repeated.

The three of them gathered gormlessly in a huddle, rain pelting down and soaking their clothes. It seemed to Jack that he would never be properly dry again.

"What do we do now?" Jack shouted, trying to be heard over the downpour.

"Wait here." Ember said firmly. "I don't care how wet we get. I don't care what happens, we are not leaving this spot until Einor gets back."

As if to test her resolve, the wind appeared to pick up, throwing leaves at them like an evil poltergeist while the rain got heavier than ever. Soon, the path that they were standing on was more like a river than the compact mud it had been twenty minutes ago.

"Should we..." Jack began.

"No! We are waiting here until Einor comes back." Ember said before Jack could finish.

"Yeah, and when he does get back, I'm going to slap him. I don't care that he was the Warrior of the World or whatever, he shouldn't've just left us here."

The complaining made everyone feel a little better but not for long. The weather was unrelenting and seemed to drag all motivation from Jack's soul.

Suddenly, loud as gunfire, lightning smashed down from the heavens.

"Ember, look, this is insane. We have to get out of here. Back to the cave."

Ember stayed still, thinking. She was obviously tempted. Mo took less time to decide and walked around to the back of her wheelchair and started pushing it down towards the cave. "Fine. I can get there myself." Ember said grumpily and Mo let go.

Suddenly, there was a mind-whiteningly loud crash from behind them and Jack saw a lightning bolt slam into the turning where they had all been standing moments earlier. "Run!" He shouted but there was no need, the other two were already off, making for the relative safety of the cave.

Jack managed three strides before losing his grip on the

wet leaves and falling to the ground, twisting around as he tumbled. He looked up, back towards the turning, and saw amongst the trees a tall figure watching him. In the figure's hand was a golden-rimmed Sceptre that Jack recognised at once.

Carsicus had found them!

Jack scrambled to his feet before scampering down the path. Several times he stumbled but terror kept him racing forwards, as often as not on all fours just charging onwards in any way that he could. All the time, the rain pelted down from the heavens and the wind roared.

He saw Ember and Mo leave the path and start towards the mine entrance. Gasping, he raced after them. He needed to warn them of the danger.

The cavernous entrance of the mine was dark as night, the weak light of the darkening sky outside all blocked out by the roof.

"Carsicus!" Jack panted as soon as he was through the entrance. He heard the gasps of the other two, but it was too dark to see their faces. "We need to get to the tunnels!"

"Where are they?" Mo asked desperately for it was too dark to see the back wall.

Jack tried to turn a section of the back wall into etter but felt that invisible, impenetrable barrier between him and it, blocking his powers. The Andagaldur walls couldn't be turned into etter he remembered.

Trying desperately to stay calm, he focused all his energy into turning a ball of air into etter. Suddenly, light was splayed out into the cavern. The three of them sprinted towards the central tunnel, there was something reassuring in running towards a place you had been before. As they disappeared through it, Jack returned the ball of etter back into the air it had been before.

Soon, they reached the second cavern where the metal machines were still in their positions against the wall. At the end of this space were two more tunnels. "Right hand one." Jack breathed.

The other two didn't stop and ask and Mo led the way down this tunnel. Every few seconds and Jack would turn a tiny section of air into etter, lighting their way. Each time he turned a new section into etter, he would return the previous one to air, hiding the path that they had chosen from Carsicus.

The passage that they were following deviated from side to side. Several times, Jack glanced over his shoulder expecting to see Carsicus behind him, golden sceptre about to fire but each time, he saw only darkness.

Eventually, the tunnel that they were following opened into another open space although this was much smaller than the others.

"There's nowhere else to go." Mo said suddenly. The words made Jack stop in his tracks. He looked around and saw that it was true. There were no tunnels leading off from this space.

No one said anything but all were wondering the same thing. Would Carsicus find them?

Jack extinguished the final ball of etter that he had made, plunging all of them into total darkness. He heard a whimper and then saw why – through the tunnel that they had just run, there was now a dim golden light that was getting brighter and brighter. There was no doubt about it, Carsicus was coming towards them.

Jack, Ember and Mo all withdrew to the deepest corner of the dome, but they knew it was pointless, once Carsicus reached them there was nothing they could do. As Jack knew, the Andagaldur rock of the cave couldn't be turned to etter and you could not pass through it even in the Deep. It could only be broken by sceptre fire.

The gold light simply got brighter and brighter until Carsicus was standing there before them in the doorway. A murderous, blood-chilling look on his face.

"There's no Lord Alectus to save you now, boy. It's over so come out of your little hidey hole, and we can make this quick."

Trying to catch Carsicus off guard, Jack made a decision, he drew as much energy as he could from the air, turning it into a beam of etter that he fired at Carsicus like a bullet. Carsicus deflected it easily with his Sceptre. "So there you are." He smiled, his voice dripping with sadistic pleasure.

Still with his sick smile, he fired a golden beam at where Jack lay, missing him by inches. Suddenly, there was a cracking sound above Jack which he didn't understand. He saw Carsicus' face become distorted with confusion then horrified realisation.

Another loud crack, this time shaking the floor. Jack now saw that above him, fissures were opening in the rock and there was a roar as one of the fissures suddenly broadened, and water began firing down into the cavern like a waterfall.

In his excitement, Carsicus had made a catastrophic mistake. He had just given the trio a way out. He had just used his own weapon to cut an escape route for his prey.

Jack forced himself into the Deep. He raced over to Mo and Ember, taking both their hands, and carrying them out through the hole that Carsicus had blasted open.

He looked back and saw that Carsicus was enlarged and monochrome, moving in slow motion. A sudden urge to use this chance to recapture Carsicus filled Jack's gut, but he resisted, without the crown, he was no match for Carsicus in a fight in the Deep and couldn't risk Carsicus reacting in time and dropping into the Deep as well. So, Jack continued racing upwards through the water, he was aware that he wasn't swimming, at least definitely not in the normal way, but going upwards nevertheless.

Just as they burst out of the water into the fresh air, Jack looked back and saw that Carsicus had just entered the Deep, he was now colourful and a normal size once more.

The sight gave Jack a frantic, feral energy and he forced himself down into the second level of the Deep but now he could feel himself tiring. Desperately, Jack pulled the other two to the bank and into the forest as far as he could before collapsing in a thicket of bushes. He felt himself leave the Deep entirely. The world returned to its normal size and colour. They could only hide here and wait, hoping that Carsicus wouldn't be able to find them.

So, the three of them lay in total silence, watching as the small, dense ball of etter, which was Carsicus in the Deep, rocketed out of the river and began zooming from side to side in search of them. It passed no more than five feet from where they lay but Jack realised that in the enlarged, monochrome world that Carsicus was seeing, the three of them would be even better camouflaged than normal. So long as none of them moved, they were all but invisible.

The ball of etter zipped away, further downriver. It was just on the edge of their vision when it morphed into Carsicus once more. He then began to prowl down the river, away from where they were, thinking that they had managed to get further from the cave.

"Let's go deeper into the forest." Ember whispered. "He will keep looking for us along the river, the further we can get from there the better."

As quickly and quietly as he could, Jack got to his feet, but his legs and arms felt impossibly heavy, the effort of entering the second level of the Deep had drained him. He only managed a few tired steps before coming to a rest and trying to get his breath back. Sensing Jack's need, Mo put a strong arm around his shoulders and helped his friend further into the forest.

The sky darkened as they walked, from overcast day to overcast night. Eventually, they came to a stop. "This seems as good a place as any." Ember said and Jack saw that they had reached a place where the trees were particularly close together and the undergrowth thick.

"Mo and I will do guard duty tonight." Said Ember as they all crawled into the nearest thicket. "Don't try and be the hero Jack, get some sleep."

Jack had no problem taking those words to heart and was in a deep slumber before he could answer.

CHAPTER 10: WRAITHS

When Jack woke the next morning, he was surprised to find himself refreshed and alert.

"Morning!" Smiled Mo who was on watch.

"Alright." Jack replied, looking to his right and seeing Ember deeply asleep. She let out a loud snore and several birds from a nearby tree took flight. The two boys couldn't help but laugh. Jack looked up, tracking the birds, and saw that although the sky was still grey, it was less ominous and oppressive than the day before.

Ember let out another snore, even louder than the one before. This time, it was powerful enough to wake her and she jerked upright in her chair. "What are you two sniggering at?" She asked as she saw the boys exchanging smiles.

"Nothing." They both replied a little too quickly. She eyed them suspiciously but didn't say any more.

"What's that in the distance?" Jack asked, pointing back upriver, back towards where they had started the day before.

"Teraturt." Ember stated.

"But we were only supposed to get a little way beyond Teraturt yesterday and we must be five miles away!" Jack said.

"At least." Replied Ember "And it would probably more like ten if we were to follow the river back."

"How did we get so far?" Jack asked, amazed.

"We made good speed through the tunnel I guess, it was far more direct than any other route that we could have taken. And we probably got in another mile and a half after escaping Carsicus."

"Awesome." Jack grinned.

Seeing as they had made good progress the day before, Ember suggested that they spend an hour scavenging food and water.

"You stay here and collect food. Jack and I will head back to the river and fill up the water bottles." Mo said. Seeing Ember ready to argue, Mo quickly added. "You will make too much noise going through the forest. I mean, Jack is hardly any quieter but at least he can enter the Deep so has the best chance of escaping Carsicus if he spots us."

Ember reluctantly agreed and started collecting food.

Mo and Jack snuck through the forest towards the river. They stopped twenty metres or so from its banks and lay prone on the floor, scanning the forest on either side for any golden glimmer from Carsicus.

Several times, Jack caught a golden glimmer out of the corner of his eye and looked frightenedly towards it but each time it was only an autumnal leaf falling onto the loamy forest floor. Eventually, the two boys worked up the confidence to begin sliding on their bellies towards the lake. It was Mo who went the whole way to the river and filled up the bottles whilst Jack stayed hidden, watching for any sign of Carsicus.

There was a tremendous amount of relief in the air, even from Mo, when the final bottle was filled, and they could slip back into the relative safety of the forest. On their journey back, the grey sky cracked open like the mine roof the day before and, like the mineshaft, blue seeped through the broadening fissures but, instead of water, this was sunny sky. By the time that they arrived back, Jack had never seen a day look less overcast.

"I have just finished, I think. I ate my share whilst I was collecting." Said Ember. "Although I need some water to wash it down."

Mo handed Ember the bottles and sat next to Jack, both eating with enthusiasm, suddenly realising just how hungry they were. Jack hardly noticed the abrupt return of his diet to the same as he had eaten for a month whilst in the Wilderness.

"Should we get going then?" Jack asked as he finished his food. "We ended up going way further than expected yesterday. If we can keep up a decent pace, we should be able to get there even before the two weeks that Einor was hoping for."

"Yeah I would love to get there faster than Einor thought we could. Really show him." Said Ember with alarming conviction. "Then when he arrives, I can give him a good dressing down." She continued.

"I suppose we have to get back to the river. We don't want to get lost." Jack said, dreading the thought of the tension that being close to the river brought him, knowing that Carsicus was somewhere along it, searching for them...

"No, I don't think we do actually." Said Ember "I found a path while gathering the food and it led in the right direction. It should be more direct as well."

"But Dr. Nabielle said..."

"I really could not care less about what Dr. Nabielle said right now, it was her idea for Einor to go with us and look how that has turned out."

Mo looked thoughtful. "I say we follow this path that Ember found. If it goes wrong, we can always come back here and start again but I really want to reach the University in less than two weeks. And really show Einor as Ember says."

"Ok." Said Jack. "Lead the way then Ember."

The path was only a few minutes walk from where they had camped. It was not immediately obvious as it was far smaller than the path they had begun along the day before and there was undergrowth across it, like it had once been a well-maintained road that had since fallen into disrepair.

"Perfect." Mo smiled. "Easy to walk along and there is unlikely to be anyone just strolling along it."

They made good progress throughout the morning and the path continued dead straight in the direction that Mo and Ember insisted was the right one. It was almost too good to be true.

At midday, they stopped for lunch. As they ate, Mo was of course fidgeting, rubbing his shoe up and down on the dirt floor, digging into the softness.

"Hey, look at this!" He said suddenly.

"What is it?"

"Metal I think, yeah look it definitely is."

"Looks like a rod to me." Jack observed.

"OH!" Said Ember, "This must be an old track for the carts from the mine. I bet that there are metal rails the whole way under this path, and it leads the whole way from the mine to Scholar's City."

"That would explain why it is so straight." Mo added.

All Jack could do was nod and wonder at their luck; they had stumbled across a path that drew a ruler straight line to where they wanted to get to. Something did bother him though. "Why would Einor not just bring us along this path in the first place?"

The other two looked at each other. No one could find an answer. "Maybe he didn't know it was here." Said Mo but his voice was more hopeful than confident.

Soon, lunch was over and they continued down the path. The sun was now out and the climate under the trees couldn't have been any more pleasant for walking.

"Some music now and it would be perfect." Jack said dreamily.

"How about this?

He escaped Carsicus yesterday...

J – A – C – K

University, he's on his way,

J – A – C – K

Hooray, Hooray for

J – A – C – K"

Mo sang, and every time he spelt Jack's name, he would form the letters with his arms like a cheerleader.

"I hope you appreciate that you are an embarrassment not only to yourself but to all of earth." Jack replied, feeling thoroughly uncomfortable.

Mo only grinned with more life than ever.

"He escaped Carscisu yes..." Mo began again.

"Shut up. I think I heard something." Ember whispered suddenly and Mo went quiet.

However, nothing moved and the wood remained quiet.

"Did you just do that to stop me singing?" Mo asked a few moments later.

"No." Ember replied tersely, and Jack was certain that she had heard something, or at least thought she had.

There were no more jump scares though throughout the day and when it began to get dark, Jack (who was first on lookout) wasn't expecting to see anything other than squirrels or hear anything except Ember's snoring.

The darkness came quickly under the thick trees and soon, Jack couldn't see much beyond the end of his arm. Mo and Ember found sleep quickly. They had agreed that each was to have four hours lookout duty and eight hours sleep so Jack got comfortable expecting a boring but straightforward watch.

The forest floor muffled all sound so even the scampering of squirrels was dulled and soothing and soon, Jack found himself feeling tired from a day of walking, every moment his brain began to drift from the job at hand, he could feel his eyelids easing their way towards each other, towards sleep...

Before long, Jack found himself resting in that place just before sleep where you see without seeing and thoughts become long and easy to lose yourself in.

Suddenly, he felt a strange tingling in his back that quickly spread to his fingertips. He felt as though he was being watched. Like some twisted dream, a shape emerged from a tree, it was upright and huge with yellow demon eyes. For a moment it stood still, eyes boring into Jack like torturous drills escaped from Hades while he sat there looking back, too terrified to scream. Then it turned and now that the yellow eyes couldn't be seen, the outline of the creature was hard to distinguish from the trees around it but Jack could have sworn he saw it clambering away on all fours.

Jack stood on unsteady legs and edged his way towards the others before waking them. His terrified trembling causing him to shake them far harder than he meant. Both jerked awake.

When they sat up, Jack finally let out the breath that he hadn't even realised he was holding. For several minutes, it was all he could do to suck oxygen in, trying to calm himself.

"Is he having a heart attack?" Mo asked concernedly.

Jack shook his head and eventually managed to gasp the words "Demon ... Demon eyes."

The other two exchanged horrified looks. "Just relax, there isn't anything out there." Ember said soothingly, allowing Jack to relax just enough to speak again.

"It was over there." He said pointing. "I saw yellow eyes and the outline of something..." Jack gasped. Then, suddenly he rasped the word "wraith... wraith... wraith." He didn't know where the word came from but knew that that was what he had seen.

Mo and Ember stared hard in the direction Jack had pointed. "There's nothing there." Mo said decisively.

How could they not understand the fear that the wraith had brought? Jack could think of nothing else...

"We should all stay awake tonight though." Said Ember and Jack gasped his gratitude. "None of us will be able to get to sleep anyway."

For the rest of the night, the three of them pressed as close to each other as they could. The autumn wood that had seemed so beautiful to walk through during the day was now an enemy in and of itself, the trees helping demons conceal themselves while the blanket of leaves was designed to make the approach of monsters as quiet as possible.

However, when the pale pink rays of dawn broke through, there had been no more scares.

As the day brightened, one thought ruthlessly dominated Jack's thoughts. Why had he frozen? During their time in the Wilderness, he had bravely fought every monster that had threatened the camp so why had he frozen so badly this time? How had he suddenly turned into a coward?

Jack was so lost in thought that Ember had to shout to get his attention. "Are you ok for Mo and I to go and gather food? Or do you want one of us to stay with you?"

"G … go. I'll be fine." Jack said, aware of his voice breaking as he spoke.

Ember looked at him uncertainly but left with Mo to go and collect food nevertheless. Jack stayed stock still looking into the distance wondering what had happened during the night.

When the others returned, Jack still hadn't moved. When Ember offered him food, a vision of the yellow eyes he had seen flashed in his brain and suddenly the thought of food made Jack's stomach turn and he refused any. "Well we will save some." Ember said calmly, "I am sure you will be hungry in a bit."

Then, the other two started packing up. Jack wanted to go and help but every time he tried to get to his feet, the yellow eyes shot into his brain once more and he felt an irresistible urge to stay where he was.

"C'mon, let's get a move on. We should be able to make good progress today." Mo said happily. The tone of his words brought Jack slightly more to his senses and he found his feet.

Mo set the tempo, striding through the forest. As Jack hurried after him, he found that the freshness of the morning air and the exercise of quick walking made him more sensible. He started to think clearly again. It hadn't been surprising that he had been terrified of the eyes, they had been so unexpected and menacing. Next time, he would deal with them better. He would not let his guard down again.

At midday, Jack made sure to eat plenty of food which did even more than the walk for returning his critical faculties and he felt almost back to normal. Understandably, a bit tired, a little on edge, but nothing he couldn't deal with.

As evening began to deepen and they came to a halt, he offered to take first watch. Ember and Mo looked closely at him but Jack insisted that he was fine and would wake them if he saw anything.

But as the daylight faded, he found his mind wondering to the yellow eyes of the Wraith once more. He could not hold any other thoughts, as if they were too scared to enter his brain at the same time as the Wraith. When the forest became night dark again, Jack's visions of the yellow eyes became clearer and clearer and the terror that they brought with them mounted.

His heart hammered and Jack could hardly summon the courage to keep his eyes open.

Suddenly, a hand touched his shoulder. Jack screamed until the hand clamped over his mouth.

"Shut up you clown." Came Mo's voice. "You weren't answering when I was trying to talk to you so I had to get your attention somehow."

"Th... th... thank you." Jack stammered.

"You alright?" Mo asked.

Jack could only nod.

"Have you seen anything else?"

Jack wanted to tell Mo about the yellow eyes that filled his mind, that haunted every thought but couldn't find the words so just gasped. "Not... not in the forest."

Mo's eyes were full of worry and concern. "Get some sleep. You will feel better in the morning."

But as Jack lay on the floor, the yellow eyes prevented him from sleeping, from resting. They were always watching, waiting for his guard to be lowered.

When Ember offered him breakfast, it seemed to Jack that the nuts and berries were crawling and alive like maggots. Again, his stomach rolled at the sight of them and it was all he could do to stop himself being sick.

As they walked that day, Jack couldn't escape the yellow

eyes. He didn't eat lunch even though he could feel how hungry and tired he was, the concept of food revolted him.

When Ember and Mo stopped for the night, Jack lay in a foetal position on the floor, shivering and terrified. His mind thinking of the yellow eyes that only grew more vivid in the darkness.

The next morning, it seemed to Jack that the sun never rose. Everything was dark. Everything except the yellow eyes that filled his mind. He hardly knew that he was walking, was oblivious to the fact that he was staggering onwards.

He stopped abruptly.

"Stop!" He shouted drunkenly at the forest. "Stop!" He yelled again at the yellow eyes that filled his mind.

Mo was quick to cover Jack's mouth again to prevent him from shouting and letting the whole forest know where they were.

Ember looked terrified but when she spoke, her voice was clear and logical. "We should stop here. Jack needs rest. There is no need to rush."

Mo and Ember spent the afternoon building a bed for Jack and helping him in. Several times, Mo had to cover Jack's mouth as he started shouting again at the yellow eyes. Mo took advantage of one of these outbursts to force some water and food down Jack's throat. It caused him to cough and splutter, but he did manage to drink and eat a little.

The meal, minimal as it was, revived Jack's normal self a bit and just before he tried to go to sleep, he said something to the others.

"What if the mine didn't close because of a collapse and what if Einor didn't forget about this path?"

"What do you mean?"

"What if there is something in this forest that terrified

the miners away? What if Einor made us stay out of the woods because there was something in here more dangerous than Carsicus?"

The other two looked at each other. "Jack, did you see something?" Ember asked but Jack was already asleep, trying to keep the yellow eyes out of his dream.

It was only in the morning that Jack heard something that broke into his consciousness. It was Mo saying, "During the night, I think I saw what Jack saw. I saw yellow eyes." Jack felt delighted at the words. He knew that they meant that Mo would soon be joining him.

Where would Mo be joining him?

Jack wasn't sure where he was going but knew that he was nearly there.

That morning, neither Ember nor Mo suggested that they go any further while Jack lay corpse-like in the bed that they had made. "He just needs rest." They said to each other and themselves all through the day but neither believed it, every minute that ticked by, he was getting weaker and weaker.

As he lay in his terrified, unsleeping state that night, Jack began to feel things moving towards him in the dark. He didn't have to open his eyes to know that wraiths were in a ring, closing in on them.

He heard Mo shout and Ember scream. For a moment, this brought some of his old self back and Jack began to fight the yellow eyes that filled his brain, but they quickly overpowered him and Jack found himself lying contentedly backwards. Knowing that wraiths were coming to get him. He finally knew what lay at the end of his journey... he too would become a wraith.

Skeletal arms wrapped around him, and Jack felt himself being lifted off the ground. Ember and Mo were still shouting and screaming, fighting the wraiths as best they could. Why could they not understand that the wraiths were family that they were about to join?

Ember and Mo went quiet and the wraith holding him started to run. Jack could also feel the other wraiths running alongside him, carrying Mo and Ember with them towards their home.

For several hours, they crashed through the forest.

Eventually, they stopped and for the first time since the day before, Jack's eyelids opened. He saw that they were in a clearing. The perimeter was composed of a few hundred wraiths. In the middle was a short stocky woman.

"Welcome, welcome to your new home. My name is Tyshah." She said, spreading her arms.

"What do you want?" Mo spat.

"I want you to join my family." Said Tyshah. At these words, Jack felt a warmth in his heart towards her. He wanted to join her family.

"What do you mean join your family?" Mo replied viciously.

"Become wraiths like all my other children." Tyshah said excitedly. "Oh look, this one has already started." She gasped, crossing over to Jack and drawing her hand across his face. "Two or three days more and he will become one of us!"

"What do you have to gain from this?" Ember asked.

"Nothing, nothing, I just like watching the process. It is so beautiful if you know what to look for. Twelve years ago, I created my first wraith knowing that it would be the first of many, the start of a family. I let him roam through the forest, waiting for unsuspecting prey and soon my family began to grow. You see, the moment that the yellow eyes of the Wraith meet yours, it plants a part of itself inside you. First comes the fear that consumes you, then you stop wanting to resist the fear and just fade away, let the Wraith take over your soul..."

Tyshah's words made Jack happy, confirmed that he would soon cease to exist, and his body would become a Wraith like the others.

"I must take my children to hunt but don't worry, we will be back soon, I wouldn't miss your turning for the world, my child." Tyshah said, looking hungrily at Jack who could only stare vacantly back.

Without another word, Tyshah turned and scampered off into the woods, the Wraiths following in a pack behind her. Jack could hear Mo struggling against his bonds. He tried to speak to the others a few times, convince them that joining Tyshah would be good but the gag across his mouth muffled them beyond comprehension.

Eventually, they heard noises. Ember whimpered, expecting the immediate return of the wraiths and Tyshah. But, as the noises grew closer, Jack was able to hear particular voices. They were male voices.

CHAPTER 11:
ENGELIAL

"Quickly then you lot. We want to press on today, try and get to Scholar's City before evening." Came the earthy voice of one of the men. Somehow, the honest, hard-working tone made Jack's mind clearer again. It was the total opposite of the dark magic of the yellow eyes.

"MMMM!!!!" Mo began making as much noise as he could through his gag.

"What was that?" Asked the earthy voice.

"It might be a wraith!" Replied another voice.

"Don't be silly. There are no such things as wraiths."

"MMMM!!!!" Mo moaned again.

"Still, we need to get on." Said the earthy voice. "Doubtless just some strange animal."

Jack heard footsteps going away.

Suddenly, there was a deafening crash as Ember slammed a branch into the metal side of her wheelchair.

One of the men screamed and bolted away shouting "Wraiths! Wraiths! Wraiths!"

"Charlie, you go after that muppet. George, you come with me to see what made that noise."

Soon, the two men emerged into the clearing in the forest where Jack, Ember and Mo were tied up.

"Well what have we here?" Asked the taller of the two men and Jack realised that it was the one with the earthy voice.

"University students sir." Said Ember quickly.

"And what are University students doing tied up in the middle of a wood?"

"It is a challenge sir; at dawn we were tied up and left here and we have to get back to the University before nightfall."

Both men broke into smiles. "I remember doing a similar challenge when I was at University although I must admit I was a fair bit older than you three."

"Please sir, if you untie us then we will be back long before evening, we might even be able to break the record of fastest time back." Said Mo, cottoning on to Ember's story.

"You have yourself a deal." Smiled the earthy man. "On one condition, when we arrive at the University, you clean the stables."

"Deal!" Said Mo and Ember enthusiastically.

"You must be keen on getting that record. My name is Raleigh, by the way."

Soon, the three of them had been untied and were being helped through the forest. Raleigh explained that he was the master of horses for Lady Engelial who was on her way to the University. George, Charlie, and Miles (the one who had run off) were his apprentices. Raleigh's voice again had the effect of recovering Jack's normal thought process a little, but he was too tired to understand all that was going on around him.

As they walked, Jack became aware of the sound of flowing water.

"The river!" Said Ember excitedly and Jack realised that this Lady Engelial must be going along the riverbanks to the University. He realised as well that if they were with the large crowd of people escorting Lady Engelial to the University,

Carsicus would have a hard time spotting them and an even harder time getting to them.

Lady Engelial's escort was huge, if Jack hadn't known better, he would have thought that it was an army. She had at least fifty guards, various high-ranking people to aid her in every eventuality besides huge numbers of cooks, stableboys, and other helpers.

"There you are." Said a grumpy voice as the five of them reached the large group. "We've been waiting for you before we set off. What took you so long?"

"These two stableboys wanted to go a bit further away so that no one could hear them doing their business." Said Raleigh, indicating Mo and Jack. Ember had wheeled herself away and pretended not to know them.

The owner of the grumpy voice shook his head in a disapproval.

Once it had been shouted through the group that everyone was there and ready to march, they continued down the River towards the University. They made good progress for several hours.

Suddenly, just as they turned a meander of the river, the yellow eyes that had faked surrender into the deepest corner of Jack's mind launched an ambush. They leered over him, holding his gaze, his thoughts. But Jack managed to remember the earthy voice and the river and, in his head, the nature of Arcane did battle with the yellow eyes of the Wraith inside him.

The ferocity of the battle within his skull caused Jack to drop to his knees. He felt Mo's strong arm wrap across his shoulders to support him and still the battle raged.

Then, he felt Ember draw close to him. "Jack." She whispered. "We are almost there. Just look."

Jack forced his eyelids open and saw a blot on the horizon. "That's Scholar's City." Ember breathed.

Jack managed a harsh, raggedy intake of breath and tried to force himself to his feet. With Mo's support, he managed to get upright once more.

Mo half-pushed, half-carried Jack along the riverbank towards the blot on the horizon. All Jack could do was try and keep his eyes open, struggle to force the yellow eyes from his brain.

He didn't notice when the forest thinned and then stopped, giving way to green floodplain. Then, for the first time in several hours, Jack looked up and saw that only a short distance further downriver, houses stood on either side of the river.

"Scholar's City." Mo said happily. "C'mon mate, you can do this."

The happiness of seeing the finishing line of their journey drove the yellow eyes to the very back of his mind. For the first time, he noticed the day's blue sky and cool breeze.

Scholar's City grew very quickly and before Jack knew it, the first house was a stone's throw from where he stood.

"Dr. Nabielle said that the safe house was on this side of the river." Ember said, looking hopelessly at the rows and rows of houses to their left. "Number 24, East High Road."

Jack leant against Mo's arm, wondering how they could possibly find the house. The doubt left an opening for the yellow eyes which rose like a viper and stared him down once more.

Jack let out a noise between a scream and a groan. He felt his legs turn to jelly and only Mo's quick reactions prevented him from collapsing onto the floor.

"We need to get him to the safe house." Mo said urgently and he and Ember looked more frantically at the houses but had no clue where East High Road was.

"You are holding up the queue, what've you stopped for?" Barked the owner of the grumpy voice. "And what's wrong with him?" He asked, jerking a bony pink finger at Jack.

"Nothing, he's fine." Mo replied.

"Well keep moving then. Lady Engelial wants time to change before having dinner."

"'course she does." Said the earthy voice of Raleigh, who had just caught up with them.

"You should show a bit more respect to the Lady."

"Make me." Raleigh returned and that was the end of the conversation. "You sure he is alright?" Raleigh asked, nodding at Jack, his voice properly concerned.

"We are all just very tired. We haven't slept for two days." Said Ember, yawning.

Raleigh smiled. "I understand. I was a Uni student once as well. Tell you what, you don't have to clean out the stables today, just make sure to come and find me and do it another day."

"Thank you." Mo beamed.

"Well, see you around." Said Raleigh, turning to go just as Jack let out another moan.

"Sorry, do you know where East High Road is?" Ember called after him.

"Yeah, just follow the left turn here and it's the third turning on the right."

"Thanks again." Ember called after him. Mo was already half-guiding, half-pulling Jack down the left turning.

"One... Two... Three." He counted as they passed the roads on the right. "This is the one!" He muttered and Jack opened his eyes just enough to see a sign saying 'East High Road.' They soon reached number 24, a squat wooden bungalow.

Ember pulled the key from the back of her wheelchair and unlocked the door before helping Mo carry Jack through the doorway. The bedroom was at the end of the main corridor. Jack felt a thump as he was dropped onto the bed.

Finally, they had reached Scholar's City. But at what cost?

As Jack lay in bed, the battle continued to rage in his head, tearing him apart. He knew that this wasn't how it normally went. Normally, the wraith grew stronger and stronger until it took over its host. It was not used to being fought. But Jack was certain that the fight between the wraith and all that was good would tear him apart leaving who knew what.

There was a rhythmic tap on the door but with his head aching like it was, the sound seemed loud as cannon fire. Mo and Ember both bolted for the door.

Jack heard the door swing open and Ember gasp, "Einor!"

"This way." Mo growled and seconds later, he burst into the room where Jack lay, Einor just behind him.

"What happened?" Einor challenged.

"Wraiths." Mo replied.

"Can you fix him?" Ember asked.

"Maybe."

"It is your fault he is like this." Mo stated. "You fix him, or I'll make you regret the day that you were born."

But Einor was already working on Jack and too focused on his patient to listen to Mo's threats. He pulled Jack's eyelids open and leant in so close that they were nearly eyeball to eyeball. Jack saw Einor's face turn from concerned to terrified.

"He is a long way gone but there is still some hope." Said Einor. He pulled Jack's jaw open and poured water down it. Just like in the forest, it made him cough and splutter, but some found its way down his throat, and he felt a little better

"You two light a fire and keep him warm. Try and get some food down him if you can but the main thing is you keep him warm."

"Where are you going?"

"To get the only thing that might just save him."

"Ok. But if you wander off and go looking for Briar instead, I will find and I will kill you." Said Mo. But Einor had already gone.

Ember and Mo got busy throwing the wood that was stacked up around the fireplace into the furnace and Ember managed to get a spark from the flint that lay next to the fireplace. The spark was soon taken up by the wood and spread quickly. The heat poured into the room and Jack began to feel his muscles again, started to feel connected to his body once more.

"Closer." He managed to gasp. Ember and Mo looked at each other, it was the first word that he had spoken for days.

Mo grabbed the bottom of the bed and began to pull with all his might and, with plenty of squeaking, edged the bed to the fireside.

"Do you reckon you can drink something?" Ember asked.

Jack nodded and Mo put the water to his mouth and Jack allowed it to trickle down his throat. Then, he patted the bed on either side of him.

Mo and Ember got what he meant and both sat down on the bed, helping keep Jack warm. Jack swam in and out of consciousness and it felt like only a few moments until they heard the door swing open again, marking Einor's return.

For a second, Jack thought that Einor had forgotten to bring anything back with him but then noticed a small sachet of crushed green leaves.

"Is that everything you need?" Ember asked, sounding

surprised.

Einor grunted that it was. "Just need to dissolve them in some boiling water."

Mo went to get up and help but Einor shook his head, "No, you two both stay there." So, they watched along with Jack as Einor began heating a small metal pot above the flames that now took up the entire fireplace. Every few seconds, he would sprinkle a thimble of the green leaves into the pot and stir it.

Eventually, the sachet was empty.

Bracing himself, Jack forced his mouth open. Einor looked surprised that he didn't have to force Jack's jaw open and poured the liquid into his mouth.

Jack was aware of Mo and Ember's close attention as he swallowed as much as he could. He blinked. Then became vividly aware of the sensation of warmth that flowed from his mouth to his stomach. The heat seeped left and right, backwards and forwards, up and down through his veins into his body.

"Do you feel better?" Ember asked nervously.

"Yeah!" Jack smiled, getting up so quickly that he nearly pushed Ember and Mo off the bed. He did one quick lap around the room appreciating his strength like he never had before.

He saw that Mo and Ember were looking at him, incredulous.

"I feel fine." He exploded, excitement making his voice ten times louder than he had meant. "Should we go and explore?"

"Not quite yet you lunatic." Mo laughed. "Let's make sure you are definitely better before doing anything like that."

There was something so familiar in Mo's crooked grin that brought Jack to his senses, and he took a seat on the bed. "Thank you." He said to Einor.

"Thank you!" Ember exclaimed. "It is because of him you were in that state in the first place, that you nearly became a … a … a wraith! I think he has got some explaining to do."

"Fair enough." Einor sighed, slipping into the chair in the corner of the room. "I did slip off into Teraturt for a little bit."

"To do what?" Ember probed.

"Does it really matter?"

"Yes."

"Well you can probably guess can't you Miss. Genius."

"I think we all can, but I want to hear you **SAY IT!**" Ember replied, her voice rising to a shout.

"Fine! I went to go and get some Briar. There, I said it."

"Hmm…" Ember acknowledged in her most disapproving manner.

Jack saw Einor's nose twitch with irritation. Ember, noticing as well, crossed her arms. "Stupid kids." Einor growled as he turned and walked away.

For the rest of the afternoon, Jack filled the other two in on what he had felt in the forest, the constant internal battle between himself and the wraith. Ember had an expression of terror throughout and even Mo looked slightly concerned but lying in a comfortable bed with the warmth of whatever it was that Einor had given him made the whole experience feel no more substantial than a dream to Jack.

"Should we go cook?" Mo asked once Jack had finished the story.

"Ok." Ember replied quickly.

"Jack?" Mo asked.

"I dunno, still feeling a little bit rough actually mate."

"Yes, of course you do." Ember said, pushing herself off the bed and into her wheelchair. "You just stay there."

Just as Mo left the room, Jack winked at him and saw his friend break into a wide smile.

"Einor! Dinner's ready." Mo shouted an hour later. There was silence throughout the house. "Einor?"

"Oh for goodness sakes!" Ember exclaimed.

Jack helped Mo check every room in the house, but both didn't look with much expectation, just hope that Einor hadn't left them. But he had. Of course he had.

Throughout dinner, Ember maintained a steady silence that Jack knew stemmed from resentment towards the missing person on the four-man table.

Einor still hadn't returned when the three of them decided that it was time for bed. Ember insisted that Jack sleep in the actual bed while Mo and herself slept in separate bundles of anything soft that they could find. Jack hadn't put up any resistance although he had made himself promise that from tomorrow, he wouldn't let the others do all the work thinking that he still needed to recover because he felt really pretty good.

CHAPTER 12:
ACROSS THE RIVER

Jack woke unexpectedly at midnight. He sat up and stretched, wondering why he had woken.

Soft footsteps approached down the hallway. Silently, Jack got out of bed cursing himself for not finding Sauris and keeping it next to his bed.

The footsteps stopped and the door swung open. A huge man entered the room. "Ah, Jack you are awake." Einor's voice said, and Jack sighed with relief. "How are you feeling?"

"Good."

"Ok, excellent. Do you think you are strong enough for a walk?"

"A walk?"

"Yeah. There's some stuff I wanted you to see."

"Like what?"

"The other side of this town."

"Should I wake the others?"

"Mo, yes. Ember, no."

"Why?"

"I don't want to spend the whole evening getting patronised by a little girl and anyway I think that you and Mo will gain more from seeing the other side of this town."

Jack paused for a moment. "Sorry, I can't. I'm not going to

leave Ember out of anything Mo and I are doing."

"Fine, it's you that needs to see this really so let the other two sleep."

Moments later, Alectus and Jack were out into the night. It was warm and the moon was shining bright, lighting their path. They made their way towards the river, retracing the steps that Jack had staggered earlier that day.

Several times, they passed people but every time that they drew close, the people would draw their jackets up their face and cross the path so that they couldn't be identified.

After the fifth or sixth person had done the exact same thing, Jack had to turn to Einor and ask, "what are they all doing?"

"They don't want to be seen coming from the bridges, do they?" Einor replied and Jack was alarmed to hear more contempt in Einor's voice than he had ever heard before, which was saying something.

"Why not?"

"It's one in the morning. They aren't going to the poor bit of town to do charity work are they?"

"So what are they going there to do?"

"Use your imagination. Yeah, they are going to be doing all that and worse." Einor spat on to the floor of the nice bit of town.

They passed two more people on the bridge and again, both of them distanced themselves and hid their faces.

As soon as they were on the other side of the bridge, Jack noticed that the houses were closer together. A horrific stench rose into his nose causing him to splutter.

"That's the sewage." Einor growled.

On this half of town, there were more people out. But,

instead of slinking into the shadows, they didn't move as Einor and Jack approached except to turn their downbeat, hungry eyes towards the two strangers. Sometimes, Einor would go to them, Jack following closely behind, and give them some money. On a few occasions, Einor sat down and spoke with them for a while. Jack realised that when Einor was talking to these strangers, his voice wasn't its usual growling, menacing tones but instead soothing and understanding.

Jack thought of the times before when Einor had strayed from his normal tough guy persona and spoken softly, when he had been talking of Dr. Nabielle and when he had been thinking of his childhood.

"Do you know why I have brought you here?" Einor whispered to Jack as they moved down a particularly dark, ominous street.

"No."

"The kids up at the University, the ones whose mummy's and daddy's paid more money to send their kids to University than anyone here sees in a lifetime, those kids sometimes like to have a bit of fun of an evening, to see who is the bravest, they walk through the nice new bit of town and come here to smash stuff up after dark."

"Why doesn't anyone do anything about it?"

"The police couldn't care less about what happens on this side of the river. They sure as hell aren't going to risk their lives coming to check out some vandalism down here. Especially not when they know it is the sons and daughters of their boss smashing the place up."

Jack felt such a deep sadness at the way of the world, at the resentment in Einor's voice, at the selfishness of the kids up at the University.

"Surely it isn't all the people at the University." Jack said, needing some thimble of hope.

"No. But even the ones who don't get involved aren't interested in stopping it."

Jack sighed deeply.

"Which is why I brought you here. I want you to promise me that not only will you not get involved in it. You will try and stop it."

"Of course I promise." Jack said firmly, looking Einor dead in the eye.

Suddenly, there was the sound of smashing glass. "Was that some of the students?" Jack asked but Einor had already shot off, his silhouette bounding like an apex predator towards the sound. A sense of vulnerability swam through Jack's veins, and he sprinted after Einor as fast as his legs could carry him.

The scene was only just around the corner, a group of two dozen all on horseback were in a tight knot in front of a grey, concrete building. Two of the group shoved their way through the window that they had just smashed open. Jack realised with a start that they weren't students but police.

Seconds later, the pair who had broken into the building returned, dragging a defeated man who was bone thin and dressed in rags. His greasy hair hung from his head in places while other patches were bald as though the hair had been torn off his scalp.

Just as the man was shoved onto horseback by one of the policemen, Jack saw Einor step out of the crowd, the darkness hiding his outlawed face.

"What?" Said the police officer aggressively, taking a truncheon from his belt.

"What grounds do you have for arresting that man?"

"The hospital stores were raided today; this man has a criminal record of stealing."

"But you don't have any actual evidence, do you? You are

151

just going to arrest someone innocent to be your scapegoat, to improve your numbers." Einor growled.

"I don't have to explain myself to you. Why do you care anyway?"

"Because it was me who stole the Iris."

There was a seconds pause and then the police began diving towards Einor one after the other like fish jumping into the sea. Einor, however, either darted out the way or shoved them to the side. Just before he fled, he made eye-contact with Jack and pointed in the direction of 24 East Road.

Jack turned and ran back through the Old Town, over the bridge and home. He banged loudly on the door before putting his hands to his knees and gasping for breath. Before the door had even swung open, Jack was joined in the porch outside the house by Einor.

When Mo opened the door, he looked in disbelief at Jack and Einor as they walked past him into the hallway.

"Where HAVE you been?" Ember demanded.

Einor ignored her and instead walked into the kitchen to get himself some water. Jack took the time to collapse onto the floor and explain the adventure to them. He did, however, leave out the conversation he had had with Einor about promising not to go and vandalise the Old Town. He knew that that was to be kept private.

The next day, Ember and Mo woke early, keen to explore the other half of the city.

"Can we go and see the University first?" Jack asked. "Seeing as that is why we are here."

Ember and Mo took little persuading and not long after sunrise, they had set out into the street, leaving Einor fast asleep, to find the University. Jack recalled Einor saying how the University students 'passed through the new town on their way to the bridges' so guided the other two away from the bridges to the old bit of the city.

His guess was proved correct when they found a city map showing the University only a two-minute walk along the path that they were already following.

"Race you there." Mo grinned, already running off. Jack didn't bother trying to catch him and instead watched his friend sprint away.

Then suddenly fall over.

But he fell all wrong. He didn't trip or slip, he bounced backwards!

By the time that Jack reached him, Mo was sitting up, rubbing his head. "There's something there." Mo mumbled, pointing to where he had bounced off. Now that Jack looked closely, he saw that there was a haze exactly where Mo had bounced.

Cautiously, Jack approached it with his hand out-stretched.

"No, Jack, don't be stupid, it might be electrocuted."

"There isn't any electricity in Arcane."

"Well I don't know but don't touch it."

Reluctantly, Jack returned his hand to his pocket and stepped back. He saw a blur out the corner of his eye as Mo launched a spinning kick at the invisible wall. Once more, his foot bounced off.

The trio all looked at each other, bemused.

"We should do that more often." Said a voice behind them, making the three of them turn around. Two young men were walking towards them. University students, Jack realised.

"Sorry, do you know how to get in?" Ember asked in

her best Arcanian.

"Stupid Old Towners." Said one of the pair. Despite his lack of Arcanian, Jack didn't doubt that he had heard right, the superior smile and arrogant eyes of the boy spoke for themselves.

"Most animals learn that you can't just walk through but Old Towners, well they are the stupidest members of the animal kingdom."

"The world's gone soft – I can't believe that we now bother to put animals in wheelchairs." Said the first boy looking at Ember just as he passed through the barrier that had blocked Mo's path earlier. And, the second he was over the threshold, he vanished. It was lucky for the boy that he had because Jack darted forwards before Mo or Ember could stop him but, just like Mo had earlier, Jack simply bounced backwards off the transparent barrier.

Still fuming, Jack stormed off back the way that they had come, he wanted to return to East Road and ask Einor about the barrier.

It only took them half as long to get home as it had to reach the University such was the pace that Jack was setting in his fury. When they arrived back, Einor was up and eating breakfast.

"How come some people can get into the University and others can't?" Jack asked as soon as Einor had opened the door.

"Eileaftium." Einor replied at once, not showing any interest in Jack's lack of manners. "The dwarves were able to make it such that it only let certain people through, only those who have permission to enter the University can pass through the barrier."

"But I am going to the University, and it didn't let me through."

"You haven't started there yet. It will let you through

when it is time. Stop worrying."

"I'm not worried." Jack answered quicky. "How come we couldn't see a barrier?"

"Another of the magical properties of that material, the dwarves were able to make it so that inside was white space. Tell me what you saw through the barrier."

"More houses." Said Ember.

"A field." Replied Jack.

"Farmland." Mo answered.

They all looked at each other as though they were worried about their sanity.

Einor remained with a smug expression, "everything within the dome of Eileaftium is hidden, what you all saw was simply what you expected to see."

"But how did the Eileaftium know what we expected to see?"

"It doesn't have to; all it has to do is be full of white space. Your own brain does the rest, it doesn't believe that there is only white space there so fills in the gaps with what it thinks should be there."

"Wow." Ember said, awestruck. Jack and Mo remained looking a bit suspicious.

"So what is actually behind the Eileaftium then?" Jack asked curiously.

"How would I know? I never had the chance to go to the University, did I?" Said Einor, his tone made it clear that that was the end of the conversation.

Every night for the two weeks until University began, Jack would tell the others that he needed to go out for a walk to clear his mind, but his feet would inevitably draw him to the University, and he would sit and think what was really be-hind the barrier. Dr. Nabielle would be able to tell him, but she wasn't here.

So, instead of clearing his mind, it filled it with yet more worry and uncertainty. Just endless ideas of what could be hid-den from his view. Then there was the fact that even once he got to the University, he would somehow have to befriend the King, who would undoubtably be surrounded by the popular kids. Mo would be so much better than Jack at that with his easy smile and unbelievable athleticism. What on earth could Jack do or say to impress any of them?

CHAPTER 13:
THE MAZE

Before Jack knew it, he was waking up on the morning of his first day at the University. Mo was not only already up but had been for a run and started making porridge. Einor was nowhere to be found, Jack wanted to believe that he was in the Old Town, being the kind, good-natured person that he could be. But Jack doubted it. Since that night when he had taken Jack to the old bit of the city, Einor hadn't gone back there. Instead, he had gotten into four fights and Mo had seen him spend a whole day at a suspicious house a few streets away, presumably drinking Briar. Jack couldn't work out how Einor's two sides could belong to the same person.

By the time that Jack had managed to shake Ember awake, Mo had ladled the porridge out into bowls and started wolfing down his portion.

Each of the trio found that they had far more to do before they left than they had expected. They buzzed around the house like bees, pushing past each other looking for missing items only to remember that they had packed them the night before in a different part of their suitcase.

Eventually, innumerable heart-stopping moments and surges of relief later, Jack felt half-confident that he had everything he needed and followed Ember and Mo out of the front door.

"Where is it we need to get to again?"

"Junior Parlour." Said Ember anxiously, rummaging

around in her pocket before finding and unfolding a map.

"We walked past it yesterday, stop worrying." Mo said calmly, continuing down the street without slowing down. Ember shot him a stern glance that Mo missed entirely. Jack desperately hoped that Mo did know where he was going because Jack doubted whether he would even be able to find his way back to their house if they got lost.

Soon, the houses became older looking and Jack grew more confident that they were heading the right way.

"I'm not sure it's this way." Ember said concernedly, taking the map from her pocket, as Mo made a sharp right turn.

"Trust me." Mo sang and Ember sighed before putting the map back in her pocket and hurrying after him. It was only a few minutes until Mo said, "Yeah, look." Pointing to a yellow sign with 'Junior Parlour' written on it.

From then on, there were yellow signs every time that the group needed directing and soon Jack found himself at the edge of the dome that encircled the University. There was a shed that was cut in half by the invisible barrier. A man sat on a wooden chair next to the door of the shed, reading a book.

"Student and servants?" He enquired without looking up.

"Yeah." Said Jack as Mo made a dismissive snorting sound.

The man raised his head, looking at the trio for the first time. "Blimey, I knew that there was a youngster joining this year, but you must be what, twelve?"

"I'm fourteen." Jack replied indignantly.

"Blimey! Although, you should fit right in, most of the students here have the maturity of twelve-year-olds."

"Fourteen."

"Your two servants should go right here." Said the man, pointing to a small, grotty side street. "You go through this door; the route should be obvious from there."

"Right, ok, see you later." Jack said with a slight smile to the other two who grinned back. Ember looked as though the effort of restraining herself from hugging Jack was intense. They turned together and left him.

"Thanks." Jack said to the man, but he was far too engrossed in his book again to respond. Jack pulled open the heavy wooden door and stepped through into the surprisingly dark room. It was bare and empty except for a corridor directly in front of him.

Suddenly, Jack realised that there was a back wall and no haze through the room as would be expected if the Eileaftium barrier extended through the shed.

Nervously, Jack walked towards the corridor. After a few strides, he was certain that he had gone beyond where the barrier should be. Cautiously, he turned and walked back towards the door where he had entered before turning again and walking right to the back wall of the shed where the corridor branched from.

He was certain now, the shed tunnelled through the Eileaftium barrier. Unable to think of an excuse for waiting in the shed any longer, Jack nervously hurried into the dark corridor. He was immediately aware that the air in the corridor seemed far cooler than the shed and the Andagaldur walls of the corridor were oppressive and ominous.

Suddenly, with a booming rumble that shook the floor, something slammed down behind Jack. Terrified, Jack spun to see that a large block of Andagaldur had closed the archway between the room and the corridor. He couldn't go back.

Now, surrounded on all sides except one by walls of Andagaldur, Jack began feeling as though he was back in the mine. But there was no Carsicus this time, he reminded himself and instantly felt a lot calmer. It is always reassuring to remember that there isn't a powerful murderer chasing you.

Jack now hurried along the corridor. It was illuminated every twenty metres or so by small bundles of etter hanging from the ceiling. Jack passed a dozen or so of these bundles before coming to a junction like a serpents-tongue. Both the left and right choices were lit equally, the same size and identical in every way that Jack could see.

Just before he started rummaging around in his pockets for a coin to flip, Jack noticed that there was a small wooden sign above the right hand of the two forks. He had to get right up close, so his nose nearly touched the sign, before he was able to read it.

> Those who try for dreams at any cost,
>
> Take this way and you shall not be lost
>
> But if you should pale at this thought,
>
> Your route lies left of this board.

Jack read the rhyme several times and every time he did so, the idea of 'at any cost' made him feel more and more disquiet so he decided to take the left turn instead and for a while it seemed no different to the original tunnel, the narrow walls and low ceiling remained oppressive and the small bulbs of etter still added too little light to lift the dark atmosphere.

Suddenly, his feet began to splash on the floor and water seeped through his shoes. Looking up and squinting, Jack realised that once again, there was a fork and above one of the routes a wooden board. He crossed over to it and read.

> This left turn is only for
>
> Leaders, Captains, Generals in times of war
>
> If you need to look 'round for support,

You must take the right-hand port

Nervously, Jack peered down each of the turnings and saw that both of them had a small boat bobbing a few metres along them. Jack turned back to the sign and read it once more, he thought about the time he had spent in the Wilderness as the leader of the camp. True, it hadn't really been at war, but Jack supposed it had been close enough to count. Also, he reminded himself that he needed to think as much about what the King would have chosen as what he wanted to choose himself and it was obvious that the King at least viewed himself as a leader, even if anyone who had met him quickly learnt otherwise.

So Jack again chose the left-hand turn. With every step he took, the water rose higher and higher up his legs. By the time that he reached the boat, the water line was at Jack's waist. Carefully, he climbed into the boat and it set off along the tunnel. Now that he didn't even have any walking to distract him, Jack found himself pondering the questions he had answered so far. He thought he had done a decent job. At least, he was confident he had chosen honestly.

Just as Jack began to wonder how much longer he would be on the boat for, it began to scrape along the bottom and Jack saw, not far away at all, the water end and dry land begin once more.

Soon, the boat ground to a halt and Jack climbed over the side, again he was plunged into waist high water and had to wade his way through. He found himself standing before a third junction. This time, he peered through each of the two tunnels leading off before looking at the sign, both passageways looked broader than the ones he had journeyed through so far and both sloped upwards in similar directions, making Jack confident that this was the last decision for him to make.

The left-hand climb must be taken by

Those whose desires reach the sky

If, however, you are more content,

Continue through the right-hand ascent

Jack shrugged, of all the decisions throughout the day, this one was surely the easiest. The King was as far away from content as could be, always trying and failing to live up to the exemplary reign of his mother. As Jack took the left-hand fork, he once again felt a stab of pity for the King.

As he continued down the corridor, it continued to widen and get brighter but steeper too and soon Jack was really having to grip with his toes to stop himself slipping on the smooth stone slope. Abruptly, the corridor became level and a few moments after that, Jack was out of the corridor entirely!

He found himself in a huge circular room with a wooden floor and ceiling but glass walls. There were eight long tables, all with a handful of students in their late teens or early twenties, pointing into the centre of the room. The entrance through which Jack had just entered was at the head of one of the tables.

Curiously, Jack looked out of the windows and saw the grey silhouette of hills in the distance, then, a little closer, the Old Town, then the river seeming to run to infinity left and right. He kept moving the angle of his gaze closer and closer towards vertically down. He saw the wooden shed that he had entered through that morning, no bigger than an ant. Then, he saw something even more interesting, thick lines of Andagaldur crossing and colliding seemingly at random below him.

Jack blinked as he theorised, remembering his route from the shed into this hall and as he thought, his eyes traced the lines of the Andagaldur until he had no doubt, the lines were not lines at all but the very corridors that he had walked through all morning! Looking more closely, and with his deepened understanding, Jack saw that the maze formed by the corridors had not one but four exits on his side leading up to this glass bubble and, not only that, but the maze also stretched to the other side of the circular room he was in, and Jack guessed that there were more exits on that side, which he just couldn't see.

Again, curiously, Jack traced the route he had walked that morning and saw that the last kilometre or so, when he had been climbing up the slope, was not like the rest of the maze at all, it had an unnecessary amount of Andagaldur around it. Suddenly, his breath caught in his throat.

"No way!" He whispered to himself.

Jack had realised for the first time that the last kilometre of his walk was sculpted into a vast dragon, he had unknowingly entered through the dragon's tail and exited through its mouth. He saw also that the other three entrances to this hall were the wing of an owl, the claw of a bear and a shark's fin.

With a heart-stopping suddenness, Jack understood that this hall was not supported from the ground directly below but only by the Andagaldur statues of the different animals. At once, Jack felt as though the hall might at any moment tip backwards or forwards and fall onto the ground far below before smashing into a million pieces with him inside it.

Trying to calm himself, Jack took a seat halfway along his bench and instantly regretted it. It was too late to move now though so Jack sat stock still listening to the awkward, stuttering conversations of the people on the long tables around the room. All the tables had at least a handful of people on them. All the tables, that is, except his. But Jack didn't dare move.

As Jack continued to listen, the more relieved he felt, no one here looked like the popular kids that the King surely surrounded himself with. They were all too nervous and diffident.

Occasionally, a new person would emerge from one of the doors. All the doors, that is, except Jack's. Eventually, Jack began to theorise once more – he thought about the questions and how his answers to each of them had directed him down a particular path – and proposed to himself that the decisions each person made in the maze determined the route that they took and therefore the table that they sat at.

Eventually, a good quarter of an hour passed without anyone new arriving. Then, the main doors to the hall swung open and a very tall, very thin lady entered. She wore a high-necked black coat that went nearly the whole way from her chin to her ankles. Her eyes were small, dark, and cold, her nose upturned and proud. Close behind was a diminutive man, half a head shorter than the lady and with a rattish face.

The two of them kept their eyes upright and forwards as they walked to the table in the centre of the room.

"Welcome." Said the lady in a high, cold, unwelcoming voice as she reached the middle table. "You have all been sent here to learn a selected discipline that will be used to help the Realm move forwards. Remember that you are here to learn and that you have a great opportunity to do that here. If you choose to not work during your time here, it isn't just your-selves that are missing out but the whole Realm is not getting the benefit of improved, more educated leaders of the future. To encourage your education, or rather to discourage distrac-tions, the dome through which you entered this morning has, of this very moment, been made impregnable to each of you. It is possible of course to blast your way through with sceptre fire but guards have been stationed around the edges and if anyone is caught destroying a section of this ancient creation, they will be caught and punished *severely.* I will now hand you over to Professor Virta, my deputy head."

Jack could envisage Ember nodding thoughtfully at these words and Mo muttering "what a bundle of fun." sarcastically under his breath.

"Good evening." Said Mr. Virta, in a nasally voice as though he was ill, "congratulations on completing the maze and reaching the bubble. I am sure you are all hungry and tired so will be brief. The maze that you have passed through has been here since the reign of Ziro three thousand years ago. The choices that you made on your way through it determined your route up to the bubble here. And, therefore, lead to different tables. But the tables where you are now all sat are far more important than simply where you have your dinner. Each table is reserved for a different college. From this moment onwards, where you live and who you live with is fixed – you have all already chosen your college."

Before Jack could even turn around to see if anyone else was as confused as he was, the main doors swung open again and a host of middle-aged adults swarmed in, Jack guessed they were teachers and was proved right as they all settled into the middle table. Close behind was a large body of students. All of them were looking around the hall, seeing which new people had been added to their college and then turning to talk to their friends about it.

At once, Jack became aware that there were a disproportionate number of eyes turned towards him, presumably because he was the only one on his table.

Only a handful of the older students sat on his table, it was the least popular by far. Not even one of the students that did sit on his table sat near Jack, they all took places as close to the end of the table as they could, near the middle of the circle. Jack had a feeling that this was the same as the people at school all trying to get the back seats on the bus.

Jack's first feeling was of relief, he didn't feel up for a conversation, all he wanted was some food and an early night. Then, instantly, he felt guilty remembering that the whole reason he was here was to get close to people and glean information on the King.

Overwhelmed, he turned his eyes down to the table and sighed.

Suddenly, Jack heard two people sit down either side of him, saw flashes of blond hair out the corner of both his eyes.

"Hi!" Said two very similar voices at once.

"Umm… Hey." Jack replied nervously.

"We are your starting friends." The two voices said simultaneously.

Jack had no clue how to respond. What did 'starting friends' even mean? Maybe it was a joke, maybe this was some trick on the new kid.

Trying to join in on the fun, Jack sat back slightly and tried to force a relaxed smile onto his face.

For the first time, he got a good look at the two of them. There was no laughter hiding behind their eyes. Their identical eyes. Jack turned rapidly from one to the other, blinking.

Every tiny aspect of their faces was exactly the same, the shape, the freckles, the nose.

The only thing that was notably different was that the one on the left had long hair and was definitely a girl. Her brother was clearly a boy and yet Jack didn't know how he was so certain of this as they just looked so similar.

"We get that all the time; we are identical twins."

"You don't say." Jack replied, too surprised to worry about appearing rude. Thankfully, the twins only laughed.

"What's your name?" The girl asked, still smiling broadly

"Jack."

"We are the Ished twins." The boy smiled; he pronounced their surname like the ending of the word 'famished'. "I'm Finley, and this is Polly."

Jack gasped, in his surprise at the sameness between the two twins, he hadn't properly processed Polly's face. It was the same girl that had been in Teraturt's library when he had been there! She had been reading up on Rafiki's he remembered.

It seemed that she had remembered the exact same time at the exact same time because she gasped as well, her eyes widening in what looked like fright. It took her a moment to recover herself, "Jack, wasn't it?" She asked, holding her hand out. Jack shook it.

Something about the twins helped Jack to relax. They were easy going and funny and helped Jack forget for the time being his seemingly insurmountable mission. But the best thing about them from Jack's perspective was that they didn't make any inside jokes between just the two of them and make him remember that he had only just met them. He listened attentively as they told him about their own experience at choosing their college.

Polly admitted that she had let Finley make all the decisions in the maze (they had gone through together). This surprised Jack as he had had a building impression that Polly was the more decisive and forceful of the pair. But he didn't think he knew them well enough to push it.

They had just started talking about lessons when the door swung open and a small army of children all carrying large plates entered through into the hall.

"What's that?" Jack asked.

"Potted crab I think." Finley said, craning his neck backwards.

Before Jack could whisper back that that wasn't what he had meant, a particularly tiny child had placed the food before him.

"Thank you." Jack smiled. The child gave him a frightened glance before hurrying away. When Jack looked up, he saw that Finley and Polly were looking at him with great concern. "What's happened?" Jack asked, worried he had given himself away already.

"It's just that you aren't meant to speak to the servants, never mind thank them." Said Polly. "They are only doing their job."

"I don't think there is anything wrong with saying thank you really." Said Finley.

"But where do you draw the line?" Polly asked rhetorically. "You will give them ideas above their station, I don't want Jack to turn into one of those nutters who thinks that University places should be given out like cheap toys regardless of birth right. It should be kept amongst those who know what to do with what they learn here."

It was clear that Finley considered this the end of the conversation.

Jack couldn't bring himself to argue with the only two friends he had here, but he couldn't make himself to nod along either.

As they began eating, Polly, with occasional additional comments from Finley, explained the lessons. "It is nothing like school." She said excitedly. "You don't actually have to go to any lessons if you don't want. But if you do go, the lessons are all in big lecture halls upstairs with a lecturer and a few fourth years who help out."

"There is an upstairs?" Jack enquired.

"Yeah, did your father not explain the layout of the University to you at all?"

"Umm... we aren't really that close." Jack replied.

"Oh, sorry, I didn't mean..."

"It's fine."

Polly hurried on. "Yeah, so this is the bubble that we are in now. Everyone comes to the bubble to eat and do their lessons."

"Where do we live?"

"The colleges. That is why the table that you end up on is such a big deal." Polly explained. "The maze filters who goes to which table and then everyone from the same table goes to the same college."

"Which college are we all in?"

"Dragon."

"The best one." Smiled Finley.

At that moment, the doors swung open again and the army of children entered once more. Jack noticed that he had a different server this time, presumably the one he had thanked last time had been frightened off by his manners. So, this time, he smiled his thanks instead of vocalising it, but this seemed to terrify his new small waiter even more than the last one.

As they ate, Jack discovered that Finley, like him, was studying English, while Polly was taking Etter Studies, the subject of how people began being able to control etter and why some people could control it whilst others couldn't.

Jack tried to move the conversation away from there as fast as he could because every time it was mentioned, he thought of Errion and knew that one whisper of his adventure in the Wilderness and he would not only be under suspicion but probably thrown out of the University there and then.

Jack managed to watch his mouth throughout the meal and before long, the last of the food had been taken away. As soon as the servants had gone, there was a uniform scraping of chairs as the teachers got up and left the hall. Jack went to stand up as well, but Finley caught his arm just in time.

"We have to wait for the teachers to leave first." He whispered.

Once the teachers had gone, Jack, Finley, Polly and all the other students followed them out of the main door. The staircase down was much more manageable than the slippery slope that Jack had had to struggle up to get into the hall which wasn't surprising because this number of people trying to get down that at the same time would have been pandemonium.

Soon, they were out into the fresh night air. Jack saw to his amazement that when he glanced upwards, the sky looked hazy and he knew that it was the domed roof of Eileaftium and that what he could see wasn't there at all but just his mind accounting for the emptiness.

"Don't stare up for too long or you'll give yourself a headache." Said Finley and Jack stopped looking.

They followed a cobbled path directly away from the bubble. Every hundred metres or so, there would be two turnings on opposite sides of the path leading to two different colleges.

Polly and Finley showed little interest in the first three of these branches so when they came to the last one, Jack knew that they would also be turning. Polly led the way down the left-hand fork, up a gradual hill. The cluster of buildings was only a two-minute walk further along this path.

"Umm... this is our bit of the college." Finley said awkwardly. "You carry on just across the Quad to that lit up building there."

"Right, ok." Jack said, trying not to sound too worried that he had to leave his only friends.

"It's just because we are second-years now so live in the middle block. We'll see you in the morning." Polly said positively.

"Yeah, see you."

Alone, Jack continued across the square towards the brightly lit building at the top. He couldn't believe how nervous he felt, after everything he had done, why was he so terrified about meeting new people?

Before he knew it, his feet had taken him to the front door of the building, and he found himself knocking on the door. As soon as it swung open, he heard an excited scream.

"Oh, look how small he is!" A shrill male voice gushed. "Engelial is going to want to see this. Engelial! Engelial!" The boy shouted as he ran over to the corner of the room where a large group of people were clustered together.

The group parted in the middle and a single figure turned around. "Aw! Look at him!" She said.

Jack wanted to say something in return, but his throat appeared to be blocked so all he could do was gasp. The young lady practically glided across the room towards him. She was the most beautiful person that Jack had ever seen, clearly far too much for his brain to handle.

"Hello, I am Engelial. You must be Jack."

"Yeah... yeah... I Jack." Jack replied, noticing at once how out of breath he sounded and how high his voice seemed.

"Come and sit down." Engelial smiled. "Otto, get out of that chair. You can have Simon's seat."

A boy with spiky blond hair stood up. Jack recognised him as one of the people that had been sparring with Einor back in Edenvale. Otto, however, didn't appear interested in Jack, he was instead busy looking disgruntled at being re-moved from the big seat near the fire.

"Jack, come and sit in this chair." Engelial prompted and Jack found himself sinking into a handsome leather sofa. He snuggled himself into the far corner, making room in case anyone else wanted to sit down.

"Aww, look how he is sitting. So adorable." Said the boy who had first noticed Jack.

"I just wanted to leave some room so that someone else

could sit down." Jack said meekly.

"Aww..." The group chorused.

"Well in that case, it would be rude for no one else to join you. Dara, sit next to Jack." Said Engelial and at once, the boy who had first spoken sat on the sofa alongside Jack.

Jack spent the rest of the evening comfortably snuggled up next to the fire as the group fussed over him as though he was four rather than fourteen and he found himself not minding in the slightest. Engelial fretted over him the most, but Jack enjoyed her fussing above all the others. She laughed easily and the more that they spoke, the more certain Jack became that she was the most beautiful person that had ever, or would ever, exist.

In between their regular bouts of saying how cute Jack was, the group spoke about all sorts of things Jack had never even considered discussing, make-up, clothes, posh parties. There was no doubt in his mind that he had, by some curious twist of fate ended up in the middle of the popular group, admittedly more like a pet than a fellow member but in the cool group none the less. A small voice at the back of his mind whispered that this was didn't seem to be the circle that would bring him closest to the King, but Jack ignored it and, every time Engelial spoke, the small voice was silenced entirely.

Eventually, hours later, Engelial stood up, "I am going to bed. You must be tired." She said sympathetically to Jack who wanted to say no but found himself yawning.

Engelial turned him around by the shoulder and pointed towards the back of the room. She was so close that Jack could feel the warmth of her breath on his cheek as she spoke, "the boys' dorms are through that wooden door there. Otto is your parent I think."

"My parent?"

"An older student that is there to look after you. Although, of course, if you ever really need something, just come and find me and I will sort it."

"Thanks." Said Jack.

He noticed that Otto had stood up at the same time as Engelial. Throughout the evening, Jack knew Otto had often and subconsciously been looking in their direction and there was no doubt in his mind about who he had been glancing at.

Jack followed Otto through the doorway into a wooden room.

"We're in this one." Otto said, his voice spoke of a long, tiring day and he pushed open another door with a large bronze three hanging off it.

The room that they now entered was smaller than Jack had imagined, five beds in total, two along each side wall and one pointing towards the door from the opposite side of the room, in front of the window that had the day's rain running in tracks down it. Otto closed the blinds, blocking out the inky black night sky before propping himself up on the bed.

"So, what do you make of your first day?"

For the first time, Jack realised that he had completed his first day at university. "Loved it!" He said enthusiastically. "I was really worried before I came but everyone has just been so nice and welcoming. And I think that the maze has put me in the right college."

"Good." Otto smiled a genuine smile. "I have training early tomorrow so will turn the lights out now if that's alright with you."

"Yeah of course." Jack yawned.

"Hey, do you fancy coming and squiring for me tomorrow, about six o'clock?" Otto asked as he turned off the lights.

"Yeah, that sounds great." Jack answered, thinking about Dr. Nabielle's words telling him to get involved in everything.

"Perfect. If you come to help, I think there's a better chance of Engelial coming to watch, I reckon she's about half an hour away from adopting you as her son."

Despite the offhand voice of Otto, Jack was certain that there was more than tongue in cheek humour in his words.

For some reason, Jack just couldn't find sleep as the minutes ticked by. Three more boys quietly got into the other three beds. He heard them start to snore one by one and yet still couldn't drift off. Eventually, he grew frustrated; he was already tired and needed to get to sleep now or else he would have no chance of getting up for six o'clock tomorrow.

Not able to contain his annoyance lying down, Jack decided to return to the common room and get himself a glass of water. Silently, he threw on the dressing gown that hung on his bed and slipped from the room into the main living space. There was now only one figure there, Jack could see her silhouette in the firelight, a thick tome of a book in her hands.

"Hello." Jack ventured nervously.

The girl jumped a foot. "Just reading a magazine." She said quickly and Jack realised it was Engelial who, in a flash, had hidden the book behind a glossy, gossipy magazine.

"I was just coming down for some water." Jack said, tip-toeing towards the tap and filling his cup.

"Well, I have finished my magazine so think I will go to bed properly now. Sleep tight!" Said Engelial in her normal soft, charming voice without any hint of the fluster she had had only a few seconds before.

As soon as Engelial was out of the room, Jack couldn't resist going and looking under the magazine to see what she had really been reading. The book was even more vast than Jack had expected. '100 Era-Defining Women Overlooked by History.' Jack turned the book over in his hands several times, in three hours of conversation that evening, Engelial hadn't discussed anything more substantial than clothes but had snuck out at midnight to read a book so huge that Jack could hardly lift it.

Jack returned to bed in a trance, his mind utterly caught up in the mystery of Engelial.

CHAPTER 14: FLAIR

A firm shake woke Jack the next morning. He rubbed his eyes, trying to work the sleep out of them. Sitting up, he realised that he was no longer at 24 East Street.

"C'mon or we will be late to training." Otto said, pulling on a tee-shirt and jumper. "I got all your kit out, it's by the side of your bed."

Jack saw a pile of clothes including a thick woollen tracksuit with a dragon on the chest. Quickly, he rolled out of bed. "It's not right that I should be getting my squire's stuff ready." Said Otto as Jack pulled on his gear. Jack was relieved to see that Otto was smiling.

"I'll sort out your stuff next time." Jack promised and Otto nodded.

"Right, I need you to carry these for me." Said Otto, passing Jack a sheathed Sceptre and two large shields. Jack hoisted both the shields onto his back and felt his knees sink as he tried to support their weight.

"It's good training. We've all been in that boat." Otto said noticing Jack's struggle.

Soon, they were out of the room and then out the college entirely. They came into an open square that Finley had called the Quad the night before.

Otto led him through an archway to the left of the Quad onto a boggy field. The sun had just started to rise over the horizon.

"Good, we're the first ones here." Otto said, holding his

hand out.

Not knowing what to do, Jack shook it. Otto gave him a look of disbelief. "When I hold my hand out, my squire is meant to give me my sword, not a handshake."

Awkwardly, Jack withdrew his hand and handed the Sceptre to Otto. Grinning, Otto began swinging the Sceptre in swooping yet controlled figures of eight. Suddenly, he spun on his heel and brought the sword crashing down onto the floor, leaving a deep, narrow gash. "I wonder if Engelial will come and watch this morning?" He muttered to himself as he swung his Sceptre in a figure of eight once more.

A loud giggling sound made Jack turn and he saw a large group approaching. The man at the front was tall, even taller than Otto, with a thick black beard and handsome green eyes. Jack guessed he was older than Otto too, in his early-mid twenties.

"No one from your college wanted to come and watch?" Asked the man. "Didn't want to see their only vaguely competent member get embarrassed I guess."

The group behind the handsome man laughed together. Jack gave them all a hard stare, he had fought Carsicus and Alika, he backed himself against a bunch of students.

"And who's the kid you brought with you?" He continued.

"You know perfectly well who that is, Flair, that's Jack, you know, the one who broke your record for the youngest person to ever be accepted into the University." Said Otto, looking smug and Flair's smile lost its energy.

"He only got let in because his father is a Lord."

"So is yours you muppet. And anyway, he got let in because of his powers. Jack, go into the second level of the Deep."

Jack looked nervously at Otto, he hadn't had to enter the second level since escaping Carsicus and remembered how hard it had been then. But then he saw a look of satisfaction growing on Flair's face, clearly thinking that Jack wouldn't be able to go that deep.

With a quick breath in, Jack let his vision blur and then dragged himself from reality. When he opened his eyes, all his surroundings were monochrome except for Flair who stood before him with a taunting expression. Jack gritted his teeth and then let his vision blur again, let his mind go loose and then dragged himself down, down, he was falling and when he opened his eyes again, he saw to his delight that even Flair was now monochrome and magnified, his expression just beginning to turn into one of annoyance.

Simply to prove a point, Jack remained in the second level of the Deep for as long as he could before allowing himself to float upwards into the first level and then back to the normal realm.

"Whatever." Flair spat as he joined the others in normality. "We didn't come here for this." He continued, pulling his Sceptre from its sheath.

Flair's Sceptre had a light green rim of etter around its outside.

"Jack, stand back." Said Otto, his eyes focused on Flair with laser-like concentration.

The group that had been backing Flair all retreated at once and fell totally silent. It was Flair who moved first, a feint towards Otto's right shoulder who slipped easily to the other side of the blade. Otto swung his Sceptre in the figure of eight shape as he had done earlier, still watching Flair with that intense, smouldering intensity. Then, he darted towards Flair's right elbow, raising his shield over his head as he closed the distance. Flair, however, stepped nimbly to the side, sweeping low with his own Sceptre to keep the fight at range. Jack had the distinct impression that Otto had anticipated nothing less, that he was just testing Flair, keeping him off balance and on edge.

The fight continued in this fashion for several minutes, both fighters testing each other's defences, searching for a weakness or a mistake.

Jack saw Flair suddenly grit his teeth and briefly glance at the crowd he had brought to watch before starting to attack with increased ferocity, stepping the speed up another gear. Otto didn't match his foe's new vigour, but Jack noticed that there was no trace of concern on Otto's face as he continued to parry and slip Flair's assaults.

Eventually, Flair began to push Otto back but still Jack was not able to spot any worry in Otto's expression. The pair moved off the flat, grass circle and onto the more slippery, muddy field around the outside.

It seemed to Jack that Flair moved with even greater aggression now, buoyed by the fact his opponent was being forced back.

After three rapid, shorter blows had been blocked by Otto, Flair swung his sword in a wide arc, looking to break through Otto's defence with shear force.

Otto got his shield up just in time and the sound of the collision rang out loudly across the field. The force caused Flair's right foot to slip on the rough ground and Otto, quick as a flash, hooked his foot around Flair's back leg and swept it from under him. With a squelch, Flair was flat on his back in the mud, looking skyward with Otto's pink Sceptre a hair's breadth from his throat.

"Too aggressive again Flair." Said Otto calmly as he took his Sceptre away from Flair and put it back in its sheath.

Flair snorted in reply before battering the hand Otto had offered him out the way. Red in the face, Flair returned to his group who gathered around him sympathetically.

"The first piece of advice I will give you, and it is one

worth remembering, is the importance of understanding your enemy and making them make the mistake." Said Otto, turning to Jack. "Flair has always been too aggressive. He knew that the ground was too slippery to try and make that attack but he can't resist."

Jack looked at the older boy in wonder. Then, suddenly, he remembered that scene on the top of the hill in Edenvale when Einor had easily handled not just Otto but two others as well.

"I didn't realise how good you are. Like if you are that amazing think about how insane Ein..." Jack caught himself just in time. Thankfully, the abruptness with which he had stopped made him start coughing and it didn't look like Otto had realised that Jack had nearly given away the fact that the man Otto believed was called Shadow was in fact the most wanted man in the entire Realm.

"What were you saying?" Otto asked.

"Sorry... I just didn't realise how good you were and how unbelievably powerful Shadow must be."

"I know!" Otto replied. "It is amazing that he isn't interested in doing competitions, I really think that he could be the Sword of the Kingdom if he wanted to. He fights just like Einor is said to have done and look what he achieved!"

"Mmm..." Jack nodded, regretting that he had ever brought up this topic and desperately wanting to move onto a different one before he said anything else stupid.

Thankfully, Otto was soon distracted by several new groups turning up, all the new groups were much smaller than the one that Flair had brought with him although they also all contained one person in their full combats with Sceptre in hand.

Jack watched as Otto sparred with each of the newcomers in turn. Several times, Otto looked to be in trouble but on each occasion, he managed to find some way of coming out on top. Jack enjoyed the different battles and looking at how the different styles matched up. He was so engrossed in Otto's final battle that he didn't notice Engelial approach from their College.

Unfortunately for Otto, however, he did notice Engelial's arrival and instantly his focus went, his blocks were a fraction slower, and it was clear that he was overthinking everything. His partner who, until this point, had been able to do no more than defend now took the initiative and began moving forward and pressing his attacks.

One of the opponent's thrusts found Otto's ribs and Jack could tell from Otto's grunt that although the armour protected him from serious damage, he had been winded. Thankfully though, it seemed to be the wake-up blow that Otto needed and he began to fight with his normal calculating but natural style and before long, his opponent was back to focusing all his energy on defending himself without any room for aggression.

Mere moments after that point and he was down. Otto had won his last sparring session to make it seven from seven.

Engelial gave him a brief round of applause but didn't look too interested.

"Do you really enjoy this Jack, or did he just force you to come?" She asked.

"I love it!" Jack grinned. "It's so interesting." And before he could stop himself, Jack found himself explaining all his thoughts from the sparring sessions that he had just seen.

"It's great that you enjoy watching it so much." Said Engelial. "But please don't think about taking it up yourself. It's much too dangerous."

Jack longed to tell her about all that he had accomplished since arriving on Arcane, to explain every detail about how he had fought Carsicus' Rafiki before battling Carsicus himself.

But, just about, he managed to keep a lid on it.

"No, I am happy just squiring for now." Jack said to her in his most reassuring voice.

"Good. This morning, I didn't get to finish my makeup before coming down to watch! I wouldn't have bothered normally but I wanted to check that Otto wasn't getting you to do something horrid like run laps or do press-ups."

"No one could possibly tell you haven't finished your make-up; you look stunning." Otto beamed and Jack realised that he had been left out of the conversation for longer than was fair.

Engelial smiled slightly at him, but it was more of a 'nice try but stop it' smile than a genuine display of happiness or pleasure.

Otto must have noticed because his expression sunk like a stone.

"I want to have a word with Jack and need to get back in time to finish getting ready so do you mind putting your own stuff away, Otto?" Engelial asked.

Jack watched Otto sigh but all he answered was, "yeah, that's fine. See you later."

"Come on you." Engelial smiled at Jack and together they headed back to the college. "Have you looked at your timetable yet?" She asked.

"No." Jack replied guiltily. "I haven't missed anything have I?"

"Yeah loads of stuff." Engelial replied.

Jack stopped in horror. Why hadn't he checked his timetable the day before?

"Ohhhh I am only joking." Said Engelial in her softest voice. "That look on your face was adorable. You must be the cutest person EVER!"

Jack blushed.

"Anyway, I am happy that you haven't seen your time-table yet because it means that I get to give you a nice surprise."

"What's that?"

"Your first lesson is English and guess who your Teaching Assistant is?"

"You?"

"That's right, it will be so much fun." Beamed Engelial, pushing the door open as they entered their college. As soon as they were in the college antechamber, Engelial pulled a mirror from her coat pocket "Right, I need to go and finish my make-up and do my hair again, that's one of the many problems with going outside, it always messes my hair up so I will see you here again in half an hour or so."

"Ok." Jack smiled and they went off in their different directions once into the lounge.

When Jack got back to his room, he noticed that there was a pink letter sticking out from under the pillow of his freshly made bed.

Jack,

Come to the Servants door at midnight so that Mo and I can hear all about your first couple of days!

Love,

Ember and Mo (who is definitely not your servant)

Jack grinned broadly, today was looking good, first he had a lesson with Engelial and that evening, he was going to see his two best friends again and get to tell them all about his first two days.

Keen to get on with his day, Jack arrived in the antechamber ten minutes before he needed to, leaning against the handsome wooden back wall, and looking out into the common room. The door to the girls' quarters swung open, and Jack watched, expecting to see Engelial emerge but instead, it was the blond hair of Polly that came through the door.

As she crossed through the common room, Polly kept her head looking downwards, trying to avoid everyone's attention but that only made Jack observe her more closely. Just before she reached the antechamber, Polly looked nervously over both her shoulders like prey checking its tail for a predator. She was so preoccupied with looking behind her that she walked straight into Jack, who couldn't get out of the way in the miniscule entrance.

Polly jumped a foot and gave a squeak and all the eyes in the common room turned towards her. With a terrified look at Jack, she muttered something about going to the library and scurried out into the Quad. Jack watched her turn left out of the Quad, in the direction that Otto had gone that morning for sparring.

"Girls don't like it when you watch them." Said Engelial in his ear.

Jack spun around already protesting. "No, I wasn't looking at her like that!"

"I know." Laughed Engelial, messing up Jack's hair the same way that Jack usually messed up Tom's. "Although you two would make a great couple."

"No way, she is like twenty."

"She's seventeen. Anyway, there is nothing wrong with being twenty." Said Engelial. "Thirty on the other hand..." She said to herself with a shudder.

"Hadn't we better get going?" Jack asked.

Engelial nodded and before Jack knew it, he was being led

out through the right-hand side of the Quad towards the main hall that he had entered through the maze the day before. He struggled to believe that had been only yesterday.

As they turned the corner, Jack saw the vast structure in daylight for the first time. It was as he had predicted; the giant glass sphere was supported by eight vast legs of Andagaldur, each of them carved into the shape of a different creature. The Dragon was the closest to Jack, but he saw that the others were an Owl, Bear, Shark, Trout, Tiger, Eagle and Raptor.

"C'mon. You were the one who was worried about being late." Called Engelial playfully and Jack suddenly realised that he had been standing rooted to the spot, awestruck by the mindboggling superstructure before him. Still half in a daze, Jack followed Engelial into the main entrance and up the flight of wide stairs.

They passed the door that led into the main hall where Jack had eaten the night before and into a wooden corridor that was reminiscent of the inside of Ziro's Wall far away to the East.

Engelial pointed to the first door, "That is the library through there. Full of weirdo's and boring old books."

"How many libraries are there?" Jack asked curiously.

"That's the only one."

Jack stopped dead. There was no way that Polly had been going to the library, she had been heading a hundred and eighty degrees the wrong way.

Trying not to sound too interested Jack asked, "what is through the left-hand arch leading out of the Quad?"

"Just that horrid muddy field where Otto was sparring this morning and the Old Tower."

"What's the Old Tower?"

"It's just a tower, silly. I think that it was built so they could teach astronomy or something boring like that, but no one wanted to do that obviously so no one goes up there now. It is made all out of Andagaldur so you can't get in unless you have the key. Anyway, we are through here." Said Engelial, pushing open a door on their left.

They entered a large wooden room with three steep, sloping sides. Chairs were in spacious rows along these sides. The fourth side was glass and Jack could see far into the distance, the green hills nearby rolling into the deeper green of forest with spread into the horizon.

The hall was already half full. Just as Jack spotted the King, sitting in the front row, Engelial said "we will sit here, in the back corner. Please move." She added coldly to a group of frightened first years who were seated nearby. All four of them looked at her, first with indignation but quickly resignation and they hurriedly packed their pencil cases back into their bags before scurrying off.

Jack watched them awkwardly, wanting to apologise for throwing them out of their seats but he had a feeling that Engelial wouldn't approve of such meekness so instead remained silent. He could think of no excuse to move closer to the King so instead sat down next to Engelial. Dara, the long-haired fourth year who had been the first to greet Jack in the common room, arrived minutes later.

"Dara." Engelial called, "come and sit with us."

"But we are the teaching assistants." Dara said quickly, "We need to spread out through the room so we can help as many people as possible."

Engelial looked at him in disbelief, then said in a voice totally devoid of its usual charm and elegance, "I told you to sit."

Head bowed, Dara came straight over to them and sat down between Engelial and Jack. Engelial smiled again and it was as if her change in tone had never happened.

After Dara, only a few more people trickled in before a blind rolled down in front of the far glass wall and a woman with hair stuck up all over the place stood up from the front row and turned to face the class.

Immediately, Jack heard giggling and knew the reason. He turned anyway and saw Dara pulling his own hair in odd directions. Jack gave a wet smile but quickly turned back to focus on the lecture.

"Welcome to the most curious of all the subjects taught here at the University. I am Professor Clara, the lead lecturer of English. The study of English dates back to at least the reign of Ziro three thousand years ago. Before which, of course there was no history..."

The slight uplift in tone before the tailing off left Jack wondering if there was more that Professor Clara wanted to say but couldn't, especially not with the King present.

"This writing has often been found in places rumoured to be associated with the mythical stories of the Crown and Amulet. As a result, many doubted whether this study would be allowed to continue but the King has sagely decided to allow it to be taught and even registered himself on the course." Said Professor Clara with a small bow to the King who sat in the front row.

"I am sure that there are many here already with a firm grasp of the history around English as well as the language itself, but we will start at the beginning, the first worksheet is attached to the bottom of your desk, the teaching assistants will go around the hall and check if anyone requires any help."

Disinterestedly, Engelial reached under her desk and flipped a square of wood over and Jack was surprised to see a worksheet in front of her. He felt under his own desk and realised that there was an identical bit under his, he pulled the latch it was sitting on and it swung forwards. Everyone else in the hall did the same before starting to get on with the work.

Professor Clara immediately went over to the King to see if he needed any help. Jack expected him to snap and yell that he was the King and didn't need any assistance with anything ever but clearly someone had warned Professor Clara of his ego and she managed to avoid his wroth.

Jack struggled to focus, partly because the worksheet was so easy that he kept overcomplicating everything but mostly because of the incessant chatting of Engelial. Dara genuinely seemed to want to go around the room and give people a hand, but Engelial barely paused for breath as she gossiped and gossiped and gossiped. Soon, Jack gave up on the work, accepting that there wasn't anything on there he didn't already know and tuned in to Engelial and Dara's conversation.

"It's a total waste of time if you ask me." Engelial said haughtily and Dara nodded with a sombre expression.

"What's a total waste of time?" Jack enquired.

"Sceptre battles. Particularly Ziro's tournament. It's wet and cold and muddy." Engelial replied with a dramatic shiver.

"What is Ziro's tournament?"

"Are you serious? Lord Alectus' son, Otto's squire, doesn't know about Ziro's tournament?"

Annoyed with himself that he was once again looking out of place, Jack attempted to pull his cutest, most innocent face as he shook his head.

Engelial at once went from suspicious to sympathetic and began in her softest voice, "Ziro's tournament, named after Arcane's first King of course, is where each of the eight college's puts forwards one boy and one girl and they all compete in a knockout tournament to see who the best is. The eight boys are Otto and all the others who were sparring with him this morning. Normally, the boy's tournament is during the first term and the girl's is during the second term."

"Right, got it." Jack beamed.

"Can't believe that Otto hadn't explained to his own squire about the tournament." Engelial muttered with a disbelieving smirk.

"When does it start?"

Engelial shrugged. "Soon. Far too soon if you ask me."

Jack only realised that it was the end of the lesson when everyone else began standing up.

"Well that was pointless." Said Engelial as they made their way out of the hall.

"Only because you were talking all through it." Jack replied before he could stop himself.

There was a moments awkward pause before Engelial began to laugh. "You are too cute Jack. But really all these lectures are a waste of time for us. I mean why bother stressing out and learning all this stuff when you could just marry someone powerful and get everything that you want that way? In all honesty, if you are as pretty as me, there is no point in learning."

Jack had to use all his self-restraint to stop himself telling Engelial that he had found the book she had been reading the night before and knew that this blasé approach to learning was nothing but a façade. And a thin one at that.

As they sat in the common room that afternoon (Jack had no lessons), Jack found himself getting more and more irate as Engelial continued talking and talking and talking to her friends about the most frivolous, immaterial subjects imaginable. He wanted to ask her interesting questions about anything substantial but whenever he tried to pursue that line of questioning, he was instantly shut off. He didn't dare ask her directly about the book after she had tried so desperately to conceal it from him the night before.

Eventually, not able to take it anymore, Jack had said that he wanted to go and explore the college a little bit.

"We will take you." Engelial said excitedly.

"I'd prefer to go by myself if that's ok." Jack answered. "I remember places better if I have to find them by myself."

"Oh, ok then."

Once out of the common room and into the Quad, Jack immediately exited through the left archway, keen to have a look at the Old Tower that Engelial had mentioned, seeing as apparently that was the only thing in the direction that Polly had tried to sneak off that morning.

He passed the place where he had watched Otto spar that morning and saw, not far away, a squat Andagaldur structure.

As Jack crossed over to the bleak tower, he couldn't help wondering why it had been left standing for so long instead of being replaced by something nicer looking. When he reached the base of the tower, he saw that it was made from perfectly smooth Andagaldur, he even entered the Deep to magnify everything but still the surface was smooth as the surface of the lake, making the tower impossible to climb.

By the time he had gotten back, the common room had emptied. "People started heading for bed already?" Jack asked Otto who was reclined on one of the large sofas around the edges of the room.

Otto raised an eyebrow. "Bed? This early? What do you think this, an old people's home?"

"So where's everyone gone?"

"To get changed and do make-up or whatever people like that do, I don't know."

Over the next couple of hours, the common room began to fill up once more as people emerged from their rooms in their nicest clothes with their hair all different, which Jack found slightly annoying as he had just started being able to put names to faces and now people didn't look quite the same as they normally did.

The group of Engelial's friends came to sit with Jack and Otto, fawning over Jack once more who was just beginning to find it slightly annoying. Engelial was the last to arrive, "What's the point?" One of her friends whispered as Engelial approached, "who in their right mind would give any of us a second look when she looks like *that*?" And there was a communal sigh of agreement.

"Should we head off?" Engelial asked and there was some nodding of heads, but most people just got to their feet and followed her without the need for acknowledgment. "I heard that Bear College were hosting tonight, so we will head there." Engelial said as she walked and the group followed her out of the Quad, towards the glass bubble but, before they got there, they turned left off the main path and went up towards the large wooden college at the top of the hill.

The door had been left open and music came booming through. Engelial led the way in and there was much excited screaming and cheering as they all arrived, which Jack thought was as much just making noise for the sake of it as a genuine expression of joy at seeing them. Engelial headed towards a cluster of plump sofas at the back of the party. As soon as the people sitting there saw her coming, they picked their drinks up and went off somewhere else.

"Dara, you sit here and save these sofas for us, and look after this for me, it's too hot to dance with it on." She said, taking off the shawl from around her shoulders. "Ok you, it's time to dance." She said to Jack taking him by the shoulder into the mass of people.

Before he knew what was happening, a grin had spread across his face and Jack found himself dancing more easily even than on the Darkest Day Dance. He was delighted to see that Engelial was smiling too, not just with her mouth but her eyes as well and all the contradictions of her character seemed to fade away and for again, Jack could convince himself that this was the real her; kind and beautiful and happy.

Jack was so lost in the fun that when his eyes watched Flair and his group from Raptor College join the party, his brain hardly registered it. Flair soon joined the others, dancing with one of the girls from his group that Jack didn't recognise.

Half an hour later, although it felt like a blink of an eye for Jack, Flair was starting to look bored, he had stopped dancing a while before and started leaning against a far wall, watching the crowd with aloof superiority in his eyes. Curious, Jack began trying to move with Engelial towards him.

"...dumb music." Flair muttered, "full of first-years."

"We don't have to be here." One of the others suggested. "We could head down to Old Town."

Flair's expression didn't change as he continued looking through his nose at everyone dancing.

"Fine." He spat suddenly.

Jack watched them go with frustration, he remembered his promise to Einor that he would try and stop any of the University students from going down to the Old Town but wanted nothing more than to keep dancing with Engelial.

"I need to go to the bathroom." He said, abruptly stepping away from Engelial.

"Don't keep me waiting too long, I was enjoying our little dance." She said, messing up Jack's hair maternally.

The loud obnoxious voices of Flair and his friends made them easy to follow from a distance and Jack made sure to stay out of sight in case one of them turned around. A sense of curiosity began to build as he followed them, he was interested to see how they got out of the dome that was meant to be impenetrable.

The group headed along the main path towards the bubble, a few students walked in zig-zag lines in the other direction and Jack tried to avoid drawing their attention to him but judging by the state of them, they had bigger issues.

To Jack's surprise, Flair's group didn't go through the main entrance at the bottom of the stairs up to the bubble but instead went around the staircase so that the bottom of the bubble was directly above them. Just before they passed out the other side, they stopped next to one of the legs. Flair squatted down and ran his hand across the ground as though foraging for berries. Suddenly, he stood up and Jack was amazed to see a large square of earth rise with him, there was a trap door in the ground!

Flair went through first, the rest of his group following close behind. Anxious that the trap door would close and require some password or special knock to open it, Jack ran across and slid his hand underneath it just in time.

Then he waited for several long breaths, the last thing he wanted was to follow too closely and get caught all alone stalking Flair and his gang. Eventually, Jack decided it was safe enough to enter and swung himself into the darkness below. Once again, Jack found himself in a corridor of Andagaldur. Far in the distance, there was lamplight, "Flair." Jack muttered under his breath before following it.

A minute later, the lamplight began to go up a ramp, darkening Jack's surroundings so he could see no further than the end of his arm. Still, he scurried on through the corridor. Soon, he too began to climb the ramp.

The ramp then flattened, and Jack now found himself at the bottom of what appeared to be an Andagaldur well, he saw spiral stairs wrapped around the outside. The lamplight had now gone entirely and yet Jack could still see just as far, for there was another light now, silvery starlight slipped through cracks above him. Worried that he had already fallen too far behind Flair and the others, Jack hurried up the stairs.

He paused just below the top, listening attentively, just in case Flair and the others were at the top, waiting for him. As he listened, Jack heard no whispered voices or shuffling of feet but instead a muffled, metronomic sound. Like the static of an old television. Or the patter of light rain on stone walls. But it was clear night inside the dome, how could it be raining?

Tentatively, he stepped up two more stairs and peered out the top.

At once, Jack felt a sweeping of relief as he grew certain he hadn't been caught but his relief was soon replaced by curiosity, he realised that he had not been at the bottom of a well as he had supposed but instead the bottom of a tower! With a start, he worked out that he was now at the top of the Andagaldur tower he had examined only a couple of hours ago. The so called 'Old Tower'.

Jack crossed over to the edge of the rooftop and looked down, wondering where Flair could have gotten to. He looked down three of the towers' sides but there was no sign of Flair or the others.

As Jack crossed over to the fourth and final side of the roof, he noticed that there was a wet patch on the roof – but it never rained inside the dome. Squatting down, Jack examined it more closely and became certain this wasn't a random shape but instead the impression of a tridactyl foot. The image of the raven that had sprung Carsicus from jail swum into Jack's head.

The more Jack examined the shape, the more certain he became that that creature, or one exactly like it, had made the impression. After all, he knew the shape of their feet very well after trying to hold onto one whilst it had been flying away.

Just as he was about to get to his feet, Jack noticed something else only a few feet away, a patch of Andagaldur reflecting the starlight softly in contrast to the rest of the rooftop which remained Stygian black. It was a puddle and, what was more, its surface rippled as the faintest of raindrops pattered their dance on its face.

It was bizarre, why was the rain falling on only this minute section of the roof?

With more curiosity than ever, Jack continued to the small puddle and became certain that it was only on this small section of the roof that the rain was falling. He looked upwards and realised that the constellation of stars directly above him was totally different even than a few degrees to either side.

Jack reached his hand straight up, then swept it across. He hit something hard and invisible in mid-air. "I thought so!" Jack whispered to himself.

Carefully, Jack wrapped his fingers around the invisible object, which he now realised was the dome, clearly someone had cut a hole in the top so that they could get out at night. The hole was concealed from the ground by the tower which, as Engelial had said, no one ever went up unless, it seemed, they wanted to sneak out of the dome.

Jack pulled on the edges of the hole with all his might, lifting himself up until his torso was totally out of the dome and then scrambling his legs over the top as well.

Jack sat still for a few moments getting his breath back. Then he looked down, straight through the invisible dome to the tower roof two metres below. He felt his legs go wobbly as his eyes told his brain something it believed was impossible, that he was sitting on nothing. Jack quickly looked up, needing to avoid the contradiction between his eyes and brain that was now making him feel sick. Far in the distance, he saw the light of a lantern that marked Flair and his group.

The sight gave him the strength to get to his feet and start walking along the dome, which sloped downwards towards the rest of Scholar's City. It took all Jack's willpower to stop himself looking down because he knew that if he did, he would see the ground twenty metres below him. An uneasy thought crept into his mind, what if someone had managed to carve another hole out of the dome? He would fall straight through, to the ground far below.

Luckily, Jack soon reached the cobbled street where the dome met Scholar's City safely.

He had lost sight of Flair's lantern a while ago but knew where they were headed so Jack strode through the New Town towards the Old, keeping as far from people coming the other way as he could. When he had been with Einor, there had been a sense of adventure and intrigue but no more, now he was alone however, Jack began to feel a nasty edge of danger as well. He began to question, even if he managed to find Flair and the others, what could he do? They were all much older and bigger than him.

Still, he hurried on and soon found himself crossing the bridge between the two halves of town.

It appeared Flair and the others had been going more slowly than him as Jack found them just a street further on. "All of you, get five King's notes out." Flair whispered and his group all rummaged around in their pockets before pulling out their money, Jack began to wonder if he had gotten it wrong, maybe Flair and the others had come down here to help.

"Good evening sir." Said Flair, waking one of the men sleeping rough with the sole of his shoe. "We were feeling generous this evening and thought we would put some money towards a good cause."

Jack was sat too far away to make out the man's face in the darkness, but he saw him sit up hopefully as he noticed the money that the group held.

"It is mighty chilly tonight, and we thought this dump

could do with heating up."

With a smattering of giggling, Flair's gang each created a ball of etter and set their money ablaze. Jack now watched the shoulders of the beggar sag hopelessly as the money that he had dared to imagine buying him food and shelter was burnt before his eyes.

Crying out, the beggar threw himself at Flair. For a moment, it looked as though he might have the upper hand but quickly, the athleticism that Flair had developed with the advantage of his soft bed and plentiful food meant he quickly overpowered the beggar.

"Dirty scum." Flair shouted as he threw the beggar to the ground before stomping on his knee causing the beggar to yell out in pain.

Just as Flair went to continue the beating, a voice came from behind him that chilled Jack's bones. "Will you lot shut up?"

Flair stopped so suddenly it was as if he had been turned to stone for the voice held a murderous nature. Jack continued to watch, every bit as still as Flair but without doubt more terrified, for Jack knew whose the voice was.

The beggar continued to moan in pain. "Shut it." Said the voice again.

"I can't!" Gasped the man. "My knee, it hurts so bad. Can you help me please?" He begged.

From the sheath that hung at his side, Carsicus pulled out his golden Sceptre. Jack's heart thundered.

"Please no!" The man shouted as he realised what was about to happen. But it was too late. Carsicus fired the golden ball from his Sceptre, filling the narrow alleyway with a flash of blinding light, Jack's eyes adjusted just in time to see the man slump back, dead.

Flair and his group sprinted away like the wind, all of them passing Jack who remained frozen in anger and fear, watching Carsicus' handsome, high cheek-boned face that was illuminated by the golden glow of his Sceptre.

Sheathing his Sceptre, Carsicus turned his back, disappearing back down the alleyway.

Jack never remembered running back to the dome or climbing it or even dropping back through the hole onto the top of Ziro's Tower and before he knew it, Jack was passing through the door to his college.

Heart still thundering in his chest, like a hammer against an anvil, he collapsed into his bed and stared at the ceiling, hoping it had all been a dream, that Carsicus hadn't found his way to Scholar's City, but Jack knew it was true.

For several minutes, Jack lay totally still on his bed, his gaze half-turned towards the door, terrified that at any moment, it would squeak open and reveal the terrifying form of Carsicus. Suddenly, a loud gonging sound caused Jack to leap half a foot in the air.

It was the sound of the clock hitting midnight and Jack remembered for the first time since that morning that he was supposed to meet Ember and Mo at the door to the servant's quarters. He hurried out of his room and turned right, away from the common room. Only a short distance further on was a narrow set of stairs with a small black door at the bottom. The door was open already and both Ember and Mo were there waiting for him.

"He's here. Carsicus, he is here in Scholar's City." Jack said at once, exasperation in his voice.

"Well I can't say I am surprised, Dr. Nabielle said he probably would be." Ember replied sensibly and Jack at once felt a lot more relaxed to hear her calm take on things. "Still, it means we can be confident that we just need to focus on *how* he is talking to the King. Have you managed to find out anything about that?"

Without thinking, Jack found himself talking about how Polly had been acting strangely when crossing the Common Room and how she had lied about going to the library when she had, in fact, headed towards the tower. And, not only that, but the footprints that had been on the rooftop led Jack to believe that whoever was talking to Carsicus was using his Raven Rafiki to do it.

"I still think we need a lot more." Ember said as Jack finished his story.

"I dunno, seems quite positive to me. We know that Polly lied about sneaking off to the Old Tower, we can be fairly confident that whoever is talking to Carsicus is doing it from the Old Tower. I say we just keep an eye on the Tower the whole time and wait for Polly to show up." Said Mo.

"No." Ember answered firmly. "It is far too early to put all our eggs in one basket. Don't get me wrong, I think that it is possible, but we haven't even been here two full days, let's not rule anything out at this stage."

Jack sighed, "It isn't just that, you should have seen how scared Polly was when she walked straight into me and how wide her eyes went when I said that I had been up to the tower."

"I get that but it's just too early..." Ember began but at that moment, the door from the common room swung open and Otto entered through it.

"Hello." He greeted Jack, ignoring the other two.

"Hey." Jack smiled back.

"You two get out." Otto scowled at Ember and Mo. Jack watched Mo's fist clench but neither of them said anything and left through the door with their heads bowed. "They weren't bothering you I hope."

"No, no. Not at all."

"Good. I need you up at six o'clock sharp tomorrow for sparring. The Quarter Finals of Ziro's tournament are this weekend, I only saw the notice just now. I knew I shouldn't have gone out tonight." Said Otto, looking frustrated with himself.

CHAPTER 15: THE QUARTERFINALS

Jack and Otto were again the first pair to arrive for sparring. This time, Otto only won six of his seven battles. Much to Jack's annoyance, the one that he lost was against Flair.

"I shouldn't have saved Flair for the last battle, I was already tired and just couldn't keep up with his aggression this morning." Otto berated himself.

On the walk back to the college, Otto and Jack analysed every facet of Otto's performance from all his seven spars. When they arrived back, Jack was amazed at how long ago last night felt, back in the relative safety of the Dome with its hundreds of students and teachers, Carsicus felt like a very real but very distant threat. It was like being in a warm bed in a safe house while a thunderstorm raged outside but couldn't get you. Also, Jack couldn't think of anything he could have enjoyed more than watching Otto spar and analysing the bouts with him. Although they had only known each other for only one full day, Jack was beginning to feel as though Otto was the older brother that he had never had.

"You have a good eye for detail Jack, I couldn't think of anyone I would rather have as my squire." Said Otto as they sank into the comfy chairs by the fire.

"Ah, you are back already. I was wondering about coming to watch." Said Engelial, emerging from the girls' dorms. "He didn't make you run any laps this morning, did he?"

Jack shook his head but before he could reply, Otto began

speaking, his voice a little nervous, "Engelial, you know how the champions are all given one front row ticket to give to someone?"

"Yeah..."

"Well do you want a front row seat for the quarter final this weekend?"

"I'll think about it." Engelial answered in her most non-chalant tone.

"If she doesn't want it, I'll take it." Said Jack with a tongue in cheek smile.

Engelial and Otto both turned to him with a disbelieving expression and once again Jack knew that his big mouth had shown just how little he knew of this world.

"Do you not tell your squire anything?" Engelial asked Otto who shrugged as if to say that Jack's ignorance wasn't his fault.

Succumbing to Engelial as usual, Otto turned to Jack. "I don't need to give you a front row seat because you are my squire, you are already in my corner for the fight."

"Oh, right. Nice one."

"Have you checked your timetable for today?" Engelial asked Jack probingly. Feeling that this was a bit unfair, since Engelial herself had spent yesterday's lesson doing no work, Jack nevertheless dug his crumpled-up timetable out of his pocket.

"Yeah, I have got second year English all day." Jack sighed. "Suppose I should get going."

"The Second years don't have Teaching Assistants so I won't come with you but have a good day." Engelial said with a maternal smile and Jack half expected her to add that she had made him sandwiches. Otto was right, she did seem a hair's breadth away from trying to adopt him as her son.

As soon as Jack reached the door, the corners of his eyes caught the flashes of blond hair that signalled Polly and Finley's arrival.

"Hello." They said together as they started walking either side of him.

"Hi." Jack replied, trying not to look too suspicious as he made eye contact with Polly whilst thinking that she was his best guess for whoever was communicating with Carsicus from within the University.

"We heard you saying that you were on your way to the second-year English lecture, which is where I'm going." Stated Finley.

"And I am going to my Etter Studies class which is right next door. But I only have morning lessons." Smirked Polly.

"Layabout." Finley teased.

During his morning lesson, Jack sat with Finley in the middle of the room. He quickly became aware that the lecture hall was fuller than it had been the day before. He was also conscious that there was a great deal less interest being paid to the lesson itself.

"This weekend, that's what I heard!"

"Have all the college champions been chosen yet?"

"We'll have to get up early to get decent seats."

Jack couldn't hear any of the students talking about anything other than the Quarterfinals of Ziro's Tournament. It seemed that everyone had come to the lecture with the sole intention of discussing the weekend. Professor Clara tried to give the lesson from the front for a few minutes but soon gave it up as a lost cause and told them all to work in groups where, instead of working, all the students took this as a golden chance to discuss the tournament more freely.

"Never really understood the build-up to Ziro's Tournament myself." Finley whispered to Jack in an undertone that suggested not being interested in Sceptre battles was something to be kept private. "Polly can't get enough of it though, last year she insisted on being the first person to the stadium for all the battles." Said Finley with a smile.

Jack smiled back and turned to his worksheet but before he could get on with the first question, there was a tearing sound from beside him and Jack turned to see Finley had just ripped a sheet off the notepad.

Shrugging, Jack started the questions. Within ten minutes, he was finished and looked over to see if Finley needed any help. What he saw made him laugh, Finley hadn't even done a single question, instead he had turned over the bit of paper and started to draw a cartoon of Professor Clara but not in a mean way, just a funny way.

Finley looked up and grinned back and for the first time, Jack saw him clearly. He had Mo's self-confidence in his smile but he wasn't naturally incredibly athletic or extroverted like Mo was, instead Finley was just confident and happy in who he was, someone a little bit different.

An hour later, Jack and Finley met Polly downstairs for lunch and Jack got to see Polly's enthusiasm for Ziro's Tournament first-hand.

"Leonard won last year; he beat Otto in the final, but it was a really good match up, Otto just made a mistake and got caught."

"Is Leonard competing again this year?"

"No, last year was his final year which is good because it means that Otto has a much better chance of winning for Dragon College."

"What about Flair, was he in it last year?"

"Yeah, Otto beat him in the Semi-finals. One of the best

moments of my life. You should have seen his face afterwards. Never seen anyone that furious, tried to start on the referee!"

"Were they ok?" Jack asked, concerned.

"Yeah, of course, it was Dr. Nabielle so she just dropped into like the thousandth level of the Deep and took his Sceptre off of him."

"Dr. Nabielle was the referee?" Jack asked, surprised that she had never mentioned this to him before.

"Yeah, she is always the referee in case something like that happens. The most powerful teacher here by a long way."

"Very kind of you to say so, Polly." A familiar voice said from just behind Jack who spun around to see Dr. Nabielle standing before him.

Jack was at once struck by how different she looked to when he had seen her in Edenvale. Back then, she had been full of life, but she was now bent-backed and tired looking, as though she had aged a decade in a month. Of course, he couldn't say any of this to her in front of Polly and Finley but took it as confirmation that whatever she had done on her mission had not been straight forwards.

"Sorry, I don't think I know your name." Said Dr. Nabielle and it took Jack a few moments to realise that she was speaking to him and, of course, they weren't meant to already know each other.

"I'm Jack." Said Jack far too loudly.

"Dr. Nabielle." Replied the doctor with a knowing smile that made her look, just for a moment, a bit more like how she had in Edenvale. "Now I must go and sit with my esteemed colleagues."

As Dr. Nabielle sat down with the other teachers, Jack saw the Headmistresses and the Deputy Head both wrinkle their faces as if a particularly horrible smell had wafted across the table and Jack remembered Dr. Nabielle saying that all the other teachers saw her as a slightly dangerous weirdo but were forced to put up with her because she was the best at what she did, Dr. Nabielle was clearly unconcerned or didn't notice it as she continued merrily telling her terrified little waiter to pour more gravy onto her potatoes.

"Anyway, back to the tournament, last year Otto beat Flair, he was just too fast and ..."

"Sorry to interrupt." Interrupted Finley as he stifled a yawn. "But Jack and I actually have work to do this afternoon unlike some people."

Polly smiled while Jack got to his feet and left the room with Finley. "I know that we are going to be a bit early getting back but I couldn't deal with hearing about any more Sceptre battles." Finley admitted as they re-entered the lecture hall.

The rest of the lessons that week were filled with the same perpetual low-level murmuring about the tournament. The only change was that as the week flew by, the whispers became louder and louder. Indeed, by Thursday Professor Clara had given up trying to teach from the front and instead simply told them to get on with the worksheets already on their desks in groups.

Jack became convinced that he was the only one doing the work, everyone else was talking except Finley who was drawing. Since Tuesday, Finley hadn't mentioned Sceptre battles once and Jack thought that it was only fair to avoid them as a topic. Still, he hadn't had a shortage of people to discuss them with, Polly could think of nothing else, and Jack had been squiring for Otto every morning and analysing each of his sparring sessions in minute detail with him. Even Engelial seemed to be showing a vague interest.

On Friday morning, a poster was put up in the common room saying that all lessons had been cancelled as 'there was a shared belief amongst the lecturers that students would not be sufficiently focused on lessons for teaching to be worthwhile.' Otto took this as a chance to have two additional sparring sessions in the afternoon.

Then, all evening, he insisted that Jack sat with him and pour over the battles in fanatic detail. However, Jack only realised how obsessive Otto was about tomorrow when Engelial came over to say Jack should head to bed and Otto ignored her entirely. She may as well have been talking to a wall.

Suddenly, Engelial's hand had flown across and caught Otto on the cheek, finally bringing him out of his narrow-minded stupor.

"You don't ignore me. NO ONE IGNORES ME!" Engelial said, jabbing her finger at Otto's face. Her normal celestial beauty hidden beneath a mask of anger.

"Sorry Engelial." Otto said weakly. "Jack, go to bed, I'll wake you early tomorrow."

Jack looked perplexedly from Otto to Engelial and back again, amazed at what he had just witnessed. Then, still in disbelief, he made his way to bed.

When Otto woke him the next morning, Jack found the words falling out of his mouth before he had even opened his eyes. "Why did she get away with that? Why didn't anyone do anything when she hit you?"

Otto sighed. "I'll tell you out of here, when we are somewhere that no one can hear us."

Jack threw Otto's shields onto his back and picked up his sceptre and together, they left the common room, passing through the Quad and then into the field where Otto did his sparring. Jack stopped still, looking at Otto expectantly, resolutely refusing to move until he got his answer.

"Do you know who Engelial's uncle is?" Otto sighed.

"No."

"Lord Sorain." Said Otto as if that name ought to be enough.

"Sorry, I don't know who that is."

"Lord Alectus' son doesn't know who Lord Sorain is?"

Jack shook his head.

Otto checked over his shoulder nervously. "Lord Sorain is the ruler of Kulle, the hill Kingdom. And, well, no one has ever been able to prove … to prove anything … but …" Otto swallowed and seemed to lose his voice.

"What has no one been able to prove?"

Otto swallowed again. "Let's just say that people who have stood in Sorain's way, including Engelial's mother and grandfather, have tended to end up dead. Or worse."

"What do you mean worse?"

Otto checked over his shoulders again, "no, that's enough. We aren't discussing this anymore."

Still confused, but now scared as well, Jack followed Otto to where they normally sparred, his head down as he focused on carrying the weight of the shields and weapons.

"What do you think?" Otto said and Jack looked up to ask him what he meant but quickly found that he needn't ask. Where Otto usually sparred, a large wooden stadium had now been set up.

"How … How has that been built overnight?" Jack asked, awestruck.

"Dr. Nabielle." Otto replied and there was no missing the reverence in his voice. "None of the other teachers could hope to build something like this in an evening."

"Wow!" Jack sighed, running his hand along the wooden frame just to make sure it wasn't an illusion. "Where did all the wood come from to make it?"

"Ah! Corporis Metamorphosis, the ability to turn one substance to another by changing its etter composition."

"Right..."

"Dr. Nabielle is the only person here capable of Corporis Metamorphosis. I believe that there are two other people in the Kingdom capable of it, but they are both in Konungur working on the King's new palace."

Once again, Jack was struck by the realisation of just how powerful Dr. Nabielle was.

Whilst Jack had been standing in wonder at the stadium and Dr. Nabielle's ability to convert between materials, Otto had stridden on ahead, into the belly of the Stadium. Jack hurried after him.

They were the only ones there which felt to Jack even more terrifying, almost claustrophobic despite the open roof with the high walls all around him and a vast audience of chairs. Otto seemed to be feeling the tension as well, he paced the ring relentlessly, swinging his Sceptre in his standard figures of eight.

The longer that they waited alone, the more tense Otto seemed to be getting. All the frantic nervousness that had been evident last night had returned and was stronger than ever.

When the first person entered the stadium, they sat down with a crash and Otto jumped half a foot before fixing them with a furious stare.

By the time that the other competitors began to arrive, the stadium already had at least a hundred eager faces around its sides. And with every new face it seemed to Jack that Otto's anxiety rose another level. All the time, Jack kept an eye on the new arrivals, wondering if Polly and Finley would get good seats and what would happen to Otto's confidence when Engelial showed up.

When Engelial did arrive, the stem of people entering the stadium had become a trickle and Otto had stopped taking as much notice, which was a silver lining. Jack continued to watch the arrivals though, surprised that Polly at least had yet to show up. Finley had said that last year she had been the first one to all the battles to make sure that she had had a good seat. Finley himself had shown up fairly early and was sat only a few rows from the front, which again interested Jack because Finley had spent the whole week avoiding talking about Sceptre battles.

The last of the competitors to arrive was Flair who was, as usual, escorted by his gang from Raptor college. Jack could not help but notice the confidence in Flair's expression juxtaposed against Otto's nervous restlessness.

The doors to the stadium all closed together with a sudden bang and Otto give an involuntary twitch. Flair's confidence became ever more apparent.

Suddenly, Jack realised that he still hadn't seen Polly arrive. He scanned the crowd quickly several times and was certain that she wasn't there. A suggestion presented itself in his mind, everyone was here at the Quarterfinal, if Polly had wanted the perfect time to send another message to Carsicus, this was surely it.

"Champions to the centre." The Headmistress' crisp voice called out and the whole crowd went quiet. Jack could have heard a pin drop.

Otto was now shaking so badly that as he tried to walk to the centre of the ring, he banged into Jack, almost knocking him over.

"I will draw your names out one at a time to determine the fixtures."

"Flair Sjor of Raptor college."

Flair stepped forwards, barely able to contain his excitement.

"Will be facing … Ragnar Gero of Bear college."

Ragnar stepped forwards, although that was hardly necessary, no one was going to miss him towering over the others.

The Champions of Eagle and Shark were drawn together. Then the Champions of Owl and Tiger. That left Otto with Ferran, the Champion of Trout college. Jack could barely contain his grin, in a dozen spars, Ferran hadn't so much as forced Otto to get out of first gear. Otto seemed a tiny bit more relaxed but still anxiously moved from side to side.

As they had been drawn last, Otto and Jack had to wait for all the others to battle before it was their turn.

Flair was first. Jack had thought that he couldn't be any more aggressive than what he showed day in, day out at sparring. Jack was wrong.

Flair fought with brutal slashes and swipes that the raptor emblazoned on his chest would have had to admire. Ragnar blocked all Flair's attacks but being constantly on the backfoot, he had no chance to put his size and weight to his advantage. He was constantly having to move away, just trying to give himself some extra time that Flair's relentless pressure denied him.

Ragnar's size quickly became a disadvantage, the pace of the fight soon catching up with him and making his movements even slower and now Flair was landing more and more shots on the arms and torso of his opponent. Just before the bell went for the end of the first round, Dr. Nabielle slipped between the two fighters, waving her hands and the contest was over. Flair was the first Semi-finalist. And Jack was certain that he would get to the Final as well. Otto, he was less confident about.

The two champions of Eagle and Shark colleges were

evenly matched until the third round when a slip from Eagle college's Champion lost him the fight.

Next came the Owl against the Tiger. Tiger College's Champion fought just as would be expected of his college's figurehead, watching, and pacing before leaping forwards with deadly intent. Owl college's champion was far more calculating, always watching his opponent with ferocious intensity but rarely pressing the attack leading to lengthy periods of inactivity during which the crowd began to catcall and boo from the side-lines.

Suddenly, Tiger College's Champion made one of his signature leaps towards his opponent but this time, the Owl College Champion charged forwards as his adversary leapt, causing them to collide with an almighty crash. The element of surprise gave the upper hand to Owl College's Champion and seconds later, he had his Sceptre at his rival's throat causing Dr. Nabielle to dive in and halt the fight.

It was now Otto's turn.

When Jack looked closely at his friend though, he was tempted to ask Dr. Nabielle to call off the fight because Otto had turned a nasty shade of green.

"Just relax, it is no different to all the sparring sessions. It's only Ferran." Jack said, trying to reassure Otto who nodded but that might have just been a mark of how much he was shaking because Jack had a feeling that none of his words had got as far as Otto's brain.

However, the moment that Otto stepped through the ropes, Jack saw his ribs expand like a balloon as he sucked in the morning air. And, suddenly, he stopped shaking.

"Water." He said calmly to Jack who hurriedly passed him the bottle. Otto took one quick swig then swung his Sceptre in a controlled figure of eight.

"Round One!" Called Dr. Nabielle and before Jack could

blink, Otto was striding across the ring like Einor.

Jack noticed something of Einor's style in Otto's fighting to an extent he hadn't seen before. The jinks and jerks from side-to-side were lightning fast and Ferran was swinging at thin air before getting caught short and sharp by several clean blows from Otto's Sceptre.

It had seemed like Dr. Nabielle was about to stop it when the bell went for the end of the first round.

As it turned out, it would have made little difference if she had stopped proceedings because Ferran quit on his stool.

Otto was through to the Semi-finals!

Back in the common room, Otto was a hero for the evening. For the first time, he was even more in the limelight than Engelial. Jack was again in the curious position of being the closest person to the most popular person in the room which he quickly decided was a great place to be, everyone was excessively pleasant towards him and yet he had few eyes on him throughout the evening, no one refusing to let him go to bed because they wanted to celebrate with him all night long.

Jack decided to make the most of this fortuitous position and slipped off to bed early, he was hoping that Ember and Mo would still be making his bed so that he could tell them about Polly not being at the Quarterfinal but, even more than that, he wanted to see his best friends again. It was great being a bit of a celebrity amongst people older than him but there was far less substance in it than his friendship with Mo and Ember.

Unfortunately, the dorm was empty when Jack entered so he found a spare bit of paper and wrote a small note on it.

Ember and Mo,

I have some more to tell you, when can you meet?

Leave a note here, letting me know.

Jack then tucked the slip of paper so that it just stuck out from the corner of his pillow, not suspicious enough for any of the other boys to notice it but when Ember and Mo made his bed, they would find it for sure.

Throughout Sunday, Jack would spend at most twenty minutes in the common room before making some excuse and returning to his room, hoping to find a letter from Ember and Mo but, time after time, he was left disappointed.

By six in the evening, Jack was beginning to wonder whether the servants had Sunday's off. Based on everything that he had seen up to this point, Jack strongly doubted it, but it seemed the only answer. And then, finally, Jack returned to his room to find a freshly made bed with a different letter sticking out of the pillowcase.

Go through the Servants door at the end of the corridor at midnight, Mo will be there to meet you

Jack couldn't help but feel a little short-changed at the brevity of the letter but contented himself with the knowledge that in a few short hours, he would see his friends again.

As Jack sat in the common room that evening and watched the clock slowly tick onwards, he was every bit as restless as Otto had been the day before.

Eventually, Jack thought that it was late enough for him to head to bed without too many eyebrows being raised so he left the room quietly and climbed onto his soft mattress. Surprisingly, Jack found that he was quite tired despite the early hour and his bed was just so irresistibly comfortable.

Jack woke with a start. He had no way of knowing what the time was, but it was dark and everyone else was snoring. Kicking himself, Jack hurriedly got dressed in the dark, trying to force his legs into a jumper and arms into his trousers.

Finally properly clothed, Jack rushed out into the common room. The clock said that it was half past midnight. Jack tiptoed through the corridor and down the narrow, dark set of stairs to the Servants door.

It was already open; Mo was standing there looking unimpressed.

"C'mon quickly." He muttered as Jack grinned at him.

Then, unable to contain himself any longer, Mo broke into his standard wide grin and gave Jack a spine-crushing hug. Jack couldn't put into words how good it felt to be in Mo's company again.

They found Ember in the darkest corner of the corridor on the way to the kitchens. She also brought Jack into a tight embrace before he had the chance to say hello.

"Right, what was it you wanted to tell us?" Ember asked, returning to her normal crisp, effective manner.

"Well while everyone was watching the Quarter Finals, I think Polly must have been out sending a message to Carsicus."

"Really? How?" Ember asked, looking excited.

"She didn't turn up at all and Finley said that last year, she was the first to all the battles to get a good seat!"

Both Ember and Mo continued to look at him expectantly.

"Oh, was that it?" Asked Mo when it began to get awkward.

"Yeah."

"That doesn't prove anything Jack, she might have just

been ill or something."

"But she looked normal today."

"Even so, her not turning up to a match is hardly evidence."

Jack sighed, he guessed that Ember was, as normal, right. But that didn't stop him feeling certain in his gut that Polly was the one talking to Carsicus, he just hadn't been able to prove it.

"We just need something more concrete, that's all. You are right that all the clues are pointing towards Polly but there is only really your word at the moment." Said Ember, obviously feeling that she had been a little too blunt towards Jack. "I'm not saying that I don't trust your judgement but let's keep digging a little longer until we find some less anecdotal." She continued

"Fine." Jack sighed.

"Anything else to say about that?"

"Nope." Jack replied with a shake of his head.

"Well in that case how has your first week of University been?" Ember asked.

"Amazing but I have to admit, I have really missed you guys."

"Pathetic." Mo laughed, "we have been what a hundred metres away and only for a week anyway."

"What about you guys?" Jack asked curiously.

"Not too bad so far. We've been really busy and early mornings suck but other than that … alright. Although I have to do Engelial's room tomorrow." Ember said with a shiver.

"What's wrong with Engelial?"

"There hasn't been one person who has come back from tidying her room who wasn't crying. I don't know what she says to them, no one is even willing to tell everyone else what she has done."

Jack wanted to dismiss everything that Ember was saying as hyperbole but found his throat refusing to pass the words as he remembered her aggression towards Dara, her hitting of Otto and everything that Otto had told Jack earlier that morning.

CHAPTER 16:
SCHOLAR'S
CITY SNOW

Jack found that the next three weeks swept by in an almost unnerving fashion. Every morning, he was squiring for Otto. His lessons were of course child's play and he spent them whispering with Finley in an undertone or sitting with Engelial and Dara. In the evening, he would spread his homework on the floor and do it really slowly, making some mistakes along the way whilst Engelial would watch over him, frequently saying that he was working far too hard. When he was in her company, everything that Ember had told him seemed impossible and even the evidence of Engelial's other side, that Jack had seen first-hand, was unbelievable.

What Jack had found he enjoyed most of all though was the moments in between when he would sit with Polly and Finley in the corner of the common room. He told Mo and Ember that this was so he could keep an eye on Polly, but he knew in his heart of hearts that was untrue – Jack just liked the ease of the twins' company, the casual teasing from Finley as he drew funny caricatures of the others in the common room and even Polly with her excitement towards Ziro's tournament.

Then, Wednesday of the fourth week, just as Jack had truly settled into the Universities rhythm of life, Mr. Virta, the deputy head, had come into the common room as they were preparing to go to lessons and told them instead to go to the main hall in the Bubble.

At once, almost everyone in the common room broke into large grins including Polly and Finley.

"What are you smiling at?" Jack asked.

"You really don't know *anything* do you?" Teased Finley as he put away his drawing. "I think, outside the bubble, it must be snowing."

"What's that got to do with anything?"

"It's a tradition as old as the University itself" began Finley dramatically, "the dome is taken down and we are all allowed out into the city on the first weekend of snow."

Finley's guess proved to be correct as Mr. Virta explained in his nasally, weasel-like voice that all the students were indeed going to be allowed out into the town that weekend.

"What is there to do in the city?" Jack asked Finley as they made their way to lessons.

"What d'you want to do is the real question."

Jack shrugged.

"Alright then Mr. Boring, I'll come up with what *I* think you'll enjoy." Smiled Finley.

Thursday and Friday of that week, Jack tried to wheedle Finley's plans for the weekend out of him but to no avail, Finley just smiled enigmatically back and told Jack jokingly to pay attention to the lesson whilst he planned his weekend of fun. Engelial had said that she wanted to go shopping so Jack had a custom-made excuse to not spend his weekend with her and Otto had hinted that he wanted to do some more training so Jack had bargained that they would do some early Saturday morning but after that, he was planning on enjoying this weekend.

Soon Saturday dawned and Jack donned his kit and went

to sparring with Otto. Otto would happily have stayed all day but once his other training partners and Jack had all made it clear that they wanted to leave, he let them go. Jack suspected Otto would spend the day tagging along with Engelial's group getting thoroughly bored.

When Jack got back to the college, Finley was up wearing his biggest grin. "Time for Scholar's City to meet Jack" he said. "Where's Polly? We need to get out of here before Engelial comes downstairs and sees her favourite little cutie."

"Geroff" Jack complained as Finley started rubbing his head saying, 'who's a cutie?' in a high-pitched voice.

"What are you doing?" Polly asked as she arrived, saving Jack from Finley for the moment.

They left the Dome through the same shed that Jack had entered through on his first day, "I can't believe it was only a few weeks ago that I didn't know anyone here, didn't have any friends at all away from home."

"Well, I'd say that you know people now, not so sure about the friend bit." Finley laughed and Jack smiled amusedly back, accepting he had set Finley up for that one.

"Jack." Said a familiar voice as soon as he left the Dome and Jack turned to see Mo leaning on the invisible wall. "Your father wants to see you."

"Alectus is in Scholar's City?" Jack asked, sounding surprised.

"Yeah." Said Mo slowly.

"That one of your servants?" Polly asked.

Jack nodded as Mo snorted softly. "You want to learn some respect for your superior's boy." She told him coldly.

"Where's my father?" Jack asked quickly before Mo could voice a reply that, Jack was sure, would be less than respectful.

"This way." Said Mo with none of his usual upbeat energy.

Jack turned to Finley whose face had dropped, "I really need to see my father, I don't know what he wants with me, but it must be important for him to come all this way and tell me to my face." Jack said and Finley nodded, and Jack knew he understood but was disappointed nevertheless. "We can do everything you had planned tomorrow, I promise." Jack said. Finley nodded again.

With an apologetic look, Jack went to catch up with Mo who had already started walking off.

"Hey, how're you doing?" Jack asked once they were out of the twin's earshot.

"Yeah not too bad." Mo shrugged, carrying on walking. There wasn't any cold in Mo's voice but there was none of his usual genial vigour.

"Any idea why Alectus has come here?" Jack asked, "probably trying to control us again, I still can't believe how you got around it last time." Jack laughed.

"Alectus isn't actually here, I just said that because Einor and Dr. Nabielle wanted to have a meeting, but I couldn't say that in front of your new best friends."

"They aren't my new... is that why you aren't smiling?"

"No, it's just that it's not fair that you've been having a great time investigating the King and being front row for all the Sceptre Battles and having fun with all the Uni students while me and Ember have been busy scrubbing pans and making beds."

"Hey that's not my fault." Jack said defensively.

"Yeah I know, sorry, I'm not mad at you, it's just so boring what we are doing and the other servants, Errion help me they are dull. It's not their fault but they've been servants their whole lives and their parents were and then their parents were and none of them have done much other than what we are doing now." Mo ranted. "And then there's just getting treated like you need to go around telling all the students how wonderful they are the whole time."

Slightly guiltily, Jack realised he had hardly thought of how Mo and Ember were getting on, every time that they had met, it had been those two asking the questions.

"Anyway, we're in here," Mo said, leading Jack into a small pub but sounding much more like his normal self now that his rant was done.

Sure enough, seated in a dark corner in the back of the pub, Jack saw Ember, Einor and Dr. Nabielle. Ember and Dr. Nabielle burst into wide smiles when they saw the boys while Einor maintained his usual stony face. "So then Jack how've you been?" Dr. Nabielle asked.

"Good. I've made a lot of progress on the King situation..." Jack said, wanting to tell Dr. Nabielle all about what he had discovered so far but she held up a hand and Jack fell quiet.

"I'm glad to hear it but I wanted to know how *you* were."

"Yeah all good." Jack said, not wanting to annoy Mo by going on about how good a time he had been having but Mo just smiled and told him to get on with it. Dr. Nabielle watched Jack with a kind expression on her face as he ran through the exciting stories and happy memories he had already collected. She took a particular interest in his friendship with the Ished twins, explaining that the Ished family had always been ardent supporters of the Kaofrelsi. At this point, Jack couldn't hold himself back and he began to tell Dr. Nabielle and Einor about the way out of the Dome and how Polly had missed the Quarterfinals of Ziro's Tournament. Dr. Nabielle agreed with Ember that although it was more than passing queer, it wasn't nearly enough to go off.

Suddenly, Mo choked on his drink and began cackling with laughter. "The Ished twins, their names" he managed to gasp in between breaths.

"What about their names?"

It was Ember who answered, rolling her eyes, "if you shorten Finley to Fin and Polly to Pol, their names are Finished and Polished."

And Mo began shaking with laughter again, "you've made friends with Finished and Polished." He cackled.

"Other than Finished and Polished, and Otto of course, is there anyone else you have been spending time with?" Dr. Nabielle asked, ignoring Mo.

Flushing with embarrassment, Jack nodded "well she has more been spending time with me than the other way around but Engelial."

Einor snorted loudly "that girl, pretty as a picture and as nice as a dagger up your..."

Dr. Nabielle coughed loudly to quieten Einor.

"Why do you hate her?" Jack asked curiously.

"Oh she's nice enough to people she wants things from I'm sure, you've undoubtably had a fine time with her but behind closed doors... the way she treats servants... I wouldn't have taken that job for a million King's notes."

"What job?"

"I was one of Engelial's guards a couple of times."

"Why?"

"To get close to her uncle, Lord Sorain, and try to put a blade between his shoulders and chin. I never managed it." Einor said regretfully.

"Why'd you want to kill Lord Sorain?"

"Anyone with a sense of dignity should want to kill Lord Sorain. He takes kids from their families aged about ten or eleven and trains them to be killers. It was one of those kids, Vermhell was his name, that beat me and did this." And again,

Einor revealed the scar that ran from his shoulder to his wrist. "And there's the other reason…" At this, Einor's face spasmed and he went quiet "but I can't talk about that." He said quietly and Jack was willing to bet this was the same incident that had made him fall silent in Edenvale, when he had spoken of killing the one person who had meant anything to him.

Jack spent the rest of the afternoon talking with the others but even as evening began to set in, he would have happily stayed there for hours more. "It's past time you returned to the Dome." Said Dr. Nabielle, and Jack knew better than to argue.

Sunday, Jack woke in a frantic panic. He couldn't breathe or see! Someone was pressing a pillow down on his face. Then, as suddenly as it had started, the pillow was removed and Jack saw Finley's smiling face.

"YOU NUTJOB! YOU COULD HAVE KILLED ME!" Jack bellowed at once.

"Well you didn't wake up when I was throwing bits of cereal at you, so I had to try something a bit more extreme."

Jack looked and sure enough, there were pieces of cereal all over his bed. "You could have shaken me you know."

"Today's meant to be about fun, where is the fun in shaking someone awake?"

"Git." Jack complained as he stood up and three pieces of cereal that had been stuck to him fell to the floor.

"Who was shouting?" Otto asked tiredly from his bed.

"Me but it wasn't anything important." Jack replied. "Go back to sleep." And Otto grunted and did as Jack had suggested.

As he got changed, Jack found several more bits of cereal stuck to him which didn't improve his mood. "Whatever you have planned for today, it had better be good." He warned Finley.

"Or what?" Finley teased.

The two boys met Polly in the quad and left through the Shed just as they had yesterday.

Jack had been so surprised to see Mo the day before that he hadn't really looked around Scholar's City properly. It was beautiful. Not as spectacular as the Rainbow City away East, but quiet and mythical and Jack had trouble believing he was really there, it felt more as though he was lost in a book than walking through a real place. Polly and Finley must have felt the same because neither of them spoke for several minutes.

They went not towards the bridges or the forest but instead up in the direction of the wall. "Where are we going?" Jack asked after a time.

"Well the *first* place that we are going is to get the best hot chocolate in the Realm." Said Finley and moments later, they were sat outside a handsome wooden building with mugs of hot chocolate as tall as Jack's forearm but four times as wide.

"What do you know of Carsicus and Lord Sorain?" Jack asked after his first sip, warmth and richness flowing through him. He watched Polly closely as he said Carsicus' name, but she didn't twitch or give any indication of alarm, instead just asking, "why do you want to know?"

"Yesterday, my father, Lord Alectus, mentioned Sorain and Carsicus a few times but wouldn't give me any details about them. What he did say was that your family knew them both well."

"Jack, listen closely, it is very important that you don't go gossiping too loudly about this to anyone." Finley said, leaning in. "If I tell you this now, please stop asking questions, I don't want you to get hurt."

"Lord Sorain is our father's liege lord; our family serve him the same way he serves the King. As for Carsicus, he spent time at court growing up, like most of the sons of the Lords, and become good friends with Sorain's son – Flair."

Jack choked on his hot chocolate.

"So Sorain is Flair's father and Engelial's uncle making Flair and Engelial... cousins." He gasped.

With an almost imperceptible nod of the head, Finley agreed, "best not to remind either of them of that fact though."

"As I say, our father served Lord Sorain, he wouldn't hear a word against him. That was until Carsicus became consul of the Kaofrelsi after his father's death. Since Flair and Carsicus had been such good friends at court, Carsicus became almost a second son to Sorain. Our father has always been good at not seeing what he didn't want to and pretended not to notice Sorain's more... immoral actions. But once Sorain and Carsicus began working together, he could deny them no longer. He went to Sorain, just to discuss the matter with him. We haven't seen him since. Hopefully, Sorain has only imprisoned him."

"I'm so sorry." Jack said and they all fell into silence. But a thought arose in Jack's mind – it made more sense than ever for Polly to be the link between the King and Carsicus for if Carsicus and Sorain had her father hostage, they could make her do whatever they needed.

"It's ok, you weren't to know." Finley said gently rubbing Jack's shoulder. "Today is meant to be about fun though so let's put it behind us for now, we have places to be."

The three of them continued through Scholar's City until the buildings began to thin and Finley led them into another pub, this one more worn down than the two that Jack had been to already.

"Three King's secrets please." Said Finley to the barman who smiled and disappeared. Jack stood wondering what a King's secret was. Then, suddenly, there was a rumble, and a hole began to open in the floor, revealing a wooden staircase.

"Down we go." Smiled Finley and Jack followed him below before, suddenly, finding himself on the top row of what appeared to be a theatre. Sure enough, plenty of the seats were already filled.

More people came into the theatre and when it was almost full, the lights began to dim, and the curtains pulled back and... there was no one there! There were a few piles of clothes but that was it.

Jack felt Finley tug on his arm, "c'mon" he whispered. Suddenly, Jack understood, "uh uh, no way." He whispered back but Finley pulled him to his feet and Jack found himself making his way to the stage, aware that Polly was coming as well.

Finley pointed out one pile of clothes to Jack, "those ones are yours" he said before pulling on his own, Polly began to get into a set a bit further along and others from the audience came down to get into the rest of the costumes.

Before Jack knew it, they were ready to start. "What do I do?" He whispered frantically to Finley.

"Whatever comes naturally, it's like Jazz." Finley smiled back.

And suddenly, Jack was having the best hour of his life! It was better even than that night where Engelial had taught him to dance. Jack just found himself slipping into this character he was playing and reacting to what the others did. There was no script, no director, just two lives happening together at once – one where Jack was playing with his two friends and one where his character was living as well. The best part was at the end when all the other actors left and it was just him, Finley and Polly and at that moment, Jack felt more alive than he ever had before, which was strange. He could taste the air and feel every fibre of his being and believed this moment could stretch on forever. Then it ended. But Jack knew that even if that moment couldn't go on forever, the memory of it could.

The crowd cheered and Finley pushed Jack out to the front to get his own round of applause, "you were fantastic." He whispered.

"A true natural." Some old man agreed.

Jack couldn't stop talking about the play as they walked back, even when Finley started throwing snowballs and a huge snowball fight broke out, Jack kept talking. "You're turning into Finley." Polly joked later. Jack didn't see that as a bad thing in the slightest.

As Jack walked into the common room, he was aware of the snow that had tangled in his hair beginning to melt and draw cold lines down his face. Quick as he could, he started towards the showers but before he got there, a strong hand took his shoulder and Jack turned to look up at Otto.

"Semi-finals are this weekend. The Headmistress just told us. And guess what…"

"What?"

"The squires are also allowed to invite someone to watch the Semi-finals!"

A fully formed plan appeared in Jack's head as if his subconscious had been waiting for this exact opportunity. He could invite Polly, if she refused, he would be even more certain that she was the one communicating with Carsicus.

Later that evening, he found Polly sitting with Finley on two large brown sofas. Both had blank, discarded worksheets in front of them.

"Hey." Jack smiled.

"Horse!" Finley beamed.

"What?"

"Oh, you were saying hello, sorry I thought we were playing word association game." Finley said as though that were a reasonable assumption.

Shaking his head, Jack continued, "Otto just told me that the Semi-finals of Ziro's tournament are this weekend."

Finley let out a frustrated, playful groan.

"And I was wondering…" Jack began, turning towards Polly "whether you wanted to be my front row guest?"

Polly froze, which was all the confirmation that Jack needed but he decided to keep going anyway in case more information could be gleaned from the situation. "Ababa." Polly stammered. "I'm sorry but I just don't think I can."

"Why not?" Jack probed.

"I just don't think it would be right."

"But why not?"

"Jack, I said no. Drop it." Polly answered forcefully and Finley looked more than a little taken aback.

"But I thought you would want…" Finley began.

"Shut up." Polly growled. "I'm going to bed." She stropped before storming off up the stairs to the girls' bedrooms.

"Well, in that case, do you fancy a front-row seat?" Jack asked Finley.

Finley, to Jack's surprise, looked over the moon. "Definitely." He grinned. "And I will be able to give you the perfect present to say thank you."

"No you really don't have to." Jack protested quickly.

"Wait until you see what it is before refusing it." Finley smiled.

When he went to bed that evening, Jack suspected he might have just had the best day of his life so far.

CHAPTER 17: REC-TREC CLUES

Before Jack knew it, he was waking up on Saturday morning, the day of the Semi-finals. It was the first truly cold day of the year, and the blades of grass all wore coats of ice.

"Going to have to watch my footing today." Said Otto as he met Jack in the common room.

Of course, Otto insisted that they arrive at the stadium ages before everyone else and Jack noticed, to his great relief, that Otto seemed a lot more relaxed than for the Quarterfinals. Jack on the other hand, couldn't help but feel a little restless. Polly never showed up and, certain as he was that she was the one communicating with Carsicus, it was unnerving to have her able to do what she wanted whilst everyone else was at the tournament.

This time, Otto was drawn against the Champion of Shark College, whose name Jack had learnt was Hippos.

Otto was simply too good for Hippos and soon the fight was stopped, and Otto was through to the final. Although, during the fight, Hippos' sceptre had torn a deep gash into Otto's shield.

The fight between Flair and the champion of Owl College was a mirror image of the first battle. Even though neither of the fights had lasted any more than five minutes, the crowd was enthused by the outcome, they had the final that they wanted, Flair against Otto.

Beaming, Otto crossed over to Jack. "Would you mind terribly finding a spare shield to replace this one?"

"That is the job of a squire I suppose." Jack grinned back. "See you in the common room in ten."

Jack hurried off to a small room at the back of the stadium where the spare equipment was kept. As he walked through the stadium there was a constant groaning, creaking sound above him as the audience got up to leave. Jack heard them start to file out of the stadium.

Just as he went to open the door, Jack caught a flash of movement out the corner of his eye. It was a blur of blond hair coming from the bubble. Just before he could be certain that it was Polly, a huge body of people passed in front of him, all on their way from the stadium back to their colleges

Forgetting his task, Jack began pushing people aside, trying to force his way towards the bubble. Suddenly, he was through the crowd. But the person coming from this way had gone.

Jack let out his frustration by kicking a chunk of dirt out the ground.

Suddenly, he realised that there was still the potential for something to be gained and charged towards the secret tunnel that led up to the Old Tower like his life depended on it.

When he reached the trapdoor, there was a fresh footprint in the icy grass, it looked to Jack as though it couldn't have been more than a few minutes old. He didn't want to waste time looking too closely at it but was certain that it was a girl's print. There was no evidence it was Polly's, but Jack would have gambled all he owned that it was.

Aware that he had already wasted too much time, Jack sprinted along the tunnel and up the stairs to the top of the tower and saw through the hole that had been cut out of the dome the unmistakable shape of the raven that had broken Carsicus out of jail. The creature was flying across the hills, towards the forest to the South of Scholar's City.

Surprised that it wasn't heading towards the Old Town where Jack had seen Carsicus a few weeks before and aware that this was the best chance he would have to overhear some conversation, Jack pulled himself onto the roof of the Dome and once more began to run along it but now heading towards the forest instead of the rest of Scholar's City.

Refusing to look down, Jack jogged along the barrier until he found himself touching down on the outskirts of the forest. The adrenaline still pumping around his system, Jack now began to run through the forest, wishing that he had Mo's incredible stamina.

Soon, the trees began to get closer together and block out the sun's hopeful rays. Jack started moving more quietly between the darkest shadows between trees hoping that the Raven had not travelled too much further.

Suddenly, he heard a voice.

"What does she mean he isn't going to do it? The King does as I tell him!" Roared the voice and Jack knew that it was Carsicus. Jack began to move silently towards him.

The raven remained silent but staring straight at Carsicus and Jack realised that it was sending images to Carsicus' brain through the same type of links that existed between Jack and Halmer. Eventually, Carsicus gave a dismissive grunt. "I really hadn't wanted to do this because it makes it more likely she is caught, but I have a pair of Rec-Trec's. Give this one to her next time you meet."

The raven squawked its acceptance and then half-turned away before looking back towards Carsicus. Jack was surprised to find himself reading the body language of a Raven and realising that it was nervous about telling Carsicus something.

Once more, the Raven began its eye contact and started sending its roll of images into Carsicus' brain.

As Jack peered around the side of the tree, he saw Carsicus turning purple with rage. The raven squawked once more and Carsicus looked apoplectic, swelling up like a balloon. With a growl of anger, he threw something that sailed only centimetres from Jack's right-hand shoulder.

Carsicus took several deep breaths and calmed himself a little.

"That was stupid. I shouldn't have thrown that. Find it and bring it to me. If I lose that, the plan is set back a month and our Glorious Leader is running low on patience."

Mind blown at the wonderful stroke of luck that fate had delivered his way, Jack crept silent as a shadow to the black box that Carscius had thrown. He picked it up and saw that it was one of the pair of Rec-Trec's.

It read simply; 'This is Carsicus. Glorious Leader growing impatient. If the King continues refusing to listen to us, start preparations for Plan B.'

Suddenly, there was crashing behind him as the Raven came looking for the Rec-Trec, Jack dropped it where he was and dived behind a tree before pulling himself along in an army crawl away from the bird. There was no sudden call of alarm, so Jack decided that he had escaped unnoticed but carried on lying low whilst putting more distance between himself and the raven.

Eventually, he decided that he was safe enough to stand back up and he began running back towards the University.

His brain was so excited whilst building a plan that it didn't seem to have the spare capacity to be scared as Jack climbed back along the invisible Eileaftium dome and back through the tower. He danced back to his college.

"Where have you been?" Dana asked as he let Jack in.

"Finding a spare shield for Otto." Jack lied quickly. He wasn't interested in the celebrations that were raging in the common room, he needed to speak with Mo and Ember now.

However, he wasn't even halfway across the common room before he was halted by Finley. "Jack, your present." He smiled, handing Jack a piece of paper.

Jack glanced down and saw that it was a drawing of the battle between Otto and Hippos, he saw himself in Otto's corner mid-shout. Jack shook himself. There was no time to waste. "Thanks very much." He said to Finley briefly before continuing to his room.

Jack's luck clearly hadn't run out because when he opened the door to his sleeping quarters, he saw immediately that Mo and Ember were there alone, making the beds.

"Why do you look so delighted?" Mo asked teasingly.

"Wait until you hear this …" Jack replied as he dropped Finley's present into his bag.

Jack first told them about how the Ished twins' father was held captive by Sorain and how Sorain saw Carsicus as a second son and then went on to the story of the raven from the moment Otto had asked him to find a spare shield.

Mo and Ember sat there with their jaws open at Jack's luck.

"You know what that means …" Ember said.

"We know exactly what is written on the Rec-Trec of whoever is talking to Carsicus. If we could just find a way of looking at Polly's Rec-Trec…" Mo said hungrily.

"There is something that makes me unsure that it is Polly…" Ember began, and the two boys groaned. "How did she end up in the same college as Jack?"

"Mmm.." Jack hummed in acknowledgement. He gasped. "She didn't make the choices in the maze alone though, Finley made a lot of the decisions and she just sort of followed."

The three of them all shared meaningful looks. Even Ember now seemed convinced.

CHAPTER 18:
FIN ISHED

Once again, time began to slide by like sand through a timer and before Jack knew it, people were discussing arrangements for going back at Midwinter. Several times, he had attempted to find some excuse to look at Polly's Rec-Trec, but none had worked out.

"We are going to head back in two weeks' time." Polly and Finley told Jack in the common room that evening.

"I wouldn't do that." Otto said pleasantly as he arrived. "You would miss the Final of Ziro's Tournament."

Polly and Finley nodded meekly, they had always been intimidated whenever Engelial or Otto had come to speak to Jack. When Jack had asked them about it, they had always mumbled something about 'popular fourth-years'.

"Are you looking forwards to the final?" Finley asked Otto with a nervy grin.

"Certainly. Now, if you would let me borrow Jack for a bit, I need to talk to him about tactics."

"Of course." Polly and Finley said in unison.

The next week passed the fastest of them all. Jack felt as though he had barely had time to blink before finding himself just seven days out from the final of Ziro's Tournament. He put it down to the fact that he had been relentlessly busy squiring for Otto in the early morning before having lessons all day and then talking tactics with Otto into the night. The highlight of the week was still to come though when he found a small note posted inside his pillow.

Jack,

Come to the Servants door at midnight. We have a plan.

Jack couldn't help but check the back of the note and hope that there was something more written there, but he was disappointed. The meeting at midnight would have to suffice.

Otto and the others all fell asleep early and, determined not to be late for his meeting with Mo and Ember again, Jack forced himself out of bed and into the common room. It was empty except for one person.

"Hello." Jack ventured.

There was a flash of movement before Engelial said "Jack, what a nice surprise, I was just about to head for bed."

"Ok, see you tomorrow." Jack replied, trying to sound relaxed and indifferent and not at all interested that once again, he had stumbled across Engelial secretly alone in the common room after everyone else had gone to bed.

Once Engelial had gone, Jack of course went immediately over to where she had been sitting and this time was not in the least surprised to find a vast book with the title;

A Study of the Great, Early Rulers

Jack once again soon found himself pondering the mystery of Engelial. The maternal side that she always showed towards him, the absurd arrogance towards strangers and friends alike, the narcissistic violence when she didn't get her way. Her interest in great female rulers when she was alone juxtaposed against her loud opinions in front of her friends that 'In all honesty there is no point in girls who look like me learning'.

The chiming of the clock made Jack nearly leap out of his skin. He realised with a start that it was midnight and scrambled from his chair before dashing down the corridor to the servant's door.

The moment that he arrived; Mo pulled it open whispering "do you want to make any more noise coming down here?"

"Sorry."

"Have you heard about the final of Ziro's tournament?" Came Ember's straight-to-the-point voice from the shadows.

"Yes of course, it's next weekend. Why?"

"It is the perfect chance for us to get a look at Polly's Rec-Trec. You invite her to be your front-row guest for the final and Mo and I can use the time to go and look at her Rec-Trec."

"What if she just says no again..."

"I don't think she would dare if you asked her in front of other people. Especially if you asked her in Engelial's presence."

"Why not?"

"From everything you have said, Engelial seems to think of you as her son, or her little brother at least. A slight on you is a slight on her and I don't think Polly would dare do that."

"Why not?"

As if in answer, they heard the door between the girl's rooms and the servant's quarters swung open. "Who was in charge of sorting out my room?" Engelial demanded.

Jack heard a whimper of acknowledgement from someone in the kitchen.

"You were told, I suppose, that I take *warm* milk before bed."

Another whimper of acknowledgement

"Well this was absolutely stone cold." Ember shouted and Jack heard the smashing of a glass. "One of you peasants get me a warm glass of milk."

"I'll do it." Said the servant who had whimpered.

"No, you won't. From this moment you are fired. Go and find work somewhere else."

The door slammed as Engelial left to go back to her room. Jack looked at the other two, totally speechless. He had seen a nastier side to Engelial before but what he had just heard, he didn't think possible.

"She does that most nights." Ember said with loathing in her voice.

"Morning you." Engelial said charmingly when she met Jack in the common room the next day.

"Hello." Jack answered through gritted teeth.

"Are you ok?"

"Just feeling a bit ill." Jack replied truthfully.

"Aww poppet, go and lie down."

Jack grunted his acknowledgement. He returned to his room rubbing his stomach. It was true he was under the weather; he had felt sick to the pit of his stomach from the moment he had heard Engelial's outburst the night before. It was as though the guilt he felt at being associated with Engelial was an infection his body was fighting.

He had wanted to go and see if the girl that Engelial had shouted at was ok, but Mo and Ember insisted that he return to his dorm, his presence would not be appreciated by the other servants. Looking back on it now, Jack knew that they were right.

The only thing that made Jack feel slightly happier all day was the knowledge that they now had a plan to get eyes on to Polly's Rec-Trec.

Jack was alone in the darkness of his room for most of the day as it was a Wednesday, and Jack didn't have any lessons on Wednesday's. He didn't want to be around people at the moment, he felt as though the only people whose characters he could trust were Mo and Ember and, surprisingly, Finley – Engelial's multifacetedness had wrecked his faith that people were who they appeared to be.

About mid-afternoon, Engelial came into his room, Jack quickly slid the tracking-compass he had been playing with into his pocket, "I was wondering if you wanted some food?" She asked and Jack realised for the first time that he hadn't eaten all day.

"I'm not hungry." He said dismissively, not willing to accept anything from Engelial.

"Well do you at least want to come to my room, if you are feeling unwell, someone should at least be looking after you."

"Ok." Jack said briefly, reluctant to agree with anything that Engelial suggested but quickly deciding that it might be worth having a look around the dorms, see if he could find any more clues on Polly.

The girl's dorms were identical to the boy's except that they smelt nicer.

Engelial led him into a room with a large bronze five on the front. As they talked, the depravity of Engelial towards the servant girl began to feel more and more as though Jack had witnessed it in a dream, his brain no longer accepting it as a plausible turn of events, just like how it filled in the blankness of the Dome from the outside.

Suddenly, Jack spotted a familiar flash of blond hair out the corner of his eye through the open door. It was Polly.

"Hey, where are you off to?" Jack called to her.

"Just for a little walk." Polly replied nervously and Jack noticed that her eyes flicked anxiously towards Engelial.

"Um… Enjoy it." Jack smiled. "Oh, just before you go, I have something to ask you."

"Ok…" Polly said, looking more nervous than ever.

"Would you like to be my front-row guest for the final of the tournament?"

Polly's eyes again flicked nervously towards Engelial; her face seemed to spasm. Jack noticed a defeated look pass behind her eyes as she realised that she had no choice. "Of course." She answered in a voice that was less disappointed than Jack had expected.

"Nice one."

Polly left without saying anything else.

"Ok you, you seem well enough to me so I suggest you should head back to your room." Said Engelial and there was no doubt in Jack's mind that this wasn't a suggestion at all.

Smiling goodbye, Jack left Engelial's room. He was just about to head back to his own room when he noticed that one of the doors was open a crack, it was number 4. Jack replayed spotting Polly in the corridor and grew certain that this was the room that she had left from.

He knew that they had a plan in place to look at Polly's Rec-Trec, but this was too good an opportunity to pass up…

Quietly, Jack peered into the room. It was empty. He entered silent as a shadow. He knew instantly which bed was Polly's as there was a picture of her parents on her bedside table and both parents looked just like their children.

Jack turned the picture around, stupidly it made him feel much guiltier about looking through Polly's possessions.

Trying not to make it too untidy, Jack began going through the backpack that was next to Polly's bed. He found nothing but just before he shut it back up, he took the tracking compass from his back pocket and slid the blue tracking diamond into the front of her bag.

The door to the girl's dorms creaked open.

Panicking, Jack threw Polly's possessions back into the suitcase and kicked it back under her bed just as Polly opened the door to her room.

"What are you doing here?" She asked Jack breathlessly.

"I needed a word with you."

"But you knew I had just gone out for a walk."

"I thought you said you had just come back from a walk." Jack lied unconvincingly.

"Right, what did you want to talk to me about?"

Jack's mind was blank.

"What you are going to wear to the final."

"Oh, I'm not sure. You know that I don't care about that sort of thing. I'm not Engelial."

"Right, yeah, well see you later then." Jack said, moving towards the door.

Straight away, Polly noticed that the pictures of her parents had been turned around. Jack kicked himself for forgetting as Polly eyed him with deep suspicion.

As soon as Jack was in his own room, he collapsed onto his bed. What had he done?

For the remainder of the week, whenever Polly saw Jack, she would ignore him completely. Whenever he entered the common room, she would vanish into her room leaving Jack to talk with Finley alone. Admittedly, Jack had little time to do that as Otto insisted on spending time pouring over tactics and combinations whilst Engelial demanded he sit with her so that she could tell all her friends how he had been poorly and recovered so quickly. "It is because you are so very healthy." She told him adoringly.

Eventually, it was Saturday morning and the final of Ziro's Tournament. Otto and Jack woke up at exactly six o'clock, at least an hour and half before daybreak. Still, they lost no time crossing the muddy field to the Stadium. As the minutes ticked by, Jack was forced to watch Otto get steadily more tense. Whatever was going on in his head, his anxiety was clearly far beyond what he had shown up to this point.

"What are you nervous about?" Jack asked. "You fight Flair every day."

"It's not Flair that bothers me." Otto said, swinging his sceptre in sweeping figures of eight as though trying to battle the air itself. "It is everyone watching. I don't want to make myself look like an idiot. Particularly not in front of ..." Otto stopped dead, clearly thinking that he had said too much.

"In front of who?" Jack probed because he had noticed that whilst they were talking, Otto had seemed to relax a little.

"My father." Otto grimaced. "I don't want to make myself look like an idiot in front of my father."

"Why not?"

"He doesn't care about people who aren't useful to him."

"What d'you mean?"

"My father runs the Arcanian army. He has no time to waste on people that can't pull their own weight."

"But you're his son."

"That doesn't matter to some people. Duty first, that's his motto. It should be duty only." Otto growled, pirouetting and dancing with his sceptre so fast that it became a blur.

Jack didn't ask any more questions but was extremely pleased to note that Otto was looking much more relaxed now that he had admitted to Jack the reason for his nerves.

Jack didn't recognise the first person to arrive in the Stadium, he was a tall, thick shouldered man in a black coat. Jack accidently made eye contact with the man and saw that he had cold, hard features and a scar running along his right cheek.

"Are you my son's squire?" The man asked Jack.

"Yes sir."

"It is not sir; it is Field Marshal Smith. Has my son not taught his squire the proper way to address service personal?"

"No. Sorry father." Otto said, his eyes on the ground.

"Look at me when you are talking." Said Field Marshal Smith. "Now keep practicing. I don't want to see my son beaten in the final again."

Any nervousness that Jack had helped rid Otto of was now back in full force and Otto began shaking so badly that he nearly dropped his sceptre. His father gave a derisive snort. "Wouldn't have gotten close to the final in my day. Real warriors we were then. Your mother was too soft on you. I told her at the time what would happen."

Jack was an inch away from telling Otto's father to shut his mouth, Field Marshal or not, but just about kept a lid on it, guessing that an argument between his squire and his father was the last thing that Otto's frayed nerves needed.

Soon, Field Marshall Smith was not the only person on the front row that Jack didn't recognise, two other men took seats on the other side of the row. Jack could guess who one of the men was – his green eyes familiar – it was Flair's father, Lord Sorain. The other man was thin and tall and white as chalk. Upon seeing the two new arrivals Mr. Virta hurried over to them. "Lord Sorain, an honour, your son is a credit to the school and yourself. And Vermhell, a Warrior of the World for all the students here to look up to."

Jack regarded the two new arrivals closely, Lord Sorain who had murdered his own sister and father and maybe the Ished twins' father as well and Vermhell, the only person to defeat Einor in battle.

Jack was so lost in his thoughts that he jumped a foot when the doors swung suddenly shut and then remembered himself and where they were. He quickly put the thoughts to the back of his mind. He had a job to do.

Dr. Nabielle called Flair and Otto into the centre of the ring. It seemed to Jack that either Otto had shrunk or Flair had grown as Flair now towered over Otto like he never had before.

"C'mon Otto." Jack whispered, "It's just like at sparring."

His words seemed in vain though because Otto was still shaking when Jack stepped out of the ring, leaving the two fighters alone.

The bell went for the first round and instantly, Otto's shoulders dropped, he swung his sceptre in a figure of eight and Jack saw that he was ready to fight. Jack felt his own shoulders drop as he managed to relax for the first time in an hour.

The match began with deadly intensity, Otto and Flair so experienced with each other's styles that there was no feeling out process necessary. Flair's signature ferocity amplified by the occasion. Several times, both fighters put together combinations that caused the other to stagger backwards but every time, they just about managed to survive the onslaught.

A particularly savage swing from Flair skimmed Otto's

helmet as the bell rang and for five seconds after they had stopped fighting, both men stared each other down before turning and taking a seat on their stools.

The crowd began to murmur again, and it was only then that Jack realised that it had, until that point, been silent.

"Water." Otto gasped and Jack helped pour some down his throat. Once he had drunk, Otto turned and looked at Jack expectantly.

"Oh, right." Jack said, suddenly remembering that Otto was expecting an external view of the fight.

Rapidly, Jack replayed parts of the battle in his head. "Don't get drawn into his fight." Jack said. "He wants that violent blood bath in the close range. Don't give it to him. One, two blocks in there and then step out, he will follow you. Then, as he is coming in, hit the body. Let's just focus on slowing him down this round."

Otto nodded and stood up just as the bell went for the start of the second round.

Flair, already on his feet, charged across the ring towards Otto. Nimbly, Otto danced to the side, moving towards the middle of the ring, where there was more room for him to move. The last thing that anyone wanted against Flair was to be trapped in the corner.

Flair swung two huge downwards thrusts towards both sides of Otto's head. Otto blocked them before darting backwards and swinging at Flair's body armour as he closed the range. The force of the strike caused the whole stadium to tremble and Flair to grunt loudly.

This only made Flair more aggressive though and he pressed the fight again, only for Otto to block his strikes then step quickly backwards and again hit the body as Flair closed the range.

A cleverer fighter than Flair would have at this point

changed tactics, but Flair only got more and more livid, falling deeper and deeper into Jack's plan.

By the time that the bell went at the end of round two, Flair was growling like a feral animal and swinging indiscriminately. His breath, mingled in with the growling, was now tortured and irregular.

As Otto spun around to return to his stool, Flair slashed at the back of his head. Otto, seeing the blur out the corner of his eye somehow reacted in time to block the thrust. Both men let their Sceptre's fall to their sides and stared at each other with such intensity that Jack wouldn't have been surprised to see sparks flying.

It was Otto who turned away first. He had a huge grin on his face.

"Flair is exhausted. He has nothing left." Otto said as soon as he got back to the stool. But, instead of sitting down, he leant casually against the ropes.

"Why aren't you sitting down?"

"I don't need to. I feel ok. Look at how tired Flair is." Otto said, nodding and Jack saw that Flair was collapsed on his chair, having to be held in place by his corner all the while being berated by Dr. Nabielle for attacking after the bell. "If he looks across and sees me standing up, he might not even bother coming out this round." Otto continued.

"So are you going to continue doing what you did last round this round as well?" Jack asked.

Otto shook his head. "I don't need to. He is done, the rest of this fight is a formality."

When the third round began, Flair didn't come charging out towards Otto. Instead, he stood like a limp puppet in his own corner, snarling his hatred. Otto crossed the ring to him and, with a barbaric growl, Flair just threw himself at Otto.

Otto swung his Sceptre across, blocking Flair's thrust and then, using Flair's own momentum, threw him to the floor. An instant later, the pink point of Otto's Sceptre was hovering over Flair's throat.

"Stop!" Yelled Dr. Nabielle. "The fight is over. Otto is the School Champion!"

Jack sprinted over the stack of spare equipment towards Otto, almost clearing him off his feet with a hug that resembled a rugby tackle. "Great plan Jack." Otto whispered as they embraced.

The next to reach Otto was Engelial. She spread her arms out wide and Otto spread his too, expecting a hug and looking dead pleased with himself. Instead, Engelial brought her hands closer together, wrapping them around Otto's face and bringing him in to a full-on mouth-to-mouth kiss.

When she withdrew, Otto stood frozen in disbelief, his eyes round and large as saucers. Clearly her kiss had done what all of Flair's most brutal strikes had failed to do.

Several other people shook Otto's hand and embraced him but all the while he stood there in a daze. Engelial stood a little way off with a smile just playing on her face.

Jack, however, couldn't stand to wait around any longer. He left the spare equipment in a pile in the corner of the ring, confident that Otto would not notice or care. Jack needed to go and find Mo and Ember, needed to see if they had managed to find Polly's Rec-Trec.

Jack found himself humming with joy as he turned the corner from the field into the Quad.

He froze.

A body lay in the middle of the Quad.

It was Finley.

Jack raced over to him. He felt for a pulse. There wasn't

one.

"Finley." Jack said, shaking him. "Finley!" He shouted but Finley didn't stir.

Jack felt sick to the bottom of his stomach.

He was vaguely aware of a stampede of people running into the Quad to see what the shouting had been about, but Jack didn't care.

"What's that in his hand?" A voice asked.

Feeling as though he was in a dream, and his arm was impossibly heavy, Jack wriggled a piece of paper from Finley's hand.

> *Freedom for my life,*
>
> *My life for Freedom.*
>
> This boy tried to find out
>
> who I was.
>
> I killed him.

CHAPTER 19: BACK TO EDENVALE

Jack never knew how he got to bed that night. His memory didn't start working again until the next day. The only thing he could recall vividly from the night were Polly's horrendous, tearing screams when she had seen Finley's lifeless body. The screams themselves had seemed to rip apart Jack's carefully constructed timeline that pointed to Polly as the villain.

The person who had killed Finley was undoubtably the same person that was talking to Carsicus and that person could not be Polly. Jack would never forget the surprise and stomach-turning torment in her face at the sight of her dead twin.

All lessons were cancelled for the last week and the students allowed to leave for their Midwinter break immediately. No one celebrated this fact or even seemed to acknowledge it.

King Taigal had given the order for the cart network to be set up again just for today so that everyone could get home easily. The whole school left the University as one, and Jack had never heard such a large group of people so silent. There was no hint of a smile on anyone's face. Even the nature around them seemed to be muted as a mark of respect.

As they walked, Jack reflected that Finley had been one of the only people, maybe the only person, that he had befriended not to help his mission but simply because he wanted to. Finley had been kind and funny and relentlessly hopeful.

In simpler times, Jack was certain that they would have been friends for life.

As it was, Jack blamed himself for Finley's death. If he had been more switched on to finding the person who was talking with Carsicus, he might have found them sooner and Finley would still be alive, complaining with tongue in cheek about Polly forcing him to come to the final of Ziro's Tournament.

Depressed, Jack kicked a lump of dirt out of the ground, but it was half-hearted. He was in too much pain to be angry.

With a stabbing feeling, like a knife had been plunged through his ribs, Jack saw Polly walking nearby, her expression distant. There were grey bags under her red eyes and Jack guessed that she had cried out the first wave of pain throughout the night so all that was left now was an empty, unfeeling shell of a person.

Jack looked into the forest, where he knew Carsicus was hiding and felt an overwhelming tsunami of defeat. Even if he found out who was talking to Carsicus, it was too late, Finley was dead and there was no bringing him back.

When the school reached the collection of carts that had been brought for them, Jack stepped in automatically. He was so busy drowning in guilt that he barely realised when the cart set off, never mind pausing to take in the hills that he shot past or the forest where three months ago he had escaped Carsicus and been a hair's breadth away from being turned into a Wraith. He didn't care about any of that.

When the cart stopped, it took Jack several moments to find the strength in his legs to get out. He took two steps before stumbling to a stop and sitting down heavily on the grass. He didn't feel as though he deserved to return to Edenvale with the care-free Alforn. He had been given a job to do. He had failed. And caused Finley's death.

"Come on, on your feet." A voice said from above him and Jack looked up to see Dr. Nabielle standing there. "Let's get back to Edenvale. It is only just over that hill there."

Jack looked at her, hoping that he wouldn't have to say why he had collapsed, begging that Dr. Nabielle could tell just from his eyes why he felt so much guilt that he couldn't walk.

Dr. Nabielle squatted down and put her arm across Jack's shoulders, helping him to his feet. She didn't say anything as they walked but kept her arm across Jack's shoulders even once he was walking normally again.

As soon as they entered the forest of Edenvale, Jack noticed the difference in the air underneath the thick forest roof and, despite himself, he couldn't help but feel a little bit better. The Alforn passed him, the first people Jack had seen all day who weren't in a despondent daze but normal and even hopeful looking.

Alectus was waiting outside the treehouse and the moment that he saw Jack, he sprinted at him, tying him up in a hug. But to Jack it felt cold. He had been looking forwards to seeing his father but now he couldn't seem to make himself care about anything, not even seeing the only family that he had.

"There is food inside." Said Alectus and Jack nodded mutely before entering the tree house.

"Do you want to talk about it?" Alectus asked over dinner.

Jack shook his head.

"It might help you feel better."

Jack shook his head again and they ate the rest of the food in silence.

"I'll just put the plates away and then bring out pudding." Alectus said with a smile.

Jack waited until his father was out of the room before

slipping out as well and heading straight for his bed.

When Alectus peered into the room, Jack pretended to be asleep. He knew that he wasn't going to fool anyone but at least it made it clear that he didn't want to talk.

When Jack woke the next morning, there was no moment where he forgot about Finley before remembering but an instant heartsick pain. Jack got out of bed, already dressed in his clothes from the day before and headed out on a walk to Heaven Lake not because he consciously wanted to but just because he needed to do something.

The lake seemed to him less blue, the trees surrounding it less green, the sunrise less pink as though his brain had dialled them down, unwilling or unable to appreciate them.

"He's here!" A voice yelled some time later. The sun had risen but Jack still felt the same.

"Ah, you're ok." Alectus panted, his voice trembling with relief.

Jack turned slowly to face his father, not acknowledging that he had said anything at all.

"I was worried that ... that ... that you might not be ok." Said Alectus.

Jack said nothing.

"Just talk to me so I know you are alright." Alectus pleaded on their way back to the treehouse. But still, Jack didn't speak.

Jack didn't sleep at all that night. He just existed.

The celebrations of the Alforn during the night seemed insensitive and ignorant. Jack wasn't angry at them though, he was just in disbelief, he simply didn't understand. How could they not know about Finley? Why had the world not come to a stop?

Throughout the next two days, Jack didn't try and leave his room. He just sat in the darkness, unseeing and unable to feel anything except guilt.

Just as the sun rose, on the third day, Jack drifted off into a deep sleep.

"It isn't healthy to lock him up. You are being overprotective again." Came Dr. Nabielle's uniquely intelligent voice from the hallway outside Jack's room.

"You weren't here earlier. He just wondered off; he isn't in a fit state to be allowed out by himself. Anything could have happened to him."

"Well at least let him go out and just go with him."

"He won't speak to me." Alectus said, sounding defeated and Jack felt guiltier than ever.

"Just keep trying." Said Dr. Nabielle soothingly, reassuring Alectus in the way that only she could.

Jack heard his door unlock and his father enter. "Oh, you are awake." Alectus said, surprised. "Do you want to go out for a bit, get some fresh air?"

Jack answered by getting to his feet.

He walked close to his father. Neither of them spoke and Jack just let his feet take him around Edenvale. The colours had started to come back he noticed with interest. He started to feel a little more alive. The guilt was just as strong, but a little less deep, if that made sense. It made sense to Jack.

When they got back, Jack headed straight for the shower, letting the water pound on his head, and remembering Finley but not just in a guilty way, the good things too. Once into new clothes, Jack began to feel that maybe, just maybe, there was hope again and it was a good thing that the world hadn't stopped turning.

Just to keep himself busy whilst he was feeling good, Jack began to unpack the things that had been sent back from University with him. Just when he thought he was done; Jack's fingers found a piece of loose paper in the bottom of the bag. Intrigued, he pulled it out and saw that it was the picture that Finley had given him that day after the Semi-final.

Jack had never appreciated it properly.

He had of course been busy trying to find evidence that it was Polly who was communicating with Carsicus. A dagger of guilt.

Jack quickly busied himself with analysing the picture. The level of detail was extraordinary. Jack could see each curl of hair on his head in the illustration, could identify the way in which the wind was blowing by the smallest of strokes of colour, knew exactly what was happening in the fight by the expressions of Otto and Hippos. It felt that Jack was holding some part of Finley's being which was reassuring, confirmation that Finley had, at least, had the chance to leave a mark on the world.

A firm knock on the door surprised Jack. "Come in." He said, realising with a start that it was the first time he had spoken since the night of Finley's death.

The door swung open to reveal Dr. Nabielle. Ember and Mo were behind her; Jack was pleased to see that they looked sympathetic but not pitying, sombre but not sad. They understood. "We all wanted to know whether you wanted to go for a walk." Stated Dr. Nabielle.

"Yeah." Jack replied, hiding the picture Finley had drawn him under his bed. It was private.

The four of them headed through Edenvale but not towards Heaven Lake. Not even towards Teraturt but Westward. "I thought that you said there was nothing this way." Mo said, a hint of accusation in his voice.

"Sometimes nothing is everything you need."

"Mental." Mo muttered to himself.

"Careful now." Said Dr. Nabielle as the trees began to thin.

Suddenly, Jack saw what she meant, where the trees stopped, there were no gentle rolling hills but ... nothing for a long way. Soon, they found themselves at the top of a great cliff. Nervously, Jack peered over the edge to the ground far below.

Dr. Nabielle sat and they all copied her. Now, when Jack looked out beyond, it was like a carpet of green that went on and on until it met the blue ceiling of the sky at a point an infinite distance away.

"I will leave you three for a bit." Said Dr. Nabielle. "Just head back to Alectus' when you are all done."

"When we have done what?" Mo asked but Dr. Nabielle had already entered the Deep and zoomed off before he had finished speaking.

"It was my fault." Said Jack, who knew exactly what Dr. Nabielle had meant by 'done'. "If I had been faster at finding whoever was communicating with Carsicus, Finley wouldn't have had to get involved and he would be fine."

"It wasn't your fault." Mo said at once, "it was whoever killed him and no one else's'."

"But if I had been faster ..." Jack didn't need to finish the sentence and let his gaze go out into the infinite beyond, where the sky met the ground. He didn't know how long he sat looking out, but he knew that Ember and Mo stayed there with him throughout.

Eventually, Ember wheeled to sit next to him. "You can't change the past, Jack. What's done is done. You have to keep going. Find out who killed Finley."

"But that's not going to bring him back." Jack sighed.

"No, I know that, but you have to do it for him. He trusted you, Jack. He cared about you. Do him proud."

"Yeah, I can do that I suppose." Jack nodded. He still felt guilty about Finley, he still felt pain at his death but there was something else there as well, a burning desire for justice that hadn't been there before. Jack knew that the memory of Finley would never go but he made a decision that he wasn't going to just feel guilty when he remembered Finley, he was going to feel proud as well that he had found out who had killed him.

"We are done here." Jack said calmly to the others, and they all stood up and walked back to Alectus' treehouse.

Jack got involved in the Midwinter activities of Edenvale as little as he could. He was too focused on getting back to the University and finding out exactly who had killed Finley. Mo and Ember also didn't get too entangled in the festivities although Jack knew that that was so that they could spend as much time with him as possible.

The day before they were due to return to the University, Jack steeled himself to go and see Tom, he hadn't up until this point because he was too worried that his failure and sadness would rub off on his brother but eventually Dr. Nabielle had talked him into it.

Tom was already waiting for Jack when he came, Jack assumed that Dr. Nabielle must have forewarned him. "It wasn't your fault, Jack." Said Tom straight away. There was something about Tom's innocent directness that helped his words hit harder than anyone else's.

Jack nodded and for the first time believed what everyone was telling him – it wasn't his fault. "And you have to find out who did it, who is talking to Carsicus. Finley lost his life trying to find it out, don't let his sacrifice be in vain."

This hit Jack even harder for he knew that Tom was right, if he could find out who had killed Finley, while it wouldn't bring him back, at least his death would then have meaning as well as his life.

The next day, Jack stepped into his cart, breathing deeply. He was raring to get to the University and find who had killed Finley. Again, he barely took in the rolling hills or forest that lay between Edenvale and the University. This time though, it was no deep mourning that absorbed all his attention but his sheer focus on his task.

As he sat at dinner that evening, Jack scanned every person in the room, student or lecturer and weighed up whether they fitted the bill of a murderer but none of them did. That, however, only made Jack more determined to find whoever it was. In the common room before bed, Jack was deaf to Engelial's warm glow at seeing him again and instead focused on his mission but again could not find anyone that he could see committing the evil crime he was investigating.

CHAPTER 20: A NEW SUSPECT

The next day was Jack's first full day where he didn't squire for Otto. He spent it instead in the Common Room which was full as lessons didn't start for a few more days. The feeling was one of tempered excitement. Everyone else had just come back from merry Midwinters breaks with their family and were thrilled to see their friends again at the end of the holidays. There was a slight inclination from most of them to refrain from loud jubilation as a mark of respect towards Finley but other than that, it seemed that they had all successfully put it to the back of their minds.

Jack, however, knew that he would not forget in such a hurry.

Polly hadn't been seen in the common room since returning to university. Feeling unable to work on the same joyful frequency as everyone else, Jack snuck off towards the girl's quarters. He knocked on Polly's door.

"Come in." A voice said uncertainly from the other side. Jack entered the room nervously. It was dark and Polly was alone, sitting on her bed.

"Hello Jack." She attempted to smile but her muscles failed her. "Do you need anything?"

Jack shook his head. "Not really, just some company. Can I sit on the bed?"

"Yeah, of course." Polly said, scooting over to the other

side.

They sat together quietly for a while. "What was he like growing up?" Jack asked eventually.

"Exactly like he was when he was older." Polly smiled. "Always a bit quirky and... original. If he saw everyone doing something, he would find the opposite and do that. I remember doing the school play with him one year, he was the lead of course. One of the students had spent months writing this great monologue to end the play with but Finley being Finley just came up with his own on the spot and it was perfect. It caused his first breakup though." Polly finished with a shaky laugh.

"He never told me he had had a girlfriend." Jack sighed. Polly fixed him with a look of disbelief that Jack was getting all too used to being on the wrong side of. "What?"

"Finley never had a girlfriend. He was gay."

Jack sighed again; he had known so little about Finley that he hadn't even realised how little he knew. After this, the stories about growing up with Finley rolled freely off Polly's tongue. Jack kept asking for more and saw that every anecdote Polly told, she became slightly less tired looking.

Jack only left when they heard other people going to bed and one of them entered Polly's room. Still, when he got into his own bed that night, he felt better than he had since the final of Ziro's Tournament.

The next morning, Jack ate breakfast with Engelial as usual. He felt better rested than he normally did having not had to go and do sparring with Otto in the early morning. He was feeling very awake as he threw his books into his bag and headed into the common room, motivated to get to his lesson early, get his work done and then get on with his mission.

Jack waited in the common room for a few minutes,

watching the door to the boy's quarters as usual, playing with a coin that was in his pocket. Suddenly, Jack realised what he was waiting for. He was waiting for Finley.

The abruptness of this realisation made it so much worse, he had no time to prepare for the sudden ache of loss that filled his heart.

Feeling sick, he had to run to the toilets and get his head over the sink, breathing as deeply as he could. "Are you ok?" Otto asked from behind him.

"Yeah, yeah." Jack gasped. "I'll be fine."

But he didn't feel fine as he headed to his lesson. When he arrived, Jack couldn't bring himself to sit in the middle of the room where he normally sat with Finley. Instead, he allowed himself to drift to the back of the room. He watched Professor Clara talking from the front but didn't bother listening in. There was no point now that he didn't get to talk with Finley about it.

Unable to stomach the idea of going back to the common room, Jack found his feet carrying him to the library. People in there might still look happy but at least they were quiet.

The library was bigger than Jack had expected, large tables stood in the middle of the room while vast bookcases adorned the outside. Jack chose a corridor between two of the bookcases at random and headed down it. There was only one other person there and he was faced away so Jack decided not to bother him.

Having just retrieved a book, Jack turned to go back to the tables in the middle of the room at the same time as the other boy. "Otto?" Jack asked, unable to keep the surprise out of his voice.

"Oh, hello Jack." Otto replied, already going brick-red.

"What are you doing in here?"

"Had to pick up a book for a ... ummm... friend." As Otto spoke, he moved the book so that its title was hidden by his hand.

"Right." Jack nodded.

"Ok, well, I had better get going. My friend will need his book I guess."

And with that, Otto was gone. Jack watched him go with a professional interest. Otto was the last person, except Polly, that Jack wanted to investigate in relation to Finley's murder but, at this point, there was nothing that Jack wasn't willing to do, no one he would refuse to investigate in order to get to the bottom of who was talking to Carsicus.

Jack tucked the book he had just gotten under his arm and headed straight for the common room not because he wanted to spend time around the happy students that filled it but because he was going to spend as much time as possible with Otto and see if he did anything else suspicious.

However, Jack spent the whole evening being disappointed. Otto was his normal competent, popular self. He did seem a little downbeat but the reason for that quickly became obvious when Engelial entered the room.

She looked around, smiled blandly at Otto when they made eye contact before heading over to her friends on the other side of the room. "She acts like last term never even happened." Otto told Jack dejectedly. "I have spent three years trying to get her to like me and just when I finally thought she did, she just stops even talking to me. Almost makes me wonder if she kissed me after the fight just so that she could be the hero as well for the night."

Jack didn't say so but had secretly been thinking exactly that. If everything had gone as expected after the fight, he didn't doubt that Engelial kissing Otto would have been as big a talking point as the fight itself and Engelial would have been the centre of attention again. He also knew that Engelial was plenty intelligent enough to realise this as well.

Jack shook himself; this school playground gossip was not what he needed to get involved with. He had to be completely focused on his mission.

In bed that evening, Jack couldn't help but question whether it was possible that Otto was the killer. Jack had spent as much time with him as anyone at the University and he had always been a thoroughly decent person.

The long day of lessons had been draining and before he knew it, Jack had drifted off to sleep. He dreamt that he was back in Edenvale with Mo and Ember. They were on the banks of Heaven Lake and there were two Alforn playing bargeboard in the water. The one on the right had the normal thick brown hair of the Alforn but the one on the left had blond hair, something that Jack had never seen on an Alforn before.

The two Alforn were very evenly matched, and it was several minutes until the brown haired one lost the game and fell with a splash into the water. The blond haired Alforn leapt up in celebration, spinning in the air.

For the first time, Jack saw the white haired Alforn's face.

It was Finley!

Jack jerked awake, his heart thundering at what he had just seen. It took his logical faculties several moments to catch up with his imagination, which had just been lit by his dream. Panting, Jack realised that Finley had not been reincarnated as an Alforn but it had all been a dream.

Knowing that he wasn't going to be able to get back to sleep until he had calmed down, Jack propped his pillow up against the back wall and slouched back against it. He reached for his bedside table, hoping to find the book that he had taken out of the library. Sighing, he remembered that he had left it in his bag which lay on the floor. Jack rolled out of bed, noticing at once how cold the wooden floor felt on his bare feet.

Just as he was about to get back into bed, Jack got a sudden feeling that something was a bit wrong. It took him several moments to work out exactly what it was. Then it came to him; Otto's bag was gone.

Silently, Jack pulled back the curtains of Otto's bed and saw that it was not only Otto's bag that had gone. Otto himself was nowhere to be seen!

Reluctantly, Jack got back into bed. He wanted to go out and see where Otto had gotten to but without any clues, he would just be walking around hopelessly in the dark. Instead, he contented himself with a plan, just like how he had slipped the blue crystal into Polly's bag, he was now going to put the red one in Otto's bag so he could find him if he snuck off during the night again.

Jack refused to let himself drift off all night. Instead, he lay with his eyes shut listening attentively for Otto's return. He heard the clock tick around and two people walk down the corridor but only to get water from the Common Room. Eventually, the door to their dorm swung open and Otto crept in, dropping his bag against his bed before climbing in.

Within seconds, the older boy was snoring, whatever he had been doing during his night-time excursions, it had clearly made him sleepy. Jack took his Tracking Compass from under his pillow and tiptoed over to Otto's bag and saw to his joy that Otto hadn't even bothered to close it. Jack slipped the red diamond into the front pocket before climbing into bed. He had a new suspect and a new plan.

The first thing that Jack did the next morning was scribble a note to Ember and Mo.

Ember and Mo,

Meet me at the Servants door at midnight.

Jack

The day seemed to drag horribly, Jack skipped his lessons for the first time because Otto didn't have any lectures and Jack wanted to spend as much time as possible with him. However, Otto did not give any hint about his night-time wanderings leaving Jack to feel that it was a day wasted. Still, at least he had his meeting with Ember and Mo at midnight.

Jack left for bed so early that it was quite unbelievable. But Jack didn't care. He was determined that Otto was guilty, and it would only be a few days until he had proved that beyond doubt and could leave the University never to come back so what the other students thought of him was irrelevant.

For the first time, Jack reached the door to the Servants quarters before Ember and Mo. Once, he heard footsteps behind the door and hid in the darkest corner of the corridor, but no one came through until Mo swung it open and poked his head out.

"Alright!" He smiled, every one of his crooked teeth on display.

Jack broke into his first genuine grin for a very long time.

"How are you getting on?" Ember asked, and Jack knew what she meant.

"Ok. Not great but ok. Trying to do Finley proud."

Ember nodded her understanding. "Do you want to talk about it?"

"No. Not right now. I need to tell you my plan." Jack replied. "My new suspect is Otto..." And as quickly as he could, Jack explained his evidence.

When he had finished, however, both Mo and Ember looked very sceptical. "I'm sorry but there isn't much there mate. Someone getting a book out the library secretly isn't enough to investigate them for murder. And as for sneaking out in the middle of the night, well, I imagine that plenty of Uni students do that. For all we know, he might just be part of a midnight reading group."

Ember gave Mo a stern look. "I hate to say it, but I agree with Mo on this one." Ember told Jack, spreading her hands. "There just isn't anything that really points to Otto. But..."

"You didn't see him at all though, you don't understand how weird it is for Otto to be in the library in the first place."

"Just let me finish." Said Ember. "We have a way of testing his guilt at our fingertips, Mo and I can have a look at his Rec-Trec when making the beds."

"When is your next turn in our room?" Jack asked.

"Day after tomorrow." Ember said quickly.

"Ok, in the meantime, I have put the red tracking diamond in Otto's bag. So, what I planned was that during the day, I will keep an eye on the compass and if it points anywhere odd, I will follow him and see where Otto is going and then, during the night, either one of you two can keep an eye on it."

"Ok." Ember agreed at once.

Mo rolled his eyes but nodded anyway. "The sooner we get out of this place, the better." He sighed. "I just want to get back to Edenvale."

Jack had never agreed with his best friend more.

For the next two days, Jack stuck resolutely to the plan, but the compass never indicated that Otto was anywhere other than his lessons or the common room. Mo and Ember left notes both days as well to say that Otto hadn't left the boy's dorms throughout the night.

The night before it was Ember and Mo's turn to clean

their room, Jack barely slept, he was determined that Otto was guilty, and that Ember and Mo would find the Rec-Trec confirming his guilt. He willed time to go faster but it had an annoying habit of doing the opposite of what he wanted and that night seemed to last forever.

Eventually, the sun rose and Jack, groggy but excited, went into the common room. Several times during the day, he was tempted to go and check that the clock was working properly because the hands seemed to be turning impossibly slowly.

"Hey, Jack are you free this afternoon?" Otto asked suddenly from above him.

The surprise of hearing Otto talking to him without the vaguest notion that Jack was dreaming of pointing to him as Finley's murderer made Jack nearly jump out of his skin. It took him several moments to recover himself enough to say "Yeah, I am. Why?"

"I was wondering if you fancied squiring for me for a bit, you know let out the steam of a hard week of University."

"Definitely!" Jack smiled, not only was he going to get to spend more time with his suspect, but he was also going to be able to make sure that Otto didn't walk in on Ember and Mo whilst they were searching for his Rec-Trec.

Ten minutes later and they were striding across to the green circle where Otto had spent so much time sparring the term before. The Stadium had been taken down over the break. Soon, a few of the other sparring partners turned up. Ferran, the champion of Fish college, Ragnar Gero of Bear College and Hippos were all there but, Jack noticed with interest, Flair was nowhere to be seen. "Probably given it up out of embarrassment." Otto whispered to Jack with a conspiratorial grin. Jack smiled back for a moment before remembering the main reason why he was here with Otto and becoming serious again.

As the four college champions battled, Jack couldn't help but feel that he was back in his first term at university. Before Finley's death. He found himself living each of the battles, whispering advice to Otto between rounds.

When the other three champions said that they had had enough, all of them having spent the last hour and a half getting battered by Otto, Jack didn't have to fake the excitement in his voice when he asked if Otto wanted to spar with him.

"Ah, a rite of passage." Otto had laughed. "Normally squires want to battle their champion before the end of the first term so I have been expecting this. Go and grab a sceptre and some armour from the storage cupboard."

It only took Jack a few moments to run to the shed, find his armour and a sceptre that was about the right size and return to Otto. The sceptre was not as natural a fit as Sauris but nevertheless, Jack couldn't help but feel a bubble of excitement in his stomach as he stepped towards Otto.

The fight didn't last long, Otto being a great deal bigger, faster, and more experienced than Jack. "Again." Jack said the moment that he and Otto stepped away from each other. Otto smiled an indulgent grin.

Three more times they went at it and each time, Otto proved at least one step ahead of Jack.

"No. No more." Otto laughed when Jack asked for a fifth spar. "Remember that I have already done a good hour and a half before we started."

Jack shrugged, deciding that Mo and Ember must have had time to look through everything that Otto owned. Together, they headed back to the college. Jack found a note on his bed. All it said was.

Midnight. You know where

Jack couldn't wait until midnight. Instead, as soon as the last person in his dorm had fallen asleep, Jack headed straight for the Servants Door. But every second he had to wait chipped away at his confidence that Mo and Ember had found what they had been looking for.

Therefore, Jack had braced himself for the apologetic look on Mo's face when he opened the door at just after midnight.

"It's not Otto mate, we looked through his Rec-Trec and there was nothing there that matched with what was on Carsicus'."

Jack sighed and looked at the ground. Suddenly, he realised that the wooden floor was moving. It took him another moment to realise that the floor wasn't moving at all, rather he was shaking with anger, he had been so confident that Otto was going to be guilty that Jack's disappointment at finding out he had been barking up the wrong tree hit him like a train.

"What if he had another one?" Jack shouted suddenly.

Ember and Mo looked at him concernedly. "Jack keep your voice down." Ember whispered.

"You didn't look closely enough." Shouted Jack, only getting louder and louder. "You missed one. It's your fault. You had one job and you messed it up."

"Shut up mate." Mo hissed angrily but Jack had already turned his back and was storming away, back to his dorm. He was going to look through Otto's stuff himself. He couldn't believe that Otto was innocent.

Jack swung open the door to the dorm and crossed straight over to Otto's stuff then realised with a start that Otto's bag was gone. Jack lost no time in grabbing the tracking compass from under his pillow and charging out of the college, following the red needle without much attention to what was in front of him. A dozen times, he sprinted into walls or trees, but Jack barely cared. He was going to catch Otto in the act.

Jack ran down the path towards the bubble where they ate and had their lessons but for the first time ever, he didn't go up the main staircase, instead he ran behind it and then trampled over thick undergrowth. He slowed slightly when his feet began sinking into the wet ground and thick reeds reached up to Jack's stomach.

"Who's there?" Otto's voice called from nearby, he sounded nervous.

"Jack. And your time is up. I know who you are talking to."

"What?"

"Don't pretend. I know everything."

"Jack, I don't have a clue what you are on about." Otto said, genuine confusion in his voice and for the first time, Jack began to question himself.

"Well, if you aren't doing what I think you are doing, why are you out here at night?" Jack asked, praying that Otto wouldn't be able to answer.

"I was reading." Otto replied at once.

"Is that it?"

"Well writing a bit as well."

Jack's heart sunk like a stone. Otto was genuinely perplexed by Jack's accusations. "What... Why... Why have you come out here alone to read?"

"I'm a bit embarrassed I suppose." Said Otto. "I am meant to be this tough guy who's great at Sceptre battles and son of Field Marshall Smith and I... it just... just feels wrong for anyone to know that I like reading and writing poems when the moonlight is bright enough."

"Oh." Said Jack. "I'll leave you to it."

"Well that's not quite it." Otto said hurriedly, as if he was in a rush to get his words out. "I have always enjoyed poems more than Sceptre battles. But my father never gave me a choice of paths. I told him one evening that I didn't want to go and train but wanted to read instead and, well, his reaction is what led to my broken nose. I was only six."

"I'm so sorry. I never knew."

"No it's ok. The blame isn't yours or mine. It's his. It's all his. And I am going to tell him next time I see him before throwing my Sceptre in the lake." Otto said, his voice cracking with resolution. "I've never told anyone that before, Jack. You're the only person I could even imagine telling. You are a very special person, Jack. Don't forget that."

Any pride or worth of self that Otto had given Jack, however, was soon lost as he made his way back to the college. Now that he looked back, Jack realised that the evidence he had gathered on Otto was weak at best. He had just wanted a suspect. Someone else to blame. Now, he was back where he started. He was never going to catch Finley's murderer.

The tears began to sting his eyes before Jack could hold them back and within moments, they were streaming down his cheeks onto the floor below. Jack ran into the bubble; he knew that the nearest toilets were just to the left of the main staircase. He darted in there, allowing his tears to fall in the sink.

"Who's there?" A vaguely familiar voice called from one of the cubicles.

"Jack, Jack Tourn."

"Oh." Said the voice and the door of the cubicle swung open and King Taigal stepped out. Jack hadn't been the only one crying, Taigal's eyes were red and puffy, and lines of moisture still covered his cheeks. "I am not going to do what he tells me to do anymore. I refuse."

"What who tells you to do?" Jack asked quickly.

"I... I can't tell you, but I had to tell someone, that I am not going to listen to *him* or his messenger anymore, she can go to hell as well. Goodnight, Jack."

"Goodnight, your highness." Jack said, watching the King leave. He was torn between elation and dejection; he was delighted that the King was going to stop listening to Carsicus but couldn't help feeling a little disappointed that his chances at finding Finley's killer had dropped, if the King made it clear he wasn't listening to Carsicus anymore, whoever was communicating between them would have no job and be no different from the other several hundred students at the University.

CHAPTER 21:
ENGELIAL'S FLIGHT

After discovering Otto amongst the reeds, Jack had shared an even closer bond with him. They still sparred together most mornings but now frequently, someone would make a comment in the common room and Jack and Otto would share a knowing look that wasn't seen by anyone else.

On Sunday, Jack waited guiltily in his room for the entire day so that he could apologise to Mo and Ember for shouting that they hadn't done enough to help gather evidence on Otto.

"Don't be silly." Ember said immediately as Jack began to apologise. "It just shows how badly you wanted to find out who killed... I mean... whoever did... *it.*"

"And, looking forwards, I reckon that if the King isn't going to listen to Carsicus anymore, then our job here is basically done. We can head back to Edenvale soon." Mo added.

Their words did make Jack feel a bit better, but they all agreed that they should keep their eyes and ears open until at least their meeting with Einor in two weeks time just in case the King didn't manage to keep to his new resolution.

Jack went to his lessons more to make himself look like a normal student than because he intended to take any notes or pay much attention. In the evenings, he now sat exclusively with Otto. Engelial had been distant with him ever since Jack had become more preoccupied with his task than spending time with her and Polly never came into the common room. A few times, Jack wondered about going to see her but decided against it, she knew where he was and could always come and find him if she needed to talk.

Tuesday evening of the week before they were meant to meet with Einor and tell him that the King was no longer going to listen to Carsicus, Jack was sat with Otto, Dara, and a few other members of the popular group on the largest sofas in the middle of the common room. Engelial wasn't there and without her, Otto was the only one Jack really felt comfortable with and seeing as he obviously wasn't in the mood for talking, Jack felt a little left out.

"I'm just going to head out for a walk." He said in a break of conversation.

"Enjoy yourself." Said everyone but Otto was the only one that really meant it.

Jack strode his way into the Quad and was struck that this would be one of the last times that he walked through here. But unlike the camp in the Wilderness or Edenvale away Westward, Jack knew he wasn't going to miss this place at all, the only people he cared about that he had met here were Otto and Polly, well and Finley he supposed.

And now he was thinking of Finley again, lying lifeless on the floor and Jack just buried his head in his hands and walked aimlessly forwards without caring where he ended up. He reached the edge of the Dome and bounced off. He turned right and just walked that way but before he collided with the Dome again, he heard voices.

The voices were coming from a thick set of weeds surrounding the very same lake where Jack had found Otto that night when Otto had admitted his love of poetry and ambivalence towards sceptre battles to Jack.

Jack crept towards the reeds on the other side of the lake

so that he could see the owners of the voices across the water. He saw that it was Engelial and the King!

"Just tell me who it was you were talking to." Purred Engelial, in a voice that made Jack certain she had asked him this plenty of times already. "Was it Jack?"

"What does it matter? I'm not listening to Carsicus ever again, I can't believe I let myself listen to him for so long." Replied the King sounding frustrated, and Jack saw him try to skim a pebble across the lake's surface, but it just landed with a splash and sunk. He didn't try again.

"I don't understand why you stopped talking to Carsicus. Who made you stop listening to him? I don't understand why you won't just tell me who you were talking to, I won't do anything to them, I just want to know is all."

"I can't tell you. I can't tell anyone!" Said the King, starting to get upset.

Engelial reached across and wiped a tear from under his eye. "Why not, are you trying to protect them?"

The King took a wheezy breath in and nodded.

"Did you *like* them?"

The King took another wheezy breath in and nodded again. "I can't tell you anymore." He said weakly and Engelial nodded. Clearly she thought that she had pushed it all far enough already.

Feeling elated, Jack snuck back through the weeds before sprinting towards the Quad and then through the Common Room, but he didn't go through into his room, instead he barrelled through the door and dashed down the stairs towards the Servants Quarters.

"Has anyone seen Mo and Ember?" He asked.

All the servants looked at each other bemused. "Jack! What're you doing here?" Mo asked, as both he and Ember entered the room from the other side.

"Come quick into my room." Jack said, leaving the way he had come and just as rapidly. He heard Mo and Ember following him and apologising to the other servants for the surprise.

"I thought we said we would only meet in secret!" Said Ember as soon as she entered Jack's room.

"Who cares, we are only here a few days, anyway I have something that I need to tell you, it was Engelial who was communicating between Carsicus and the King!"

"How did you work it out?"

"It was dead lucky really, I was just stumbling around, and I chanced across them at the lake. Engelial was trying to find out who it was that had stopped the King from listening to Carsicus. She thought it might have been me. It wasn't though, whoever it was that got the King to start making his own decisions, I think he has a crush on them." Said Jack. "And I doubt that is a skinny kid like me." He finished with a laugh.

"So do you reckon that it was Engelial who killed Finley?" Ember asked.

Jack's laughter died in his throat. He could barely imagine Engelial killing someone but then he remembered all her many faces and grew certain that there was no one he trusted less.

"Yes." He said "Engelial is a murderer, just like her uncle."

"What do we do now?"

"You two let Einor know everything on the Rec-Trec. I am going to go and do some sparring with Otto."

"What? Why?"

"He knows her family well, her uncle Lord Sorain particularly. I'm going to see if I can find out any more about her.

Maybe some proof that she is deeply involved with the Kaof-relsi or something."

Otto took little convincing to go and do some sparring, even though darkness was already beginning to sneak up from the horizon. As soon as they were out of the common room, Jack started his questions.

"Is there any way that Sorain and Carsicus could still be in contact?"

"No, of course not, Carsicus has been banished beyond the wall."

'Yeah, right' thought Jack.

"What evidence is there that Lord Sorain killed his sister and father?"

"Why are you asking these questions Jack? It's dangerous."

"Because I think Engelial killed Finley."

Otto stopped dead in his tracks. "You need to have some serious evidence before you start saying stuff like that." He said coldly and Jack realised that Otto still liked Engelial. In his realisation that she was behind Finley's death, Jack had forgotten that to everyone else she was still the smiley, carefree, breath-takingly beautiful young woman she had seemed on Jack's first night at the University. That night when she had treated him like he was four rather than fourteen and Jack hadn't minded a bit. That seemed like an eternity ago now. Sighing, Jack realised that Otto was not going to believe him and definitely not going to help gather evidence against Engelial.

"What the hell?" Otto said as they entered the storage shed and Jack saw what he meant, the spot where Jack always left Otto's sword was empty.

"I put it there yesterday!" Jack said at once.

"I believe you. Look at the brackets."

Jack noticed that the brackets where the sceptre was usually left had been unlocked.

"Someone has stolen it." Otto said, unnecessarily.

"Who had a set of keys?" Jack asked.

"You and me obviously, and Engelial had a set and…"

But Jack was already racing back to the college.

As soon as they entered the common room, it was obvious that something was wrong. Dara raced over to the pair of them and squeaked "thank goodness you are alright." In his nervous falsetto voice.

"What's up?" Otto demanded.

"The King was meant to have a tutoring session with Professor Clara at five. When he didn't show up all the lecturers went looking for him and they looked everywhere but he is just gone."

Jack's heart dropped to his feet.

"Is anyone else missing?" Jack demanded.

Dara's eyes started to wet with tears, taking forever to get his words out, "that's the thing…" He sniffed, "no one has seen Engelial or Polly all day."

Jack hurtled down the stairs into the servant's quarters, surprised to hear that Otto was chasing after him.

When Jack entered the servant's quarters, he saw all of them in a semi-circle around a small, anxious looking girl. He spotted Ember's wheelchair at once and went over to her and Mo.

"What's going on?" He whispered, startling the pair of them.

"Alice said someone fired a Sceptre at her." Mo said, revulsion in his voice.

"Did she say what colour the Sceptre was?" Jack asked.

"Pinky." Alice replied with a shake, overhearing him.

"Arhhh… dammit…" Jack growled as he heard Otto gasp from behind him.

"Did you see who fired it at you?" Ember asked Alice as gently as she could.

"It was too dark to see any faces but there were three of them. One of them was probably the King, he was about the right shape and size. I think another one of them was unconscious, they were being dragged along by their hair. Then there was the one that fired at me of course."

"My room now!" Jack told Ember and Mo and this time they pushed after him without apologising to the other servants.

"It's Engelial for certain, she is the only one except Otto and I who could have taken his Sceptre. She must be taking the King to Carsicus. No one has seen her or Polly all day, I would bet anything that the unconscious person Alice saw was Polly. We need to get after them." Jack said but as he went to race out of his room, Ember put a hand out to stop him.

"Let's make sure we have got this right because there are a few things that still don't add up. Firstly, why would Engelial take Polly?"

The two boys froze but just for a moment, "If Finley had any clues that it was Engelial that was the link between Carsicus and the King, he would have told Polly, and Polly was trying to work out who it was that had killed her twin, of course she was, she probably worked out it was Engelial at the same time I did, and she tried to stop them. Engelial knocked her out but couldn't risk her waking up and telling everyone."

"Ok fine, but there is another thing, why would Engelial and Carsicus suddenly try and kidnap the King?"

"Because he has stopped listening to them! The only way to make him do what they want is to take him by force."

"But no one will do a thing that the King says if they can see Carsicus' sceptre at his throat." Said Ember.

"Well, they might just use him as a bargaining chip instead. We can't wait any longer though." Mo replied, getting frustrated. "We need to go and meet Einor and get after them."

All three of them looked at each other, which way would Engelial and the others have gone?

"I'm not saying that I believe what you say but I want to get to the bottom of this as much as anyone." Said Otto, making Jack jump.

Otto crossed over the room and picked his bag up. Jack guiltily thought of the red diamond that he had snuck into Otto's bag and how it should have been in Engelial's. Then, Otto brought a map out of his bag, but Jack hardly noticed.

He dove over his bed to his bedside table and scooped up his tracking compass.

"What are you doing?" Mo asked, a little startled.

"I put the blue tracking diamond in Polly's bag last term, when I thought it was her that was talking to Carsicus before I found…" Jack couldn't finish that sentence. "Anyway, if Polly had her bag on at the time, we will be able to follow them."

"Is the blue dial moving?" Ember asked and Jack put his eye right to it and squinted before nodding.

No one had to say any more, they all began to run after Jack who was sprinting towards the bubble. He snuck through the trap door and into the tunnel that led to Ziro's Tower. As Mo and Otto helped Ember through the hole that was carved in the top of the dome, Jack hastily typed a note on the Rec-Trec that was linked to Einor's.

'King escaped. In pursuit. Meet at the bridge we took to

the Old Town.'

The four of them then flew like the wind along the top of the dome so desperate to close the gap to Engelial that none of them even thought to look down to the ground far below or worry about another hole in the dome.

Just as they touched down, Jack glanced at his Rec-Trec and saw that Einor had acknowledged his message. Jack led them towards the bridge which was close enough to the direction that the tracking compass was pointing. Einor was already there, his great stygian sceptre by his side.

"Who was it talking to Carsicus?"

"Engelial." Jack panted back.

"That snake in the grass." Growled Einor. "Right give me the compass."

Jack handed it to him without fuss, they couldn't afford to waste more time and it made sense for Einor to take the lead anyway.

Soon, they were through the Old Town, heading North-East, towards Ziro's Wall and Jack realised that this was the closest he had been to the Wilderness since flying to Edenvale to stop Carsicus destroying the Amulet half a year ago.

Einor kept up a relentless pace as evening became night and even once darkness had set in, he refused to let up until Ember and Jack insisted that they could go no further without a rest.

Jack collapsed on the ground at once and stayed awake just long enough to hear Einor say, "I am going to send a message to Alectus and Dr. Nabielle to tell them where we are and, hopefully, they can catch up to us."

Only a few hours later, just as dawn broke, and they were on the move again. The ground was flat and easy going but there was still no sign of Engelial and the others to spur them on and the compass still pointed in the direction of Ziro's Wall.

As they walked, Jack tried to understand Engelial and Carsicus' plan, his best guess was that they were trying to reach Ziro's Wall and escape into the Wilderness. Although how they would get through the wall remained a mystery for Jack.

Soon, Jack had no spare energy for thinking and just got his head down and plodded after Einor as best he could.

The group only stopped as the sky began to blacken. Looking ahead, Jack saw that the gentle flatlands they had journeyed through all day were soon to be replaced by harsh rocky hills. "That's the Kingdom of Kulle." Said Einor pointing at the hills.

Morning of the next day out was swamped in thick, low cloud giving the harsh hills a haunted look. Once more, Einor pushed the pace as much as he could, desperate to get after Engelial and the others.

Just before midday, they found themselves standing before a narrow stone bridge across a deep ravine that with its ragged, rocky sides looked like it had been carved out of the landscape as a vengeful act of God.

A sign on the bridge read 'Kingdom of Kulle'.

Einor stopped suddenly halfway across the bridge and Jack saw why, there was an unnatural scrape on the loose rocks that covered the surface of the bridge.

Einor's investigation was suddenly interrupted by a muffled scream from the bottom of the ravine but with the thick cloud, it was impossible to see that far.

"What was that?" Jack asked, frightenedly remembering the Wraiths in the forest and terrified of meeting another Arcanian creature just as terrifying.

"No idea." Said Einor and his growling voice made everyone a little more relaxed. "All of you stay here. Don't move a step. I will go and investigate."

And with that, Einor was off the bridge and climbing down one of the ravine's rocky slopes. Soon, he too was lost to the clouds, and they were left alone on the bridge.

A few minutes passed before anyone spoke. "Do you think he is ok?" Ember asked nervously. But before anyone could respond, there was a disturbance in the fog that Jack could just make out as Einor. And he appeared to be carrying a body.

Jack began bracing himself for what he was about to see. Moments later, Einor, still with the limp body in his arms, was coming along the bridge.

It was only when he got right up close that Jack could see the body in any detail. It was a woman. Her thick brown hair was missing lumps and matted together with blood. Her forehead was lacerated with cuts too and mud had been pressed into every fold of skin. Her left eye was blackened and swollen with bruises as well as dirt.

Suddenly, Jack gasped. The woman had opened her undamaged eye and Jack knew those eyes anywhere. It was Engelial.

"What happened to you?" Jack asked at once, all his anger towards her vanishing as he remembered the kind young woman who had fussed all over him that first night at university and taught him how to dance on the second.

"I don't... I don't remember." Said Engelial. "I'm all confused. I just remember a man with a golden Sceptre seeing that I had woken up and saying that they couldn't risk wasting any time and throwing me over the side of the bridge."

"What did the man look like?" Mo asked.

"Golden." Said Engelial and Jack stared back. "He had

golden hair and a golden Sceptre and a proud face, but I didn't see any more than that before he pushed me."

Jack couldn't believe it. Was it possible that Engelial didn't know Carsicus?

CHAPTER 22: EINOR AND ENGELIAL

Engelial didn't manage to answer any more questions, she just fell back into Einor's arms halfway between passing out and falling asleep.

"Right well we need to get moving." Said Einor, letting her drop to the ground none too gently.

The others looked at him in disbelief. "What?" Einor growled. "We need to catch up to the others and she will only slow us down. If we leave her here, she'll be fine... probably."

"I'm not just leaving her here." Jack said stubbornly and the other three shook their heads in agreement.

"Idiots all of you. None of you know the first thing about the real world. She was with Carsicus helping him capture Polly and the King or have you all forgotten that?"

"But she seemed to not have a clue who Carsicus was."

"Oh for crying out loud! She was ACTING. I'm not surprised it took you six months to work out who was talking to the King if you believe everything the two-faced gits up at the University say."

"We can't leave her!" Jack shouted. "She might know something useful and besides, if she actually was in league with Carsicus, why would he throw her over a bridge?"

"Maybe she was slowing them down too much or maybe that was his plan all along, the more people he tries to smuggle through the wall, the harder it will be to go unnoticed. Either way, we need to get going."

And without another glance or word, Einor began striding away after Carsicus. Also without another word, Jack and Otto lifted Engelial's limp body and carried it between them. Neither of them could let Engelial lie on the bridge alone and bloodied even if she had been working with Carsicus.

"I really do HATE children!" Einor snarled when he checked over his shoulder a few minutes later and saw Otto and Jack a fair way behind, struggling to carry Engelial. "If we are going to have to take her with us, at least let me carry her so we won't be too much slower." He rumbled. "But if we don't manage to catch Carsicus, you're to blame."

Einor lifted Engelial onto his oxen-like shoulders so easily it was like she was made of air. Even despite her weight on his back, he remained in the lead, striding powerfully forwards in the direction pointed by the compass.

However, when the sky began to darken once more, they still had seen no sign of Carsicus and the others. The fog still lay thick across the hilltops and now it was night, Jack couldn't see too far beyond the end of his nose.

"It's too dangerous to continue tonight." Said Einor as they halted. "The last thing we need is someone falling down a ravine. Carsicus won't be able to go any farther anyway."

The group slept where they had stopped, Jack lumped some earth in a pile to use as a pillow and despite its unforgiving roughness found sleep at once. He dreamt that they spotted Carsicus a little way off and grew closer and closer but just before they reached him, they spotted something on the floor before them, a body. Jack went to investigate and saw that it was Finley just as he had found him in the Quad three months ago.

The vision made Jack wake suddenly and in cold sweats. It took him several moments to get his breathing back to normal. When he did, he was surprised to hear voices from a little distance away. One of the voices was the unmistakable growl of Einor. The other, though, he didn't recognise. Quiet as he could, Jack crept towards them.

"Wath it your big baddie uncle that introduthed you to Carthicuth then?"

"Is Carsicus who the golden boy was?" Said the other voice and Jack realised that it was Engelial but her lips were so swollen her voice sounded nothing like it normally did.

"Don't get clever with me. I know you aren't the innothent beauty you pretend to be." Einor spat. "Not that you are very pretty at the moment." He laughed vindictively.

"What do you mean?" Asked Engelial.

"Of courth you don't realith. You never did look twith at any of your thervanth. I wath your bodyguard for a few royal eventh."

"Why?"

"Trying to find a way to kill your uncle." Einor said bluntly.

"I honestly don't know Carsicus. I never met him before he tried to kill me!" Said Engelial.

"We'll talk again tomorrow. But for tonight, I am going to tie you up. I thtill don't trutht you."

Jack watched Einor tie rope unnecessarily tightly around Engelial's ankles and wrists before he walked a short distance away and went to sleep himself.

As they walked the next day, Jack's mind pondered the conversation that he had overheard. As the group crossed from rock-scared hills to softer, gentler country, Jack barely noticed. He had been so confident that Engelial had been the one orchestrating the plan, but she seemed so truthful when saying she did not even know who Carsicus was. Jack resolved to wait up that night and try to learn more.

This time, Jack still had an eye half open when Mo, Ember and Otto drifted off to sleep. He saw Einor stand up and cross over to Engelial.

"Do you thtill deny knowing Carthicuth?"

"Yes. Like I say, I didn't even know that was what he was called before you told me."

"Another thing I can't believe, when Carthicuth became Conthul, he wath in and out of Thorain's houth non-thtop."

"I wasn't allowed to even see any of the guests that came and went from the house." Said Engelial. "Sorain didn't think that girls should get involved in politics. Which was very un-fair."

"Oh yeah becauth you had thuch a hard life with your hundredth of thervanth to bully around."

"I wasn't always like that. Before Sorain became ruler, I was nice to all my servants, you can ask them." Engelial said and her eyes began to well with tears, "Sorain made me bully them like that. He said that if you treated them well, people like that would take advantage."

"Tho you were juth doing what you were told to?" Einor asked derisively.

Engelial nodded her head.

"You didn't ever try to thtand up to him though, did you?"

"Stand up to him? I was nine when he became ruler. He killed my grandfather and mother!" Yelled Engelial.

"Thut up. You will wake everyone up you idiot. And, anyway, what about at the Univerthity, Mo and Ember said that you bullied everyone there ath well. What ith your eth-cuse for that?"

"Sorain has ways of finding everything. He would know if I was treating them well and I would get into trouble."

Einor put his face right up close to Engelial's "coward." He whispered.

"I tried." Engelial shouted after him, crying properly now. "I tried." She said, crumpling and burying her head in her hands.

Before he could really think about what he was doing, Jack found himself crossing over to her and putting an arm across her shoulders. Engelial barely seemed to notice him because she kept crying and talking to herself. "I tried, I read all those books hoping that they would give me someone to emulate or some inspiration or just any way to be someone other than me. You get that Jack, don't you? You are there for me."

"Yeah, I'm here for you." Jack said as reassuringly as he could manage. He didn't doubt for a second that Engelial had told the truth, that she wanted to be a good person but was scared out of her skin of Sorain's retribution. Whether she was telling the truth about not knowing Carsicus, Jack was not so sure, he still remembered her conversation with the King.

When he went back to where he had been lying before sneaking off, Jack woke Mo and Ember and told them everything that he had overheard the last couple of nights. Both Ember and Mo looked at him slightly sceptically and Jack remembered that both of them already had a strong dislike of Engelial.

"If what Engelial is saying is true, then who *has* been communicating between the King and Carsicus, who *killed* Finley?" Mo asked probingly.

"I don't know, I just don't think it was Engelial." Said Jack.

"But the only other person who left the Dome was Polly and she can't have been the person that, you know, did *it* to

Finley."

"I know, I know, maybe it was someone else entirely and Polly just knew too much so they had to take her with them."

The other two shrugged. "Either way, I can't do another night listening out for Einor and Engelial to start talking, I need some sleep. Would you two mind sharing the watch for it tomorrow night?"

Ember and Mo both sighed, spending all day walking was tiring enough without having to spend the whole night awake but both agreed to do it nonetheless.

"Jack. Wake up." Mo whispered at midnight the next night and at once, Jack heard the voices of Engelial and Einor a short distance off. The three of them crept over to them, leaving Otto sleeping.

"Hate being back here." Einor spat, kicking a lump out of the ground as if to prove his point.

"You must have *some* good memories of here. When you were a child at least." Engelial said and Jack looked at the others slightly alarmed at how different the tone of this conversation was to the previous nights.

A scary smile spread across Einor's face, "I'm not thure if they are good memorieth. But you could never underthtand the ethitment of it. The violenth. Alwayth thomeone getting beat up on every corner or robbed. It wath tho ethiting. You feel alive. You could never underthtand."

There was a pause and Jack knew that revulsion was spreading across Engelial's face.

"You could never underthand." Said Einor. "Thath my nature. I'm wild. I jutht want to take everyoneth heart, their blood, their thpleen. Thath my nature."

"I don't believe you." Said Engelial, sounding braver

than Jack expected.

"Why ith that?"

"You didn't leave me to die on the bridge. You aren't an animal."

"You don't know anything about me." Spat Einor.

"Well tell me then."

"Fine. Like I thaid, I grew up here. I never knew my dad. My mum wathn't around much tho I thpent my time on the threeth and it wath tho ethiting. Yeah, I thpent more time in jail than at home. There wath thith one time I was about thirteen and thome punk tried to thove me about, but I beat him tho bad he had to go to hothpital. Never thaw him again. That night one of the prithon guardth banged on my door and is like 'think you're a tough guy huh, come down to the gym and we'll see'. He wath thome retired fighter. We got down to the gym, they didn't have any thceptreth of courth but they had these wooden thwordth tho we uthed them. I hit that man tho hard. Anyway, the netht day this guard took me to the houth of thome old trainer and he taught me how to amp up the violenth. Oh, you thould have theen it. I cruthed everyone."

Jack could hear a vicious joy begin to creep into Einor's voice now.

"It wath tho ethiting. The violenth. The noitheth that people tharted to make when I hit them."

"What was the name of this boxing trainer?" Engelial asked.

"Cali."

Engelial gasped.

"Yeah I know he wath your grandfather. And I don't care."

"It isn't that. I don't believe that Cali would ever teach people to hurt others."

"Well he did try and get me to thtop my violenth in the threeth but I am an animal thath what I do."

"How many times, you aren't an animal. You saved my life." Said Engelial. "And I think it is because of Cali that you did that. I think he did turn you into a good person deep down."

"Maybe, maybe he did for a time when I was young and thtupid." Growled Einor.

There was a moments pause and then Einor spoke again and this time, there was something other than his normal angry violence in his voice, there was fear.

"That was before *it* happened."

"What happened?"

"Cali's death."

"I know." Said Engelial sympathetically. "That was hard for me too. He was my grandfather and idol."

"It wath worth for me."

"Why?"

"Becauth it wath me that killed him."

There was another moments pause and Jack could feel the disbelief even from the other room.

"What? Why?" Demanded Engelial.

"It wath after one of my fights. Cali was in my corner, in dithguithe obviouthly but even tho, thomeone mutht have recognithed him because Sorain's men came and arrethted him. I followed them, trying to find thome way to break him free but there were tho many guardth it wath impothible. They took him to Sorain's palace, and I managed to thneak in after them. Cali wath taken to the top of the talletht tower. I found him there. It was jutht him and Sorain and the guardth. Sorain jutht looked at Cali, his own father, and told the guardth to take him below and torture him jutht for the thake of it. I still had my theptre on me from the fight. There wath only going to be enough time for me to fire it at one of them, Sorain or Cali."

"So you had to choose between killing the man you hated and stopping your father figure from being tortured?"

"Yeth." Said Einor and his voice broke, and Jack was startled to realise that Einor, the youngest ever Sword of the Kingdom was crying.

CHAPTER 23:
THE TRADE

"What's that?" Mo asked suddenly, pointing off in the distance. For the first time that day, Jack's mind was drawn out of the mystery of Engelial and Einor's night-time conversations. He looked as hard as he could but couldn't make out anything other than more raggedy hills.

"I have been wondering the same thing." Replied Einor. "It looks like Carsicus' raven to me."

"Is he going to get it to attack us and slow us down?" Asked Mo.

"Doubt it. That raven isn't a Rafiki for fighting. I would guess he is going to give us a message of some description."

"What sort of message?"

"How'd I know?"

Soon, even Jack could make out the shape of a raven a few hundred metres away. With a goal in sight, they made good progress and before long, the raven was within shouting distance.

"What do you want?" Einor shouted bluntly.

"Carsicus wants to strike a deal." Replied the raven in an odd, strained voice. "He is willing to give up the King in return for you giving up the chase and letting him escape beyond Ziro's Wall and into the Wilderness."

"Where would the trade take place?"

"Kulle Stadium. Tomorrow at midnight."

"Agreed." Said Einor at once.

And without another word, the raven spiralled into the sky.

"We don't need to go much further today." Said Einor. "The stadium is no more than a few hours walk. There is a small town over the next couple of hills. We will stay there tonight. Alectus should be able to meet us there tomorrow morning. The more of us there are the better, I don't trust Carsicus as far as I can throw him."

As Einor had said, after two more climbs and descents, a small village was laid out below them.

"Robbed every shop on the Highstreet." Said Einor, not boastful just a statement of facts.

It was left to Otto to knock on the door of one of the inns and ask for six beds for the night. The owner of the inn was a large man with a swarthy, dishonest face but with the presence of Einor in the company, Jack was confident that they would be safe until morning.

The first thing that they all did except Einor was to head down to the river that they had spotted on their way down to the town and bathe their feet in the cool water. Jack was surprised at how well the rest of his body had dealt with the chase, but his feet felt like fire every step he took.

Engelial was the first to suggested heading off back up to the inn. "I'll go with her." Jack sighed. Einor had told them that he still didn't trust Engelial and wanted someone to keep an eye on her the whole time.

When he entered the inn, Jack heard Einor and Engelial in conversation once again.

"Cali only liked me because I won. And I won because I am an animal." Came Einor's menacing voice from through the door.

"That's not true. That isn't who Cali was. He liked you because you were trying to be a good person. He wanted to help you."

"He did help me. He taught me how to hit. But more than that, I knew that he wouldn't care about me, nobody would care about me, if I lost so I got so scared before every fight, not about the person I was fighting but about losing because if I lost, I would have to go back to the streets and be all alone again. So I used to go in there so scared and just let that out on the person that I was fighting. That's why I won so much."

And for the first time, Jack understood the relentless pace that Einor fought at and the feral aggression he put into every stroke. For him, the cost of losing wasn't shame or even death, it was thinking no one would love or care about him ever again.

"Cali wouldn't have stopped caring about you if you had lost." Said Engelial softly.

"That's what he said, 'fight out of love for what's behind you not fear for what's in front of you'. Just wind. All of it. All words. They're just wind. Love makes you vulnerable not strong. Just as I had begun to let myself love Cali as a father, I had to kill him. And it ripped my heart apart. Never again."

"Vulnerable and strong aren't mutually exclusive. You can have both." Said Engelial.

Einor growled but didn't say any words in return.

As Jack lay in bed that night, he couldn't find sleep. Partly, he was nervous about tomorrow, whether Carsicus would stick to his word or if they were walking straight into a trap but mostly, he was feeling too strongly. And it was the last thing he could ever have imagined feeling strongly about, he was too focused on his sympathy towards Einor. Jack tried to imagine spending his whole life on the streets of a tough place like Kulle and then finally having a father figure take care of him and, just as Einor had begun to allow himself to trust and love, he had had to do something that had destroyed any faith he had begun to have in others.

When the sun did rise, Jack had only managed to sleep in a few short bursts.

"Morning!" Said a friendly voice the moment that they left the inn. Alectus was leaning against the frame of the door. Jack was interested to note that either Alectus had put on several kilograms of muscle since he had last seen him or he was wearing armour beneath his clothes. Jack noticed as well that Alectus had an Andagaldur shield on his back and his sceptre by his side.

"I don't expect trouble. Carsicus knows that he can't outrun us the whole way to the wall. He needs this trade to come off. But that doesn't mean we shouldn't prepare for it."

Jack nodded.

"We should get going." Said Alectus as night began to fall. "We can't risk being late."

Einor growled that he had heard and stood up, lifting his sceptre from the floor, and turning it in a figure of eight.

"You four stay here and guard her." Alectus said, nodding at Engelial.

Even Engelial stared at him in disbelief. "We aren't staying here!" Jack burst out. "We've chased Carsicus over a third of the Realm, you can't make us back out now. Anyway, I need to find out who killed Finley."

"Be sensible now." Said Alectus sternly. "There is no point you lot risking your necks as well, you won't be able to do much more than get in the way."

"I am finding out who killed Finley." Jack replied stubbornly.

"Where are you going?" Alectus asked suddenly as Einor began to walk towards the stadium.

"Not going to waste time listening to family arguments."

With a sigh, Alectus seemed to realise that the only way he could stop Jack and the others from going to the stadium was to guard them himself. And if there was a trap, even Einor would need back up.

"Fine. But don't go after Carsicus himself. If he tries to spring a trap, just get to safety. Don't try and be a hero."

Jack nodded but the only thing that interested him was finding out who killed Finley. Being a hero never crossed his mind.

Soon, they were in the familiar pattern of following Einor up and down the rocky hills of Kulle. The only change of course was the addition of Alectus to the group.

The stadium was nothing like the wooden one that Dr. Nabielle had built at the University. For one thing, it was at least twenty times as vast, towering so high it seemed to brush the clouds. Jack could imagine that for fights to determine the next Sword of the Kingdom, tens of thousands of spectators would cram through the broad entrances and fill the thousands of seats. But in the present, there was no one else in sight.

The lack of atmosphere became more and more unsettling as Jack continued through towards the belly of the stadium. Suddenly, the roof above him ended and Jack came to a sandy arena.

"Midnight isn't for a while yet." Said Alectus, trying to sound reassuring but Jack could hear all too clearly in his voice that the silence in the stadium was unnerving him too.

A nasty thought crept into Jack's head, what if all this was simply a way of slowing them down and giving Carsicus more of a head start? What if he was already passing through Ziro's Wall as they waited? Alectus said that Carsicus needed this trade to come off but what if he was wrong?

Suddenly, the ground shook under their feet and a tsunami of a sound wave swept around the arena.

"What was…" Jack began but he never finished because at that moment, two balls of etter dived down from the sky to the far end of the stadium. A second later, it switched into the figure of Carsicus and the King, who was muddy and beaten up looking.

"I warn you not to play any games with us Carscius." Said Alectus. "Let the King go, and we will allow you safe passage to the wall for you to leave and remain in the Wilderness for good."

Carsicus stayed smiling confidently at them and Jack knew, without a shadow of a doubt, that Carsicus did not have any intention of keeping his side of the deal.

"Arise brave soldiers of the Kaofrelsi."

Out the corner of his eyes, Jack spotted movement on both sides of the arena. He turned quickly this way and that and saw four faces he recognised. There was a man so tall and slender he seemed more a wraith than human, it was Vermhell. Next to Vermhell was a tall, broad-shouldered man with those handsome green eyes Jack had learnt to hate, Lord Sorain was here. Further along was a woman with hard black eyes and a snarl, Alika had crossed the wall into the Realm and once more regarded Jack with a look of furious hatred. Finally, there was a small blond girl… Polly stood holding Otto's sceptre.

From beside him, Einor gave a feral growl at Vermhell who smiled. "How's the arm?" he asked.

Einor didn't answer him but just pulled his sceptre from

its sheath.

"Engelial, don't be a stupid girl. Put that sceptre down on the ground." Said Lord Sorain.

"The only place this sceptre is going is your neck, uncle." Said Engelial and there was a fury in her voice that even Einor had never matched as she spoke to Lord Sorain, her uncle, and murderer of her mother and grandfather.

After that, there was a moment's hesitation from both sides.

It was Alika who broke it, firing a purple ball of etter at Alectus' chest. Alectus was not to be caught unaware however and dropped into the Deep before pushing the ball of etter straight back at its first master and Alika only just slipped to the side in time.

There were the sounds of etter blasts from Jack's left and he knew that Einor and Engelial were facing off with Vermhell and Sorain.

Otto charged bravely forwards at Carsicus and they began to duel.

That left Jack, Mo and Ember against Polly who now looked hesitant. "Why?" Was all Jack could say.

Polly didn't try to respond but the look in her eyes belied her questioning of herself. With a yell, she fired a pink ball of etter from Otto's sceptre at Jack who dropped into the Deep at once and pushed it aside.

The length of the battle, Jack never knew. He could just remember blocking and firing, slipping and shooting. Polly had a definite edge in being able to drop down a little further into the Deep for a little longer, but Jack had the advantage in reactions. At one point, Jack didn't quite manage to dodge a blast from Polly's sceptre and felt it burn along the side of his ribs causing him to gasp in pain, but he managed to keep his mind on the fight and remain in the Deep.

Slowly, Polly's attacks began to come less frequently and with less aggression. Sensing her tiring, Jack began to push the action as best he could and now she was only blocking on her backfoot.

Still maintaining the intensity, Jack now began to walk her down. Polly gave one last gasp attempt and Jack just about managed to deflect the three balls of etter that were aimed at him. With her energy now gone, Polly slipped from the Deep entirely and Jack, now able to move at several times her speed, simply pulled the sceptre from her grasp, leaving her with no method of attack.

Finally able to see what was going on with everyone else, Jack looked around. Otto was desperately defending from Carsicus. Engelial was holding her own against her uncle, her teeth barred. Einor and Vermhell were both still in the normal realm and yet, even in the Deep, Jack was in disbelief at how fast they were both moving, Vermhell's whip was like lightning and Einor's sceptre a blur of devastation. Alectus and Alika were also equal but as he was watching them, a blast from Alectus' sceptre knocked Alika to the floor. But, before he was able to close the distance, there was a screaming sound and Jack saw, like a meteorite, a fantastically dense, powerful ball of etter come screaming down from the heavens. It hit the ground so hard that everyone from both sides was thrown to the ground.

Then the ball of etter became a person and Jack stopped breathing.

Now, standing before him was Haldred. And this was no memory.

Jack could only watch as Haldred dropped far, far into the Deep. He knew without a doubt that Haldred was about to fire at him and there was nothing he could do to defend himself.

The light began to come but before Jack could even

react, a second ball of etter flew down from the black, midnight sky.

Jack remained rooted, watching the two balls of etter battle with such ferocious intensity that Jack's eyes couldn't even keep up. Both were much further into the Deep even than Alectus had gone when wearing the crown under the hill far away in Edenvale.

The force of the battle only seemed to build further and further, until the power involved seemed as though it should be left only to the gods, far away from the realm of mortals.

Then there was what seemed an explosion, Jack's whole frame of view whitened for a few seconds, but he knew he was moving faster than any car on earth could manage. Just as suddenly as it had begun, the whiteness was replaced by green grass and Jack felt himself slam onto the ground.

Head ringing, he forced himself to his feet and saw Mo, Ember, Otto, Alectus, Einor, Engelial and the King also struggle upright. One figure remained motionless, Dr. Nabielle lay on the floor with all her limbs at the wrong angles and lifeless.

Einor was the first to reach her, putting his fingers to her neck for several seconds, Jack and the others watched, unable to breath for fear. "There is a pulse but it's faint. We need to get her to a hospital."

"But where are we?" Jack asked.

"The far side of Teraturt." Alectus replied. "There is a hospital in the centre." He said, pointing. "Mo, you run ahead and tell them that we are coming, Einor and I will start carrying her. The rest of you, head to Edenvale, we will meet you there."

"Edenvale!" Said the King in disbelief.

"Yes, Edenvale is real, just like Haldred your highness and, as you can see, he has returned."

CHAPTER 24: A NEW KING?

Jack and Ember led the King, Engelial and Otto towards the towering trees of Edenvale.

"So they're all true then?" The King asked weakly in blatant disbelief, "the Crown, the Amulet, Haldred, Edenvale... all of it?"

"Yes." Jack replied.

And after that there was silence, which helped Jack to realise just how big this revelation must have been for all of them, the King particularly, they had all been suddenly thrown into what they had believed were no more than ancient myths and fables.

Jack led the group into Lord Alectus' house where they waited for Alectus, Einor and Mo to return with news on Dr. Nabielle.

"She'll live." Alectus said as he entered through the door. "The doctors are looking after her now."

"What's the plan now that Haldred is back?" Jack asked.

"The plan is we wait for Dr. Nabielle to get better." Einor said firmly. "Then we can choose our next steps."

It was four days before Dr. Nabielle was released. Jack, Mo, and Ember led the others around Edenvale. "I can't believe all this was hidden just down the hill from where I sparred." Said

Otto. But it was the King who remained in the most disbelief, Jack had caught him several times pinching his own arm to check he wasn't dreaming. Engelial took the new information onboard the most easily, her lacerations began to heal, and she remained in her nicest mode, just like she had been when Jack had first met her at the University. One time, Jack had accidently come across Engelial and Einor deep in conversation; "I take back what I said about hate not making you strong." Engelial had said in an aside to Einor.

"I wasn't fighting with hate in my heart."

"No?"

"No. For the first time, I wasn't fighting with hatred for what was in front of me but rather love for what was behind me."

When Dr. Nabielle did return, she was using a cane and holding a newspaper. And she did not look happy. Before any of them could say anything, she lay the newspaper out on the table, and everyone gathered to read it.

Lord Sorain Saves the Day!

The mystery of the missing monarch has been solved! Our young King has been found by none other than his most loyal subject, Lord Sorain. The escapade lasted no more than a couple of days but had the court and most of the Realm broken with worry. There is no word yet on where the King's wanderings led him, but he has a young man's impulses, so the reader can probably use their imagination.

"But what does this mean?" Asked Jack, confused.

"It means Sorain, or his master Haldred, has managed to find a boy who looks like the King and use him as a puppet to rule the Kingdom."

"But that's absurd!" Jack exclaimed.

"Is it? Ninety-nine percent of the Realm have never seen the King up close."

"But what about everyone at court? And all the other Lords and Ladies and people in power? They will know it isn't the King"

"They will, but whether they admit it or not is another question. If Haldred and his puppet king offer them more power, more land, and more money, they might suddenly become a bit less certain of who is telling the truth."

"So, what do we do?"

"We fight back."

Epilogue

"Dad, can you walk with me to the University? There is something I need to do."

"What's that?"

"I can't tell you. It's private. I just need you to walk with me."

Three weeks later, Jack and Alectus arrived at the entrance of Scholar's City.

"Can you just wait here please?" Jack asked. "I won't be long."

Alectus nodded and Jack continued up to the University alone. He passed the Eileaftium barrier, skirted around the outside of the bubble to the quiet spot where Finley's grave was.

"It's not as good as yours were." Jack told him, pulling

a piece of paper from his pocket and unfolding it. He lay it on the ground just before the headstone of the grave. Jack stepped back and looked at the picture he had drawn of Otto and Flair fighting and, watching from the stands, was Finley, his eyes alive, his mouth wide open mid-shout, living each moment as it came.

SOCIAL MEDIA

For the latest updates as Jack, Mo and Ember continue to battle the maniacal Kaofrelsi:
Website: https://www.arcanechronicles.uk/
Email: cj@arcanechronicles.com
Youtube: https://www.youtube.com/channel/UCFFY-yNAH_521oxuialVRZ1g
Instagram: arcane.cj

Printed in Great Britain
by Amazon

76085510R00180